A
POISON
TREE

John Dolan

TENTION BOOKS

TENTION BOOKS

A POISON TREE published by Tention Publishing Limited

Tention Publishing Limited Reg. No. 8098036
Unit 4 Provender Mill, Belvedere Road,
Faversham ME13 7LD,
United Kingdom

http://www.tentionpublishing.com

A CIP catalogue record for this book
is available from the British Library

ISBN 978-0-9573256-4-7

Cover photograph copyright Becky Joy Photography

For Helen

I was angry with my friend:
I told my wrath, my wrath did end.
I was angry with my foe:
I told it not, my wrath did grow.

And I watered it in fears,
Night and morning with my tears;
And I sunned it with smiles,
And with soft deceitful wiles.

And it grew both day and night,
Till it bore an apple bright;
And my foe beheld it shine,
And he knew that it was mine,

And into my garden stole
When the night had veiled the pole:
In the morning glad I see
My foe outstretched beneath the tree.

William Blake, A Poison Tree

ASH

A church. Of all the places I might have chosen to seek refuge, I would never have guessed it would be a church.

Even in my current state I can still register the smell of damp and dust, still see the darkness in old corners, feel the desperate yearning of the supplicant who cannot pray to a god he knows does not exist.

I hear the door open and close behind me, but I don't turn around. I don't care who is there. It no longer matters.

All that concerns me now is the recording of events.

It has struck me that I have to write down all of it. I feel driven, compelled to do this. I need to be able to reassemble the fragments of my life, somehow to restore a measure of order to this chaos of my existence.

To sift the wreckage, to inspect it, to categorise, to understand.

But this is not an easy process. The shards of my mirror are many and far-flung, and sharp. My fingers and hands are bloody from their edges and angles. My mind's eye is full of images I cannot switch off; images of bodies pulsing and throbbing in innumerable acts of sexual congress. Images of anguish and pain. My brain hums like some relentless machine.

Who am I now? I need to know.

1999: PARASITE LIANA

1

DAVID

"I'm thinking of killing my wife," said Jim. "Can we talk about that for a while?"

"Sure," I replied. "Why not?"

My drinking companion looked at me for a few seconds as if he were a barrister examining some witness for evidence of his reliability. He was probably wondering just how drunk I was. Although we had both been downing beers and whisky chasers, he appeared stone-cold sober. Rather too sober in fact, rather too in control.

He gave a small shrug, sipped his beer and ran a finger across the condensation on the glass.

During the slight pause, I asked my alcohol-slowed brain to remember how and when I had first met Jim Fosse. I had the feeling it had been at some unmemorable Midlands Chamber of Commerce dinner, not unlike the one we had sat through this evening. We were hardly close friends, although he lived in Leicestershire in the next village to ours. Indeed, I knew little about this chubby American other than he came from Greensboro, North Carolina – a town with which I am completely unfamiliar – and that he was some kind of 'fixer' on international energy deals. Based on his patter, he seemed to spend a lot of time travelling to exotic places, usually in Africa or South East Asia. I gathered that he was currently retained by a Midlands-based power company, assisting them in governmental negotiations on projects in Thailand and the Philippines.

Of course the question I should have been asking myself was how we had arrived at the discussion topic of uxoricide.

Jim cleared his throat.

5

A POISON TREE

"My first wife, Carol, had the decency to poison herself with mushrooms just as she was becoming tiresome. But this one shows no signs of dying anytime soon," he drawled.

"Your first wife died of *mushroom poisoning*?"

"Yup. Accidental poisoning, I might add. I was in Nigeria at the time getting a pipeline contract closed. It came a bit of a shock. The timing was convenient as it turned out, but the *modus mori* itself was somewhat unexpected. Yes, I will always be grateful to that little helping of toxic fungus. It saved me a fortune in lawyer's fees and alimony."

"When was this?"

"Eight years ago. A year before I married Monique. I figured I'd better get back in the saddle quickly as hookers get expensive after a while. You want another drink?"

"No, I'm good," I responded.

He raised an eyebrow. "Worried about what your little woman will say?"

"I think we were talking about *your* little woman."

"Ah yes," he took a mouthful of beer. "Not so little actually. Have you met Monique?"

I shook my head.

"Shapely, she is. She has the best breasts my money could buy."

Jim's expression became serious and he put a hand on my shoulder.

"Tell me, David, are you a fan of black and white films?"

"Is this pertinent to the subject of your killing Monique?"

"Absolutely."

"Well then, I like some old films."

"Such as?"

"Um … *Casablanca*, perhaps?"

He looked pained.

"You're not into romances, then, Jim?"

A POISON TREE

"I'm more of a devotee of *film noir*, David. You know the sort of thing? The shadowy world of the femme fatale, the cynical detective, the scheming bad guy who is never short of a quip. That's my kind of world. One of moral ambivalence where nothing is as it seems and everyone has a secret."

Jim made an expansive gesture, spilling some of his beer in the process.

"Whereas today's entertainment – nay, today's *life* – is so colourful and yet so unutterably boring. Nothing is blurry or in soft focus any more. It's obvious who the good guys are, or so they would have us believe."

"Who are 'they'?" I asked.

He touched the side of his nose. "You know who 'they' are, David. Everybody knows. They are the people who want us to live law-abiding, insipid lives punctuated with mortgages, children, pensions and all the other fuckwit paraphernalia of the modern age." He paused and leaned towards me. "I hate that sort of shit. I was born in the wrong era. I should have been out there on the mean streets of Prohibition New York, going to jazz clubs, getting involved in racketeering and machine-gunning anyone who pissed me off."

"And wearing spats."

"Exactly."

We clinked glasses and drank.

The pub – The Bell – was still busy, though nobody seemed to be paying much attention to the two middle-aged businessman talking nonsense at the corner table. I couldn't remember how we had ended up there, but I was glad we had. It was my local and I could walk home afterwards and leave my car in the car park. Jim was *definitely* going to need a taxi.

"Anyway, to get back to my original subject," Jim continued. "Killing Monique."

"Sounds difficult," I proffered, noticing how thick my tongue felt.

7

"No, no, no," he said. "Killing your wife is easy. There are a gazillion ways to do it. Trust me on this. It's getting away with it that is the difficult part."

"Ah."

"That is where writers like Dashiell Hammett, Raymond Chandler, Cornell Woolrich and James M Cain were such geniuses. They had great ideas on how to escape the consequences of unacceptable behaviour. And not only that, but original, imaginative concepts on how to go about the unacceptable behaviour in the first place."

"So you're planning on doing away with your wife based on the plot of a bleak, over-stylised detective novel?"

"Maybe. Have you seen a film called *Strangers on a Train*?"

"I don't recall it."

"Released in 1951, I believe. One of Alfred Hitchcock's better efforts. Based on Patricia Highsmith's novel. A *woman*, but a good writer nonetheless," he added.

I finished my beer and contemplated what I hoped would be my final whisky. I became aware that Jim was peering at me again.

"Please continue," I said. "I am listening."

He looked doubtful but continued anyway.

"Well, the plot revolves around two strangers who meet up by chance."

"On a train I presume?"

"Shut up, David. As they talk, they discover that each of them has someone whom they'd like bumped off. Then one of them suggests they murder each other's problem people. As they explore the idea further, they realise they can arrange the timing of the killings so that the appropriate individual has a watertight alibi. Since they are 'strangers', no reasonable man would suppose they were in cahoots to carry out a double murder scheme. Indeed there would be nothing to connect them to each other at all."

"Ingenious, Jim, but where is this going?"

Jim pursed his lips in a thoughtful fashion. "It occurs to me, David, that most people would categorise us as acquaintances rather than friends. After all, we don't know each other that well, do we?"

"I suppose that's true."

"It would be better if we were complete strangers, but that is where fiction parts company with reality, I'm afraid. We have to work with what we have." Jim gave a deep sigh.

I picked up my whisky. "So what you're saying, Jim – if I've followed this correctly – is that you'd like me to kill your wife for you."

"You catch on fast." Jim knocked back his whisky and smiled at me.

"Presumably I would do this while you are out of the country on one of your business trips so that no suspicion falls on you."

He nodded before adding, "Whatever method you like, provided it's not mushroom poisoning. That would be a giveaway."

"And in return, you do what for me?"

"I kill your wife, of course."

"But I don't want Claire killed."

"Are you sure about that?"

"Quite sure, yes."

Jim scratched his chin. "Is there anybody else you'd like killed? Your wife would have been the obvious choice, but maybe there's somebody else I could take out for you."

I shook my head again.

"Oh, come *on*, David," said Jim with impatience, "you can't tell me there isn't *somebody*."

"Nobody springs to mind at present, I'm afraid." I downed my whisky.

"Well, that's disappointing."

"So how did the story end?"

"What?"

"The *Strangers on a Train* story."

"Oh, not so well." He sounded morose. "One of the guys thought the other wasn't serious, so it came as a shock when he found he had to deliver a corpse."

"He thought the other guy had been joking all along?"

"Yes."

"Hmmn. Tricky."

"Yes."

Jim drummed his fingers on the table, a faraway look in his eyes.

The Bell was starting to empty.

"You could always hire a hit man, Jim, if all else fails. Some of the places you travel to, I'm sure you could find a gun for hire."

"Without a doubt," he responded, although he didn't sound enthusiastic. "In Pakistan you could have someone disappear and still get change from fifty bucks. Although no gun would be involved. Bullets are too expensive, whereas knives are always available. The same goes for India, as a matter of fact."

"Sounds like a bargain. Even if you had to pay for their return flight to England."

Jim scrunched up his nose. "Naw, those guys operate on a strictly local basis. If I wanted the job done here I'd have to hire a real professional and they're expensive. Then you have all the aggravation of sorting out their payment in cash so that nothing can be traced through bank accounts. The money laundering regulations and the access that government and law-enforcement agencies have to your bank account records these days is shocking."

"Hard for an honest criminal to make a living, eh?" I observed, but Jim's attention was elsewhere. "Anyway, you seem to know a lot about this stuff."

He sniffed. "Maybe I just watch a lot of old films," was his response.

A POISON TREE

I waited for his face to break into a laugh and for him to tell me that he loved Monique and that he wouldn't want to harm a hair on her expensively-coiffured head, but he didn't. Instead he said, "I guess a hit man would be my last resort, but if you do change your mind about wanting your wife knocked off you will let me know, David, won't you?"

"Of course I will."

He fished a business card from his jacket pocket and handed it to me. It was white and embossed. There was no company logo. It read, *James Fosse, Consultant*, and under the name was a mobile number and an e-mail address. Anonymous and somewhat enigmatic – like the man himself.

We rose from the table and I waved goodnight to Ian who was standing behind the bar looking like his glass was half empty, as indeed it inevitably was. As usual he acknowledged the gesture with reluctance. What looked like a scowl illumined his wrinkled features. The term 'curmudgeon' might well have been coined for Ian Kenney, Proprietor and Licensee of The Bell.

As soon as the cold night air hit me I felt nausea rise in my throat and I was grateful that my front door was less than a ten-minute walk away, even after making an allowance for zig-zagging.

Jim was insistent that he did not need a taxi and was quite capable of getting himself home. There was little point in reasoning with him on the perils of driving while well over the legal limit. He struck me as a man who would have no truck with anything he regarded as petty bureaucracy.

I will say, though, that as his car left the pub car park and disappeared around the bend in the road, it didn't move like it was driven by a man who had consumed, by my count, six pints with whisky chasers. Any uninformed observer would have concluded the driver of the vehicle was rational, clear-headed and acutely aware of everything he was doing.

2

DAVID

There are days when I hate England.

Days when the sky is as grey as a corporate banker's hair; when the rain doesn't fall so much as float around in the air for days making everything damp and everyone miserable; when the pinched, mouldy faces of the children of Perfidious Albion depress my already waterlogged spirits.

On such days, my local city, Leicester, dons a cloak of sodden desperation. Its lowbrow centre, staked out by pawnbrokers, betting shops and discount stores, reeks of urban decline. Trudging through the drizzle, the locals look defeated. They clutch plastic shopping bags and drag their feet through the endless present towards a future which offers nothing different or exciting. Except maybe the release of yet another electronic gadget with even more unneeded features.

Leicester has never had much of a history – its main claim to fame being that Richard III was defeated nearby at Bosworth – yet it wears its current shabby incarnation with a degree of stubbornness.

In the 1970s and 1980s it seemed to me the city enjoyed a brief flowering, spurred on by the influx of immigrants from the Indian subcontinent and those fleeing persecution in East Africa. The new residents rejuvenated the place for a while, many bringing with them hard-headed business principles and a staunch work ethic of which the city's founding fathers would have approved. But after a while, even these new enthusiastic citizens succumbed to *Leicesteritis*, a degenerative condition which attacks the joy centres of the brain. There is only one cure: leave.

Some may say I am being unfair to dear old Leicester.

A POISON TREE

To those I say *bollocks*. Try living here for over a third of a century, then tell me how you feel about the place. I have earned my right to curse this nonentity of a Midlands city.

So why do I continue to live here?

Good question, you inquisitive bastard.

1999 did not start off as a noteworthy year, despite the surrounding media hype and the Millennium clock ticking down toward zero hour. For those of us in business we began fretting about the Millennium Bug, when the various computer software programmes that separated civilisation from anarchy might fail. More apocalyptically-minded souls started making plans to be at the rendezvous point for the alien spaceships that would take them to a new world; or to be atop a mountain for when the winds of the End of Days started to blow; or just to be pissed out of their brains in Trafalgar Square when the clocks chimed midnight.

January was, as ever, cold and miserable. I celebrated my forty-first birthday with my wife and daughter at an Indian restaurant on London Road. We were all clad in sweaters, while we munched down poppadoms, gosht dhansak lamb and vindaloo curries cooked with potatoes in hot, spicy sauces. We sat, shivering in spite of the food, surrounded by dark red pebble-dashed walls on which hung friezes of blue elephants and hunting parties. Sitar music played in the background while we and the other stalwart patrons determined we would enjoy ourselves through gritted – if not quite chattering – teeth. As is our custom we left a familial food mess on the yellow tablecloths, and smiling staff grateful for the big tip.

February was much the same; just another humdrum month in the life of David Braddock, Chief Executive Officer of Braddock Motors, a retail operation founded and still owned by my father.

A POISON TREE

My father. Edward Braddock. Ramrod-backed Englishman and former planter in post-war Malaya. Frightener of small children. Master of the cutting remark. Workaholic. Capitalist extraordinaire. Midas-touch investor. Interfering *eminence grise* in the affairs of the business whose running he had in theory delegated to me. And in February passing the sixty-nine year mark with no sign of either slowing down or becoming any closer to his only child. Age cannot wither him, it seems.

March opened with an uncomfortable meeting with the old man.

"The latest sales figures are far from impressive, David," he intoned from his leather chair in the Board Room. "That Vectra facelift and re-launch doesn't seem to have impressed many people. And I'm disappointed with how the new general manager is shaping up at the Coventry showroom."

"I'm driving over there to talk to Mark tomorrow."

"You should have done it sooner. He's far too hands-off. So are you, for that matter," he added as an acidic afterthought.

"Mark was *your* appointment, father, as I recall. Harry would have been my choice for general manager."

"Don't try to pass the buck, David. You are the CEO. I just make suggestions, which you are free to ignore. These matters are for you to decide on."

Yes, right. Like your suggestions are not meant to be taken as instructions.

As usual, I bit my tongue. I never win arguments with Edward Braddock, so there is no point in trying. I also found myself wondering for the millionth time how on earth my Thai stepmother, Nang, has managed to put up with the annoying goat for all these years, let alone love him – which she does, by the way. If I didn't owe her such a debt of gratitude for bringing me up after the premature death of my own mother in Malaya, I'd have severed ties with Braddock Senior long ago, job or no job.

"As for the sales figures, it's hard to sell new cars when half the planet thinks the world is ending in about ten months."

He snorted. "Nonsense, that's just an excuse. Whatever the newspapers might say, people are continuing to behave rationally, Millennium or no Millennium."

"*Rationally?* Do you know the bookies are taking bets on whether Armageddon will arrive at the end of December? You can get great odds. The only trouble is, you won't be around to collect your winnings. That's not stopping people from betting though. Rational behaviour, indeed."

Braddock Senior consulted his watch. "I have to go in about fifteen minutes. I have a meeting with Roger on this new property development in town."

Gratitude for small mercies.

"But I'd like to go through these sales figures in detail first."

After the old bugger had left, my PA Sandra brought me a coffee.

"It's a strong one," she said. "I thought you might need it."

"Sandra, if Claire ever runs off with her tennis coach, I'm going to marry you."

"I think my husband might have a view on that," she replied. "And I didn't know Claire had a tennis coach."

"She doesn't yet, so you've still got time to work on your husband. Start with small doses of rat poison in his food so he doesn't suspect anything."

"You are so un-PC, David."

"I try my best."

I sipped my coffee and thought about Jim Fosse and the bizarre evening I'd spent with him at The Bell the previous week. I suppose if I'd been on the ball, I could have offered my father as a candidate for a tit-for-tat murder. That would have been much more appropriate than ordering a hit on my wife.

A POISON TREE

Sunday afternoon, the hottest so far of the summer, and the village swelters under a cloudless sky. Even the thick walls of the old rectory cannot keep out the heat. From my study window I have an uninterrupted view of the surrounding fields and the Welland Valley beyond. It is a sight to calm and clear the mind, and one I have cherished since we set up home here some ten years ago. This green perspective wobbles and surges in the distant haze.

On my desk lie piles of work papers, unread. An intrusive fly buzzes aimlessly around the room before at last exiting through the open window. A trickle of sweat runs down my face, but I cannot summon the energy to wipe it away.

I can hear, though not see, Claire at work on the roses. Snatches of sentimental tunes float in from the garden. It is a huge garden, and it keeps our gardener well occupied, although Claire feels the need to 'help out' from time to time. I imagine her slim figure, dressed in white, crouched over her labours, her flame-red hair hidden from sight and bundled under the ridiculous soft hat she wears on such occasions.

At length the singing stops, and I hear her footsteps on the wooden floor. Her head appears around the door and, as expected, she is wearing the ugly hat.

"Are you still here?"

"Looks like it."

"You may as well put those papers away, it's far too hot to work."

"You seem to be managing."

"I've come in for some lemonade. Would you like some?"

"No thanks."

"I thought you were supposed to be playing golf with Max today."

16

"That's next Sunday. Assuming it's cooler. I'll fry on a golf course in this heat."

"Not if you take sensible precautions, darling. Listen, if you're not going to join me for lemonade, then take a walk down to the village, don't sit in here. And take a sun hat."

"Right."

"And you're picking up Katie from town later, remember."

"I know. I'm not wearing that loopy sun hat though."

"Do as you're told."

She vanishes in search of cold lemonade. I put on the loopy sun hat and set out into the glare.

Bewdon is a beautiful place, at least for me. Once the centre of a Saxon royal estate, and grouped around greens, the village is made up of timber-framed seventeenth-century houses, as well as brick houses of various shapes and sizes from the eighteenth and nineteenth centuries.

My family has a long association with the place. My great-great grandfather, William Ernest Braddock, provided the village with its first school in 1842. My great grandfather built various lodges in the village, all associated with hunting and horses, and came to be seen by many locals as the Squire. The next two generations continued to be associated with the good works of the village and with the local hunt, until the changing political climate made this latter association undesirable. It was only recently that my father sold his half-share in Bewdon's only pub, an oddly-angled pile of beams and brickwork, known with affection as The Bell, to which I now repair.

The interior is dark and dusty and, happily today, cool. It is also quiet. Two ancient locals nod to me as I make my way to the bar where the owner Ian, a man of few words, is fiddling with the music system.

"Fucked again," he mutters.

"Good day, Ian," I say. "A pint of your finest foaming ale, please."

"That's a bloody awful hat."

I take my pint and the hat to a table in the corner. Through the grimy window I can see the war memorial. The village looks deserted.

I feel calm now. Sometimes it is as if nothing has happened, as if things are as normal in reality as they seem to be on the surface. Some days, some hours, the whispered voices of betrayal are silent, and life goes on much as before. There are, however, the other times.

In my wallet, amongst the credit cards, notes and other detritus of affluent living, is a small, crumpled photograph of Claire, taken shortly after we met. I take it out and study it. She is standing by a narrow boat and the locks at Foxton are in the background. She looks relaxed, serene ...

A pint glass is plonked down on my table as Ian takes it upon himself to keep me company. I put away the photograph.

"I've become a Buddhist," he announces without preamble.

"Really?"

"Yes."

He looks at me in a challenging fashion, but doesn't seem inclined to elaborate further. Even the few words I've had out of him so far are more than he can usually muster by way of conversation. He takes a drink of beer and stares out of the window.

I persevere. "Why?"

"Why what?"

"Why have you become a Buddhist? I've never exactly seen you as the spiritual type, Ian."

"That's because you only look with your eyes."

"Is that you being all enigmatic and Zen?"

"Fuckin' right."

"I thought Anna looked strained over dinner," I said to Claire. "What did you think?"

"I think my sister has married an arsehole, that's what I think," she replied.

We were tidying up in the kitchen. Our guests had departed and for once we were not having a battle with Katie about her going to bed. With her exams only a few months away – and with so much riding on them – she was of late displaying adult tendencies.

"Does she talk to you about it?"

Claire sighed. "No. Anna is too loyal to Max to do that. It makes me sad. There was a time not so long ago when Anna and I used to share everything, but now she's withdrawn. She doesn't talk to Mum about it either, yet it's obvious to a blind man that she's unhappy."

"Do you think Max is playing around?"

"Of course he is. He's already got form on *that*. And he's the type to do it."

I stacked some plates in a cupboard while Claire wiped around the worktops.

"And what type is that, exactly."

"He's a *man*, darling."

"That's a bit harsh."

"Present company excepted, but most men are selfish bastards. I'm lucky I got a good one."

"Indeed you are."

It was after 2.00am when I could bear the tossing and turning no longer. I put on my dressing gown and went downstairs to the study. I thought perhaps sleep would come if I could release the pressure inside my head and set free the intrusive and repetitive sounds.

I sat at my desk, took up a pen and wrote.

A POISON TREE

I love to watch you sleeping, Claire. I love it when the night sky is cloudless and the moonlight falls across the graceful curve of your neck. Sometimes I brush away your long hair so I can look at the paleness, the opacity of your skin, and touch you gently with my lips.

You smile when you sleep. Have I ever told you that? I'm sure I must have. It is a smile of innocence, of inner beauty.

Even after twenty years together, I still have an ache in my heart when I look at you. Despite the difficulties of recent years, nothing has really changed between us, has it? I know for my part that there has never been anyone who can touch me so to the core the way you do. And I do not believe anyone would ever be able to take your place, should I lose you.

I hope I don't have to lose you.

I read the words two or three times, then I crumpled the paper into a ball and dropped it into the bin.

It is so difficult now to remember the precise order in which things happened. How life unravelled. The times, the dates.

There are occasions when I muse on Time's Arrow. Does it always move in the same direction? Or do our minds reassemble events into a sequence that makes sense, one that gives us some kind of life narrative to hold onto? For it is only if we perceive time as moving in a single direction that the concept of cause and effect makes any sense. Without this structure our actions would carry no moral significance. There would be no consequences, for consequences must follow an event, not precede it.

Without diurnal predictability we would have no gravity to our lives. Everything would float. The Hindu and Buddhist concepts of *karma* – action and its resultant impacts – would be shattered. All human relationships would fracture under the stress. To exist, we need to repeat. We need the comfort of familiarity, even if we may complain on occasion of the boredom of it all.

Time, blood and karma. Unless there is interconnectivity between the three, there is nothing to grasp. We are lost.

These fragments I have shored against my ruins.

T S Eliot knew a thing or two.

Why then Ile fit you

"Mark, we need to talk."

"I know, David," said the general manager of our Coventry showroom. "I've been expecting this discussion."

Mark Standish bowed his head forward and rubbed his hands together in a slow, deliberate fashion. He looked as dapper as he always did, but there was something rumpled about his spirit.

"You were one of our best salesmen, but recently it seems like you've lost all motivation. What's going on? Are you having trouble adjusting to the new role or is it family issues, or what? Talk to me."

"To tell you the truth, I don't know what it is. All my energy seems to have disappeared. I went to see my doctor the other day for a blood test. He thought it might be some viral thing."

"And?"

"I haven't had the test results back yet. They should be back tomorrow or the day after."

"I see."

"I'll turn this around, David, I promise. I realise I was not your first choice for this job, but I will show you I can do it."

I looked at his eager face. His words had a trace of bitterness about them, but not enough for me to challenge him on them. There was something frightened about his demeanour, and I didn't think it was my presence that was causing it. I doubted Mark was being completely transparent with me – his lack of eye contact testified to that – but there seemed little point in pursuing the matter further at present.

"You need to talk to your team, Mark. They're concerned about you. Harry even phoned me."

"I will."

"And let me know the results of your tests. If you need to take some time off, we'll organise something. We can be discreet about it. Just talk to me, for Christ's sake."

I went into the main showroom in search of Harry Dempsey. It was quiet and I found him in one of the side offices flicking through the sports pages of the *Sun*. He was wearing one of his trademark check jackets which gave him the air of a bookie's runner. This was rather appropriate considering the time and money he spent in betting shops.

"Have you talked to Mark?" he asked without preamble.

"Yes."

"I'm not trying to sabotage him, you know, David. I don't play politics. I'm just concerned." His slight lisp made it sound like *thabotage*.

"I know. He needs your support, Harry."

Since Mark had picked up the general manager's job, Harry's attitude to me had cooled. He had believed he was in pole position to take over as the boss on George's retirement, and I guess I had encouraged this belief. I suspected he had not yet forgiven me for what must have been a big blow to his ego. It was to his credit that at least in public he was showing solidarity with management.

Harry examined the oversize gold ring on his left hand. "Did he tell you he's moved out? He and Janine have separated."

Theparated.

"No, he didn't. Did he tell you?"

"No. I heard through a mutual friend. He hasn't mentioned a thing to anyone here. I've kept quiet about it. No good would come from everyone here talking about the boss' private life. I thought I'd better tell you, though."

Hathen't. Botheth. I have to stop fixating on his *thpeech* impediment.

We had a cordial – if slightly strained – exchange. Some of the old Harry reasserted itself towards the end and he offered me a couple of betting tips before I took my leave.

As I made my way out of the main door, I glanced at one of the large showroom mirrors and caught sight of Mark watching me go. His look was the sort you would give an enemy when you think he can't see you.

But perhaps that was just my guilty conscience giving me a poke.

I reached into my study bin and lifted out a scrunched-up ball of writing paper. I smoothed it out on the desktop. It read:

Claire

These days I find it hard to speak to you and I know you find it hard to speak to me – about the things that matter anyway. On the surface we are happy, but there is a deep malaise burrowing its way into us. And it has been this way for a couple of years now. We need to talk, but I don't know how to begin.

I love you very much and I don't want to lose you.

This I know I have told you, hundreds of times. But when I have spoken in the past, what I had in mind was losing you to accident or illness, not to some other cause. I never imagined you running off with someone else or my killing you.

A POISON TREE

I tapped my pen on the desk a few times. Then I tore up the paper until not a word was readable.

This is not working.

I need to be more organised or I will never sort this out.

Deep breath. Recommence. Expound.

3

DAVID

The Monday following my trip to the Coventry showroom found me in my office having a lunchtime sandwich and drinking my third coffee of the day. I was taking a break from reviewing the pricing of a proposal to one of our customers, with whom I had a meeting that afternoon. Leicester Wheels Auto Limited was not a major client, but they did buy four or five cars a year from us and the owner, Mat Hoggard, was a personal friend of mine whom I'd met through the local Chamber of Commerce. So I wanted to make sure the proposal was right.

A copy of *Madame Bovary* was open on my desk. Like most of my reading it had been recommended to me by my sister-in-law, Anna. Years before she had taken it upon herself to give me a literary education, and to my surprise I had become a voracious consumer of Russian and European novels, philosophical works and, God help me, poetry. If my former rugby-playing friends had been aware of my guilty weakness for books, they would without doubt have felt inclined to squeeze my privates in the scrum by way of a warning. At least my PA was diplomatic enough not to mention it when she found this sort of material concealed among my paperwork. It must be like finding your boss is downloading porn. Only worse.

Outside my office window the depressing vista of Frog Island stretched into the middle distance. Unlike our Leicester showroom, our HQ was not in one of the more fashionable areas of the city. Like many gold mines, our profitable business concealed itself behind a corporate façade of dirt. The God of Fiscal Prudence had sited us in a road comprising old red brick buildings many of which – like ours – sported small factory windows, the ground floor ones covered with security grills. Sad, tired hoardings advertising insurance and discount retailers clustered around the dusty structures. Some old chimneys, relics of a bygone age of manufacturing, still peppered the skyline.

Behold ye the land of cheap exhausts, tyre-changing ramps, blackened welding shops, and undercapitalised garages mutating slowly into car washes.

Directly opposite us was a shop whose sign declared *We Won't Be Beaten on Price*. It was boarded up. Obviously something else had beaten them. Life, maybe.

Ah, Leicester, *mon amour*.

My cell phone rang. Katie had put an annoying ringtone on it which sounded a bit like 'The Birdie Song', and which I had been unable to change thus far.

I picked it up. It was not a number I recognised.

"David Braddock."

The phone hissed for a couple of seconds and then a robotic voice said, "Hello, David."

"Who is this?"

"A friend."

"A friend wouldn't talk through a voice synthesiser."

There was a chuckle at the other end of the phone.

"A friend," the voice repeated.

"Whoever you are, I don't know how you got this number but I'm hanging up now."

"Not a good idea, David."

I hit the off button. If this was a practical joke, the caller would in likelihood ring back and talk to me properly. Or so I reasoned. I had had a couple of crank calls before – in business this was an occupational hazard – but never one that deployed technology to disguise the voice.

A POISON TREE

The phone rang again.

I pressed the answer button but said nothing.

"Your wife, Claire," the voice said, then paused.

I still said nothing.

"Unfaithful. Unfaithful Claire. You might want to look into it."

"Fuck off, whoever this is."

"Cheating wife. Not good. I am your friend, David. You can bet money on it."

The caller hung up.

I called back the number but got a message that the phone was switched off.

At that moment, Sandra put her head around my door.

"Would you like another coffee, David?"

She looked at me with concern.

"Are you all right? You look like you've seen a ghost."

"I'm OK. It feels a bit stuffy in here. I'm just going out for some fresh air for ten minutes."

"Fresh air around here? You'll be lucky."

I left the office and walked the hundred metres to the nearest convenience store, where I did something I hadn't done in fifteen years.

I bought a pack of Marlboro cigarettes and smoked one.

Over the next few days I rang the cell number of my mysterious caller at various times of the day and night. It was always the same message: phone switched off. I surmised the number was on a Pay-As-You-Go SIM card, a more convenient option than a public phone for weirdoes and stalkers. Untraceable. Cheap. The weapon of choice for the malicious of spirit.

I was beginning to dismiss the episode as a crank occurrence. The pack of Marlboros sitting in my desk drawer was still only missing one cigarette.

A POISON TREE

Then the letter arrived.

It was delivered to the office and labelled *Strictly Private and Confidential, Only for the Attention of David Braddock, CEO.*

Inside the envelope was a single sheet of paper which read

CLAIRE BRADDOCK IS AN UNFAITHFUL BITCH. SHE IS PLAYING YOU.

The words were made of letters cut from newspapers – tabloid ones by the looks of them – and glued onto the paper. The paper itself was an unremarkable sheet of A4 and the envelope was similarly nondescript. I looked for further clues. The address was on a sticky label, typed with word processing software. The postmark was Leicester.

I considered calling an old public school chum of mine who was in the police force and with whom I was still in touch. There may be fingerprint or DNA evidence on the envelope and the letter. The perpetrator may have licked the stamp or the gummed flap of the envelope.

I dismissed the idea immediately.

Bringing in the police would in all probability make the matter public. Furthermore, the envelope would have been handled by at least two people in my office, including Sandra. The Boys in Blue would therefore want to take fingerprints from all the office staff. And I would have to tell Claire what was going on …

No.

I needed to reason this out for myself. Forget the physical paper evidence. There was little I could glean from that. My focus should be on the motive of the letter-writer.

Someone hated me enough to take all this trouble to make me feel bad. All I had to do was figure out who. Either that, or do the sensible thing and ignore the whole charade.

A POISON TREE

I put the letter in a plastic wallet and locked it away for possible future study. A calm head was needed and my head was far from calm.

I took the Marlboros from the drawer and told Sandra I was going out for a while.

Claire was late home that evening. She'd been at a business dinner for Jael Construction, the company where she was the Chief Finance Officer.

"Sorry I'm so late, darling," she said.

"Did you get carried away discussing the latest International Financial Reporting Standards with the other bean counters? I can see how the time would fly by."

She kissed me on the forehead before looking at me with a quizzical expression.

"Have you been smoking?" she asked. "You smell of smoke."

"I nipped out to the Bell for a pint earlier. I sat outside and got chatting to some guy who was chain-smoking. I'd guess it's his cigarettes you can smell."

"You sat outside in this weather? You must be mad."

"I am mad. You know that."

"Has Katie done her business studies homework?"

"Yes, all done. I could hear Puff Daddy coming through the floor a while back, but it's gone quiet now. I haven't checked on her, but she's probably asleep." I consulted my watch. "Christ, it's twelve thirty. You *are* late."

"Do you want a drink before we turn in?"

"No, I'm good."

Claire examined me closely. "Are you all right, David? You seem a bit funny."

"Only a *bit* funny? I must be losing my touch. I used to be hilarious."

"I'm serious."

29

I gave a deep sigh to make the lie more convincing. "Bad day at work. We almost lost a big contract at the Coventry branch. I had to get involved."

"Is there still a problem with Mark? You said something a week or so back about him having a health problem?"

"No, he's OK. His blood tests were fine. I'm not sure what the problem is. Maybe it's just stress."

"He doesn't have your resilience, my darling."

"Or my happy home life, eh?"

"Obviously not. He doesn't have me."

"This is the manuscript I wanted you to have a look at," said Anna.

She handed me a sheaf of papers.

"It doesn't look like a very long book," I replied.

"I haven't given you the whole book, silly, just the opening chapters. Do you want a cappuccino?"

"Well, they'll throw us out of the coffee shop if we don't order something soon. I still don't see why you want me to read it, though. You're the literary agent."

"I wanted a second opinion before I talk to my colleagues. You have a good eye. Especially since I've been supervising your education in literary matters."

"You mean I have the same tastes in writing as you do, since you've brainwashed me."

"Now don't spoil it. It's not often I get to have a private chat with my brother-in-law these days. Shut up. I'll get our coffees and maybe a couple of naughty cakes."

While she went to the counter, I looked at the first pages of *Quiet Betrayal*.

A POISON TREE

April is not the cruellest month, Eliot got it wrong. For me it is June.

June was the month I found out. What I found out was that I was a – and even now the quaintness of the word makes me grin – cuckold. Cuck-old. A ridiculous word for a ridiculous situation, is it not? Particularly given that the man in question is almost old enough to be Emma's father. Or mine, for that matter.

My finding out was not the work of a moment. I did not stumble on them in an act of passion, did not intercept some love missive, was not informed of the affair by the other man's distraught wife. Neither was I told by my own wife. Rather it was a slow dawning, an accretion of circumstances, of small details which, finally I could not ignore. I realise now, of course, that I had been ignoring the signs, perhaps deliberately or perhaps in genuine innocence. But the affair had been going on for quite some time, over a year. In all that time Emma had protested their friendship was nothing more than that, that they were close because they were working together, that others' voiced suspicions were 'disgusting' given Aidan's age.

So I suppressed any half-formed doubts, put aside any unreasonable jealousy and thought no more of it, for a while.

Their closeness was, however, very public. At social gatherings, they were often together, as would befit work comrades. Laughing, flirting and often excluding others from their close circle, they made a sparking couple, and at times I felt glances of sympathy in my direction from our more worldly acquaintances. To these I paid no attention. These people did not understand my wife as I did. She was unusual, outgoing and bubbly, and she loved me. I was the man she came home to after her days and evenings out. And we slept together naked, as we had done for twenty years.

Such was the nature of my blindness.

A POISON TREE

Anna had returned with the drinks. There was a degree of intensity in her look. And perhaps something more.

"What do you think?"

"Speaking as a car salesman, I'd say the writing is a bit flowery and overdone. Does he keep this up for the whole novel?"

"It's not a novel," she replied. "It's a memoir."

"Anyone I know?"

"No. Do you think Claire would like it?"

I took a sip of coffee. "She's not big on romance these days, Anna."

Anna put a hand on my arm.

"Not many people are, David," she said.

4

DAVID

Piece by piece, we remember. Our youth. Our life. The things that made us.

The poet's heap of broken images. How it began.

Ah, yes. That bittersweet indulgence of memory.

Claire.

Claire – or Claire Elizabeth, to be more accurate – is the younger of the Holland sisters by a year. Her sister Anna, in fact, was my initial acquaintance in that family.

Anna and I were both twenty at the time we first met. I had just flunked out of university, much to my father's disgust, and was taking a few summer months off before joining the family firm and beginning my climb up the greasy pole of business. Anna was part-way through an English Literature degree at a redbrick university, and likely to graduate with an upper second, at least.

The Holland family were farmers from just outside Market Harborough, and were pillars of the local community. It was a matter of some chagrin to Richard and Natalie that their elder daughter had embraced vegetarianism and had, on one occasion, threatened to boycott the hunt ball which they were attending to air her feelings on the topic of fox-hunting. She was not, however, rebellious by nature – or at least no more so than any other teenager – and by the time I got to know her she had mellowed into a kind and generous-spirited young woman.

And she had style and grace about her. Her skin was pale, almost translucent. Her face was pretty rather than beautiful, with a Celtic feel to it.

But her most noticeable feature, and one she shared with her mother and sister, was a mane of fiery red hair which spilled across her shoulders and down her back.

Anna's temperament was far from fiery. I found her shy and oddly lacking in self-confidence. Later I was to discover this was the effect of being overshadowed by both an independent, outgoing and popular sister, and a forceful and flirtatious (and, it must be said, still attractive and desirable) mother. Natalie Holland would come on to me outrageously whenever I dropped by the farm, and reduce me to a stammering and crimson-faced juvenile until, finally, she would relent with a giggle, and leave me to recover my fractured dignity as best I could.

Anna's disposition, I think was more akin to that of her father Frank, a sensitive and reflective man of plump stature and ruddy complexion, who bore his wife's extrovert behaviour with resignation.

"What's it like being a vegetarian?" I asked Anna.

"I don't know," she answered. "What's it like being a carnivore?"

"An omnivore," I corrected her. "I eat anything."

"So I noticed at the buffet," she said, smiling.

We were leaning against a fence, enjoying the cool late-evening air. The barn dance was still in full swing, but we had stepped outside for a temporary respite from the caller's relentless insistence that we 'dance and enjoy, dance and enjoy'.

"I can only stand so much enjoyment before my ears start to bleed," Anna had announced.

"Seeing that your parents are lending their barn to host this cornucopia of the senses," I ventured, "I should have thought you'd have worn your perforated eardrums as a badge of honour."

In reality, my attendance at this event was something of a fluke. I was chaperoning Sally Glenister, a neighbour's daughter, who had taken a shine to a visiting Australian country-dance fan by the name of Shane. Sally, needless to say, had no intention of being chaperoned, and she and Shane spent the evening in each other's company, no doubt tentatively exploring her plans for becoming Mrs. Shane Brough: plans which, in the event, would be brought to fruition within a few years.

This left me at a loose end for the evening. Fortunately for me, Anna Holland was also at a loose end, and proceeded to befriend this stray puppy from the other side of town.

And so we became friends. Over that hot and endless summer of glorious irresponsibility, we walked the country pathways of Leicestershire and picnicked and enjoyed an ease with each other, the like of which I have not experienced before or since. The issue of romance between us never surfaced. To have even contemplated such a thought would have been to sully something fine, a noble friendship.

"Tell me, David," she said on one outing, "what are you going to do with your life?"

"Apart from running a hospital in the slums of Calcutta, you mean?"

"I'm serious." She pulled a grape from the picnic basket and threw it at me.

"Find a good woman and settle down, I suppose." I sipped at my wine. "And you?"

"Find a bad man and do the same."

I squeezed her hand, and she rested her head on my shoulder. We sat together a while against the tree, and watched in the distance the slow grind of overheated traffic through the valley. After a while she fell asleep, and a little later so did I.

Claire arrived back in the country towards the end of September, shortly before Anna was to resume her studies.

A POISON TREE

She had taken a year out after her A-levels, to travel around Australia. I recollect being in awe of someone who, at eighteen, had packed a bag and, with only a few hundred pounds in her pocket, and a promise of initial lodgings with an émigré uncle, had jumped on a plane heading east.

I can still remember my first sight of Claire.

She was sitting at the kitchen table of the Hollands' farmhouse. It was early evening and I had called round to see Anna on some errand or other. The easy familiarity I had attained over that summer, and the Hollands' welcoming generosity of spirit had accustomed me to wandering around the farm like one of the family. And so it was that I blundered in, without knocking, on Claire's homecoming.

The sunlight was slanting through the window behind her, giving her hair a luminescence like fire. Her full lips were slightly parted in mid-sentence, and her green eyes looked up in surprise at my entrance. Natalie, Frank, Anna and the two Labradors also turned to stare at me. Seeing my face beginning to redden with embarrassment, Natalie leapt in and made the introductions.

Smiling with mischief at my discomfort – as her mother had before on several occasions – Claire extended her right hand while her left hand swept back her long hair that had fallen across her face.

"Pleased to meet you, David," she parted those feminine lips revealing even, white teeth. "Anna has told me so much about you."

"Nothing good, I hope."

"Oh, no. Nothing good."

I joined them at the table while Claire recounted some of her adventures.

I hardly listened. I was too captivated by the physical aspects of the woman to concentrate on her words, try as I might.

Superficially, she was not dissimilar in appearance to Anna, although her figure and limbs were more willowy. Her face was somewhat longer than

Anna's, and she had Natalie's high cheekbones. The greenness of her eyes had a penetrating quality, and they sparkled with that sense of assurance her elder sister lacked.

Chemistry, I thought. *There is some chemistry at work here.*

Claire had flown out to Melbourne the previous autumn – she recapped for me at a later date – to stay with one of Natalie's brothers. Then, buying a Greyhound bus pass, she had visited Adelaide, Ayers Rock, Cairns, then went on to Sydney via Brisbane. In Sydney she had washed up in a youth hostel in the Kings Cross area. By this stage her money was fast running out, and she took a job house-sitting in Rose Bay. When that ended, she worked for a month in a sandwich bar before the agency she had registered with placed her as a nanny to a wealthy solicitor's three children in a large house on the North Shore. There, she had had a basement flat that she shared with a few lizards. After six months as a nanny, she had flown home via Singapore, where she stayed for a week and blew what small savings she had accumulated during her time with the lizards. She arrived back in England broke, breezy and ready for whatever life next threw at her.

It turned out to be me.

With Claire's homecoming, I felt Anna begin to fade into the background. It was as if, in some strange way, the whole family had been marking time, doing their best to fill some void in the house. Now that Claire was back, everyone could resume their normal roles, and in Anna's case this meant withdrawing into herself. For those last few days before she left for university she became diffident and shy with me. She showed no signs of resenting her sister's return, despite the attention her parents showered on the returning prodigal. On the contrary, she was at pains to make Claire feel welcome, and gave her the sort of attention she had been giving me over the summer.

Although this gave me a pang of sadness, I could not complain. It must have been obvious from an early stage that I was fascinated by Claire. What was not so obvious was why Claire should be attracted to me. Though I had an athletic build, and was fairly fit – thanks to playing regular rugby – I would not have described myself as handsome. Rugged looking, more like. I suppose I was from good local stock, and expected to inherit the family businesses, but Claire did not strike me as someone who would choose her man based on the size of his bank account.

"Why don't you ask her out?" Anna asked.

"What?"

"Why don't you just ask her out?"

"Who?"

"Oh, David," she sighed, "don't be so stupid."

"Ah." I could feel my face heating up with embarrassment.

It was our last picnic of the summer. We were sitting at the spot where we'd both fallen asleep some weeks earlier. The day was not so warm and sunny, but we'd decided to make the trip regardless.

"It is quite all right," she said with kindness, touching my hand.

"I've been dreading having this conversation."

"Why?"

"And yet –"

"You wanted to tidy things up before I went away."

"Yes."

"You're a nice man, David, a kind man. That's quite rare."

"Is it?"

She smiled. "Sisters talk, you know. Especially sisters like Claire and me. We're very close. Quite dissimilar in lots of ways – apart from the hair, of course – but we do understand one another. That same evening she met you, we had a little heart-to-heart. She asked me what the arrangement was between you and me. Didn't express any interest in you herself, not straightaway, that wouldn't have been appropriate. If I had told her we were an item, she'd have left you alone."

"She has left me alone."

"Yes." She bit into a crunchy red apple, and some of the juice ran down her chin. I handed her a napkin.

"So what did you tell her?"

"I told her that we were good friends –"

"Which we are."

"– but that was all."

We sat silent for a few minutes. I felt there was something I should say, but could not for the life of me think what it was.

At length, I said, "Are you disappointed?"

She looked at me. "About what, for goodness' sake?"

"Oh, I don't know. About the fact that I haven't made a pass at you all summer, and that I fancy your sister something rotten. Most women would be rather pissed off about that, I'd have thought."

She laughed. "Dear David, I hope we will always be friends." She kissed me on the cheek.

I continued to look at her.

"What?" she said. "What? Have I got something stuck on my teeth? What?"

"I'm waiting," I said.

"For what? I'm not kissing you again. That was a one-off."

"I want to know whether Claire fancies me."

"Why shouldn't she?"

"Well *you* don't."

She punched my shoulder. "Do your own dirty work," she said. "Now pass the wine over here."

I passed the wine. She looked relieved that we'd had the conversation, and seemed a little more like the Anna I'd first met.

I had the delicacy to wait until Anna had been back at university for two weeks before asking Claire out.

The summer by then was well and truly over.

I had begun my apprenticeship in one of the family businesses, the Braddock car dealership. I was to start at the Northampton branch, then move on to Nottingham, and finally Leicester, which was also Head Office to the property and textiles businesses.

The Braddock dynasty had begun in land ownership and shoe manufacturing during the last century, before diversifying. The shoe business itself had been sold off to a conglomerate at a handsome price during the 1960s and the proceeds reinvested, mainly in property. My father, Edward Braddock, thus came from a long line of shrewd Midlands businessmen, and he had his fingers in several local pies. He had spent the late 1940s, 1950s and early 1960s as a plantation owner in Malaya, where I was born and where my mother died. He had remarried shortly after her death. My Thai stepmother, Nang, was the one who effectively raised me. In 1964, we returned to England where my father started up a number of companies and continued to build his gold pile. He also bought a part share in a golf club just outside Marbella, and picked up a non-executive directorship on the Board of a minor quoted company. He believed all our businesses needed to pay their way. The only sentimental investment he ever made was in The Bell at Bewdon, a tribute perhaps to the many happy years that he and my stepmother had spent in the village.

A POISON TREE

A fervent believer in the Protestant work ethic, Edward Braddock was also determined that his only son was not to become a wastrel. My dropping out of university had alerted him to this possibility, and so he resolved without further ado to bring my nose into contact with the grindstone.

"You've had your last summer without responsibility, David," he had said. "It's time for you to take your place in the world. Go out and get yourself a decent haircut. You start work on Monday."

And so I joined the family firm.

Claire's plans, meantime, had altered. The intention had been that following her year in Australia she would take up a place reading mathematics at Durham University, after which she would move into finance. In the event, she decided to forego the degree and, drawing on her family's contacts, secured a position as an articled clerk in a firm of Chartered Accountants in Leicester.

We both therefore had a foot on the bottom rung of the career ladder at the time of our first evening out together, which comprised dinner at an Italian restaurant I knew in Market Harborough. A safe venue, I thought, not wishing to rush things lest I mess up. I still felt uneasy too, for reasons I could not articulate, about the fact that Claire was Anna's sister.

"I don't see you as a Chartered Accountant, Claire. I'm sorry, but I just don't. After Monty Python, it's impossible to take the profession seriously."

"The starting pay is pathetic," she told me, "but in four years I'll be qualified, then look out world."

"Yes, then you can be a lion tamer."

"At least I won't be selling second hand cars."

"O-o-o-h, catty. Anyway, they're *new* cars."

She laughed, and her eyes flashed green naughtiness. "So tell me, what went wrong with you and university."

"The same as with you and university, I expect. We weren't suited. Only you had the good sense to recognise it early."

"Travelling around Australia made me want to start making my way in the world. I don't want to give up studying and go off and become a hippy, or anything like that. I just want to start earning, give myself some independence."

"Studying to be an accountant in Leicester sounds pretty unglamorous after what you've been doing for the last year."

"Glamour isn't everything."

"I suppose you met some interesting people out there."

"Are you fishing?"

"No, just – making conversation."

She looked disbelievingly at me. "Well, yes. Especially at the hostel in Sydney. Americans, Irish, French, Canadians, and Brits, of course. Plus one guy whose family were farmers in Harare. He was gorgeous, like a young Robert Redford."

"A black Robert Redford?"

"*White* farmers. Do you have a problem with colour?" Her eyes narrowed.

"Not at all. One of my best friends at university was coloured."

"*Was.* You mean he isn't now?"

"All right, then. *Is* coloured."

"Right."

The meal arrived, and we sat in silence for a moment while the waiter topped up our wine glasses.

"So what happened to him?" I asked eventually. "Robert Redford?"

"I don't know. He and his girlfriend didn't stay long in Sydney."

"Oh, right," I said, attempting to sound casual.

She put her hand on to my forearm and squeezed it. "You're so sweet, David. Anna was right."

"Does she think I'm sweet, then?"

"No. She just thought I'd find you sweet. And she was right."

I took her hand.

"And," she went on, "I hope you're not going off to the slums of Calcutta for a while yet."

"Anna told you that!" I laughed.

"But of course. We're sisters. We tell each other everything."

"Now I do feel uncomfortable."

"Don't. There's no need. You haven't done anything you shouldn't have. Everything's fine."

"Good. I'm relieved about that."

Autumn slid into winter. Grey short days replaced grey longer days. The wet leaves fell and turned to mulch, and the Leicestershire countryside absorbed the chilling rain like a sponge.

Claire and I had some outings, on those rare dry occasions in among the days of dampness. We drove over to Warwick Castle and to Stratford. We visited the ten locks at Foxton, that marvel of nineteenth century engineering, which links the Leicestershire and Northamptonshire Union Canal with the Old Grand Union Canal. It was there that I took that first photograph of her which was to sit in my wallet for twenty years.

I do not know exactly when it was that I fell in love with her. The chronology has since perplexed me. Is there a moment, a second of refulgent time when you cross over to an altogether different existence; when something of strangeness and beauty enters your soul? I suppose there must be such an instant. Extraordinary then, that I did not mark it with some substantial entry in the diary of my life.

Perhaps I did not because my mind was distracted by an even greater enigma: Claire's affection for me. If loving was, for me, a blessing, then being loved was by degrees miraculous.

It may be, I muse now as I reflected then, the guilty secret of humankind is not that the heart hides so much darkness, but that it conceals so much light.

My old battered MG was parked in a country lay-by. I had badly miscalculated the weather, believing the early clouds would disperse. They had not. We sat listening to the machine-gun noises of torrential rain on the soft roof, and watched the deluge spattering and pouring down the windscreen in endless procession. It was too dangerous to drive. The wipers could not keep up with the cascade.

"I don't understand," I had said.

"What is there to understand?"

"You."

"Oh, I'm very simple to understand. What you see is what you get."

"Why me?"

"You just want me to tell you how wonderful you are, right?"

"I'm serious."

"Yes," her voice took on an earnest quality. "I can see that you are."

She looked away from me, into the rain-drenched middle distance and her eyes became unfocused.

"You could have a more exciting life than the one I'm offering you," I ventured.

"Are you offering me a life with you? You've known me less than three months," she said softly.

"You know I am."

"We haven't even made love yet."

"Bless you for that *yet*."

"I'm not a virgin, David."

"Thank goodness for that. I wouldn't want the responsibility."

She giggled, "Of breaking me in, you mean?"

"Exactly. And by the way I'm not either."

"You seem to think it's important to me that life is full of thrills and spills, that my chosen partner should be big, bad and dangerous to know. Why, David?"

I made a vague gesture.

"Why wouldn't I want a kind man who loves me, and who would take care of me. A gentle, honest man. A man like you."

"Claire –"

"It so happens that I love you, David Braddock. I love the way you treat me, the way you treat everyone. I love your optimism and your humility. I love the fact that for you the cup is always half-full, and that tomorrow the sun will come out; that in spite of all the evidence around you to the contrary you still think people are basically good; that you will always give someone a second chance. And we all need that at some time. We all need a second chance." She turned back to me. "Are they good enough reasons for you?"

In December the real winter began. The temperature plummeted, and all at once nothing was wet any more. Everything was frozen. Then the snow came: great soft white fluttering doves of cleansing cold. Ever since I was a child I have loved snow. It has seemed to me a conception of purity made tangible; a benevolent covering of grace across the landscape, embracing fields, trees and houses, and creating a kind of oneness.

A POISON TREE

The snow lay deep and a night wind, since departed, had piled up the crystallised whiteness into wonderful deep drifts, the first time that Claire and I made love.

We had taken a brave, or perhaps foolhardy, stroll around the farm and arrived back at the outbuildings as darkness was falling. The crisp snow crunched beneath our feet, the only sound not muffled to nothingness by the cocooning air. Our breath hung before our eyes as the lights of the farmhouse glowed ahead, offering a promise of warmth.

"Are you ready for company yet?" Claire asked.

"Am I what?"

She stopped walking and lowered her eyes for a moment, as if gathering her thoughts. Then she lifted her head, removed the glove from her right hand and touched my face.

I led her into the barn, or perhaps she led me. Either way, we knew in that moment that it was time, that we had reached a threshold from which neither of us felt inclined to turn and retrace our steps. And there, among the straw and the coldness which neither of us felt, semi-clothed, urgent and careless of discovery, our breaths a conjoined, freezing vapour, we made love to the music of silence. And afterwards, cooling, the steam rising from our bodies after that joyful release, we lay hand in hand, my lips on her brow as if in benediction.

At length, I propped myself on my elbow and stroked a stray lock of hair from her face. Her eyes held mine.

"Like the animals, eh?" I said.

"No, darling," she replied seriously, "like the angels."

Then she laughed.

Looking back, that was the first time in my life I was truly afraid. Not of commitment, or of responsibility, or even of disappointment. I had known worries, the insecurities of childhood, and the strange, sometimes neurotic concerns of the teenage years. I had known the sadness and loneliness of one that loses his mother to the unfathomable brutality of death. But this was my first experience of adult helplessness. For in that instant of love I knew both the strength and the weakness that apprehension draws from the human heart.

To find love is to grow strong, but it is also to know fear. To fear the loss of what you have found.

5

ANNA

There were days Anna Harper wished she were still Anna Holland. Today was one of those days.

Emptying the laundry basket, she had gone through the pockets of her husband Max's jeans and found a scrap of paper containing the words, *Call me baby xxx muah!*

Either Max was once more becoming careless about his liaisons or he no longer cared whether Anna found out. She didn't know which was worse.

Eight years of marriage and nothing had changed.

Anna had known Max was a womaniser before she married him, but like many women before her, she had been caught up in the passion and the romance of the moment. She had managed to convince herself that he would calm down; that the act of eating wedding cake would somehow alter his brain chemistry and convert him into a loving, faithful partner.

It took less than two years for her to be disabused of this notion when Max's affair with a married woman had turned toxic. The woman in question had taken umbrage at being discarded by Max and, at the expense of her own failing marriage, decided to go public. She had even turned up on two occasions on Anna's doorstep and proceeded to rant at her. A restraining order became necessary when the unhinged behaviour continued.

Max had promised Anna it was an aberration, and even he, self-confident though he was, had been shaken by the experience.

Things settled down and Anna swallowed her pride and decided to give her marriage another chance.

A POISON TREE

It was not long, though, before Max's eye began to rove once more. His work as a management consultant required frequent business trips out of town, so the opportunities for infidelity were many and varied.

After a while, Anna became weary of it all. She knew she should leave Max, but the shame and humiliation of her situation wore her down. She found she couldn't bring herself to discuss her marriage with her parents or her sister. It became a conversational no-go area.

Thank God, she reflected, that no children had come along. Though she would have liked a child, Anna could see that might be the final nail in the coffin of her relationship. Max was not equipped to be a father. Although he had paid lip-service to having children in the early years, those discussions – like so many others about the future – had petered out.

Inconclusive.

Like so much about her life.

Recently, and in a last-ditch effort to bring Max back into the family fold, Anna had asked her brother-in-law David to play golf with him – which he now did at least once a month, although Anna knew David was at best a lukewarm fan of golf and no great friend of her husband. But he went through the ritual for Anna's sake.

Why couldn't Max be more like David?

Anna put the washing into the machine and switched it on.

She sat at the kitchen table and allowed her thoughts to linger on her brother-in-law. Anna had recently asked him to give her his opinion on an unpublished work about infidelity. She couldn't explain to herself why she had done that and the more she considered it, the less appropriate it seemed. She rationalised that David had always been there for her as a good friend, so it was all right to meet an old friend and family member for a private lunch or coffee now and again. Wasn't it?

Infidelity.

A POISON TREE

It was everywhere about her. Two couples she knew well had recently split up over extra-marital affairs. Perhaps it was something to do with the Millennium, a feeling that everything was changing, that a new order was coming, that old allegiances and certainties were being blown away. Then again, maybe it was simply an excuse for bad behaviour.

She took a letter from one of the drawers in the kitchen cabinet and opened it. It was an unsolicited job offer from Bright Sparks Publishing. Impressed with her work, they wanted her to go to London and take up a position with them.

Anna walked through the apartment and stood out on the balcony that looked out over green fields and a branch of the Grand Union Canal. The day was overcast, but even after two years there, she still loved the view, grey clouds or not. The fields brought back the feeling of her happy childhood on her parents' farm. At Max's insistence they had taken the penthouse although it was bigger than they needed, and it had been expensive. But then, what else were they going to spend their money on?

She pushed back her red hair and looked at the letter again. If she took the job she would be ending her marriage at the same time. That worried her less than leaving her parents and sister, who had been her support over the years. But worse than missing them, she would miss seeing her brother-in-law.

And there was something not right about that.

6

CLAIRE

"Oh, I forgot to tell you. I got an A+ for my last business studies essay," announced Katie Braddock.

"Well done, sweetheart," replied her mother.

"I think it's because Mr. Jennings fancies me."

"What?"

"Well, that's not the only reason. It's mainly because I'm brilliant. But I think he fancies me too. I catch him looking at me in class."

"Are you serious, Catherine? Because if so –"

"Mum, chill out. So what if I have to run my tongue over my lips and flash him a bit of cleavage now and again? Like Dad says, *Focus on the result not the process.*"

Claire looked at her daughter with suspicion.

"You *are* winding me up, aren't you?"

Katie threw her arms around her mother's neck and giggled.

"Just a little bit. Mum, you are sooooo easy."

"You're just like your father," she sighed.

"Now you're just being nasty. Anyway, I did use one of Dad's lines in my essay."

"Which particular pearl of wisdom would that be?"

"The one about the difference between capitalism and communism?"

"Enlighten me."

"The difference is that with capitalism man exploits man, whereas with communism it's the other way round."

"I am so glad your expensive education hasn't been wasted."

A POISON TREE

"When I'm a lawyer my clients are going to *love* this sort of stuff. Now I'm going out. See you later. And there is no need to worry. I have money *and* condoms."

"That's a weight off my mind. Do you need a lift anywhere?"

"No. Tom's picking me up."

A car horn beeped three times.

"That's him now. See you later."

"Take your keys. I might be out when you get back."

Through the window, Claire watched her daughter climb into the battered Ford Fiesta and she waved to Tom. Claire wasn't worried about Tom's intentions. Tom was a nice boy. And even if he wasn't, Katie could handle him. In Katie's world, Tom was located in the *Friend Only Zone*.

Claire consulted her watch. It was just before two. David was spending his Saturday afternoon playing a round of golf with Max and wouldn't be back for hours. She took out her phone and typed an SMS: *MHUP3?*

Within a minute, a reply came back: *OK* ☺

She went upstairs, showered and reapplied her makeup. After due consideration, she put on a pair of tight-fitting jeans, black ankle-length boots and a fluffy sweater. She examined herself in the mirror. The sweater wasn't right. She changed it for a cream-coloured blouse with a low neckline. She'd have to wear a scarf with her coat, otherwise she'd freeze. March was not being the kindest of months, weather-wise.

Before she left the house, Claire rang David.

"How's it going?"

"It's going," was the response.

"I'm thinking of driving over to Market Harborough this afternoon. See if I can pick up some nice cheeses and meats from the French market stalls."

"No problem. We're only on the first hole. We'll be hours unless it decides to rain."

A POISON TREE

MHUP3. Market Harborough, usual place, 3 o'clock.

Claire had a reason to be where she would be. She had only to watch the sky. She climbed into her silver Vectra and started the engine.

Claire parked in the free car park behind Church Street, close to the centre of the town of Market Harborough. She made her way to a small tea shop in the shadow of St. Dionysius Parish Church, the large fifteenth-century structure that rose from the street and which, along with the wooden Old Grammar School beside it, fixed the character of this small market town. The old-fashioned tea shop was, in many ways, an improbable spot for a clandestine liaison. Perhaps that was why she and Jack had chosen it.

Jack Irving, the owner of Jael Construction, was already sitting at a corner table and Claire took the seat facing him.

"Tea and cakes?" he asked. "Or just tea?"

"Just tea," she replied.

She looked at him. In spite of his shock of silver-grey hair and the wrinkles around his eyes, furrowed deep by years of chain-smoking, Jack still had something boyish about him.

They ordered tea from the black-costumed waitress. Claire glanced around at the other patrons: two middle-aged ladies deep in conversation and a thin elderly man clad in tweed, his nose buried in a newspaper. No one was paying them any attention.

"It's an unexpected surprise to see you today," said Jack, in an accent that betrayed his West Country origins.

"I don't know quite what I was thinking when I SMSed you. I just wanted to see you today."

"My good fortune," he replied. "I was over at Kettering for a meeting about the estate development when I got your text, so I was in the area. Well, sort of."

"A meeting on a Saturday?"

"Sometimes when you're meeting a member of the Planning Committee, it's best to do it outside of normal working hours and away from prying eyes." He gave a roguish grin.

"I don't think I need to know about that."

"No, you don't."

The waitress arrived with the tea, and they sat in silence for a while.

Sometimes Jack reminds me so much of David, Claire thought. *He has that same gentleness. Although David doesn't have his quick temper. Or his tendency for skulduggery, for that matter.*

She wondered – and not for the first time – what on earth she was doing.

"Where is Eleanor this afternoon?" she asked.

Jack stirred with unease. "Some Church thing at St. Mark's. I don't know what exactly."

"You should take more of an interest in her church work, Jack."

"I suppose I should."

"Sorry. I'm not in a position to be giving you marital advice, am I?"

"Perhaps not." He touched her hand.

"Where are you parked?"

"Behind the Conservative Club."

"Let's drink up. Later you can drop me back in town. I need to buy some things from the market."

"OK. Where do you want to go?"

"Somewhere quiet."

"How about we drive over to Foxton Locks?"

Claire shook her head. "Too public."

A POISON TREE

The place also held memories of times with David. *Inappropriate.* So much of what she thought and felt these days was inappropriate. So much of what she *did* was inappropriate. Guilt clung to her like a limpet. Yet here she was, regardless. She could not change course. She was waiting for something to happen, but she did not know what.

"Then let's just drive out into the countryside and find somewhere. Yes?"

"Yes."

Jack drove west out of the town until he found a secluded country lane, out of sight from the main road. He switched off the engine, reached across and took Claire in his arms. She held him and stroked his hair.

"Let's sit in the back seat," she said. "We'll be more comfortable."

"Are you all right, Claire?" he asked, concerned.

"Of course I am. I'm here with you."

When Jack dropped her off back in Market Harborough, the first spots of rain were starting to fall.

Claire made her way around the market quickly. The muffled stallholders blew on their hands and stomped, determined to see out the hours, to chase down those last sales. They were a hardy bunch. Gusts of wind flicked the hanging plastic sheets. Money changed hands and disappeared into leather belt wallets. Organic produce, cake and homemade biscuits found their way into shopping bags. The clock on the church tower registered five o'clock and the sky darkened appreciably. The weather deities decided it was time for everyone to call it a day and volleys of water began to drench the shoppers.

David would be home by now, or on his way home. Claire made one final purchase, a bottle of apple juice, and hurried back to her car.

She looked at herself in the rear view mirror. The face was familiar but the eyes that stared back at her were those of a stranger. It was another

A POISON TREE

Claire that sat in the car. A Claire that had secrets, that dwelled in a different world – a constricted world that contained only Jack and the potential of shameful discovery. While the real Claire was ostensibly a happily-married professional woman, *this* Claire was no such thing. She was a creature of the shadows, a betrayer of those who loved her.

Her eyes filled with tears.

The deluge beat on the car roof and the streets ran with water.

Claire switched on the windscreen wipers, but the rain was too heavy.

She could not see where she was going.

7

DAVID

The pathology of suspicion must be an interesting study, if you have the stomach for it.

The germ of disquiet, once planted, inveigles its way into your consciousness and starts to connect new neural pathways in the most insidious fashion. The term *affair* jumps out at you from newspaper articles and television shows, as if you had never encountered it before. Your objectivity erodes away. Something flutters around inside you. Your ears become more attuned to the nuances of words. You begin analysing your partner's choice of phrase. Trivial events assume an air of importance. The ground under your feet is suddenly less solid.

Despite the fact that I received no further unpleasant phone calls or any more anonymous letters about Claire, my mind inaugurated subtle departures from its normal routines.

My internal dialogue moved away from the question of who might want to poison my peace of mind, and turned towards the issue of whether there might be any truth in the noxious assertion that whispered to me in the moments of silence. I started to take more of an interest in my wife's casual remarks, her references to individuals.

Had the red flag of disloyalty been raised at any other time in our marriage, I should have paid it scant regard. But I recognised, through the haze of uncertainty, that over the last couple of years a distance had grown between Claire and me. There were many things we no longer discussed, although on the surface we continued as before. I wondered whether complacency over our marriage had disabled my critical faculties.

A POISON TREE

The frequency of our lovemaking had declined. Our conversations had become focused on everyday matters, the triviality of routine.

I found myself looking at the framed photographs of our Registry Office wedding. The eyes of the happy couple were bright and disingenuous. Some scales had fallen from those eyes in the years since.

And yet I *knew* Claire. I knew the kind, feeling person she was. But like all knowledge, conjecture sits at the base of the pyramid. We only know what we assume we know. Some assumptions are buried so deep in our subconscious that we no longer see them: they are part of our programming. That Claire and I would be together forever was not something I had ever questioned. It was a catechism.

I put aside the manuscript that Anna had given me after I read the phrase, *I was a fool to trust her so completely*. Like the comet that the ancients took as a sign of evil days to come, it seemed portentous. I placed *Madame Bovary* back on the bookshelf for the same reason. *The Adventures of Sherlock Holmes* seemed a safer choice.

I repeated to myself I was being asinine. Claire was a busy woman. She juggled a career and a household. How the hell could she find the time to conduct an affair? And with whom for God's sake?

It could be someone she met through work, the synthesised voice told me. *Have you noticed how many late meetings she goes to these days?*

She's never stayed away overnight, I replied.

Not yet, maybe, said the voice.

Braddock Motors' business was booming. The January turnover figures turned out to be a blip. Sales of the revamped Vectra were good regardless of the car experts' concerns about build quality. In popularity it was challenging Ford's UK dominance. The management at Vauxhall's Luton plant was cock-a-hoop. Our upmarket ranges were also performing well, and already it looked as though this year's bonuses were going to be good. Even the Old Bugger appeared happy – or as happy as he ever gets. Perhaps the world would not to end in December.

Not everything has gone smoothly in Braddock Land, however. I had to sack Mark from his position as general manager at Coventry. Despite his promises of improvement, his performance at work had deteriorated with rapidity. He was like a different person. All the old sparkle had gone. I tried to offer him his old job back, but I guess the step-down was too much of a humiliation for him. Mark seemed to have aged in a matter of months. He never did discuss the break-up of his marriage and for me to have raised it would have been yet another kick in the genitals. His bitterness was only too evident. He packed up and left without a goodbye.

I installed Harry as acting general manager to give me some time to think and to see how he coped before making his position permanent. That did not go down too well either.

"Have you lost confidence in me too, David?" Harry sounded exasperated.

"For God's sake, Harry," I responded with some heat. "I've just let Mark go. Let's not act with indecent haste on this. Certain people are convinced I set Mark up to fail from the start so that you could get the job. Cut me some slack. And while you're about it, lose that fucking check jacket. It's a grey or blue suit from Monday."

He muttered something about 'short odds', but took the job anyway.

That weekend, Claire, Katie and I had dinner at my father's.

As usual it was a stilted affair. Nang and the other two ladies tried their best to keep the tone light, but it was always a struggle.

My father sat at the head of the table bemoaning the state of the nation following the recent bomb explosions in Brixton and Brick Lane. Behind him on the wall hung the Braddock coat of arms, an ermine shield with an engrailed line and, at the centre, a large oak. Our motto reads, *A Fructibus Cognoscitur Arbor* – 'The tree is known by its fruit'. I've always hated the pomposity of it. Furthermore, given that Nang had suffered two miscarriages before giving up on having children, the sight of that every day must serve to keep that wound open. My father is one insensitive bastard.

To give him his due, though, he does have a soft spot for Katie, and they talked at length about how her studies were going while Claire and Nang chattered about some new dress shop that was opening in town.

Eventually Edward Braddock remembered I was at the table.

"What are your thoughts on the new Zafira, David?" he asked.

So we talked about cars. Again.

"Where would you like me to file this business card, David?" Sandra asked me. "Should I file him under your personal section, or what?"

She handed me a white embossed card. *James Fosse, Consultant.*

"We don't have a 'psycho' category, do we?"

"Not yet. Do you want me to start one?"

"Just joshing. He's an American guy I met at the Chamber of Commerce. He has a rather black sense of humour. The sort usually reserved for Brits."

"OK, I'll put him under 'Chamber of Commerce'."

"Let me just enter him in my phone contacts first."

I chucked my briefcase on the bed and changed out of my suit. I was wacked. It had been a long day at work.

As I wandered downstairs, Claire announced, "We're having a family night in. The weather's filthy anyway. I've ordered pizza for us all and Katie has chosen a DVD."

"Sounds great," I replied. "What are we watching?"

Katie handed me the DVD case.

"It's a comedy. *Throw Momma from the Train* with Danny DeVito and Billy Crystal."

"What's it about?"

"It's kind of a funny remake of Hitchcock's *Strangers on a Train*. You know, that *film noir* stuff? Danny DeVito offers to kill Billy Crystal's ex-wife if he'll kill his mother in return."

"Sounds like a barrel of laughs."

The doorbell rang twice.

"That's either the pizza boy or the postman," remarked Claire.

"The postman?" I asked.

"The postman always rings twice," said Katie and Claire together.

Katie had fallen asleep on her bed. Her study notes were strewn around her, and Aerosmith's 'I Don't Want to Miss a Thing' was playing on her music system.

I tucked her into bed, kissed her and switched off the music and the lights. She didn't stir. Katie looked so much like Claire sometimes, it was uncanny. She didn't seem to have acquired any of my features at all. Lucky girl.

The house was quiet. It was gone eleven and Claire had another late dinner.

I opened the French windows from my study and wandered out into the garden. The sky was black and starless, but the night was unseasonably warm. I lit a Marlboro and took a long draw on it. I had recently confessed to my family my return to the ranks of smokers, and they were *not* happy about it. I consoled them with the promise that I would only smoke a few cigarettes a day and I would never smoke in their presence. Claire had bought a large bottle of mouthwash and left it by my sink in our bathroom.

A POISON TREE

Somehow over the weeks I had managed to push my suspicions about Claire into the back of my mind. She was going out a lot, but I knew that Jael Construction was doing brisk business and that the big, new estate development at Kettering must be taking up a lot of time. Claire, unlike many CFOs, got involved in some of the commercial negotiation aspects of the building projects, and that meant out-of-hours meetings. The wheels of capitalism continued to turn outside of the Monday to Friday routine. I remembered Jim Fosse telling me the international power business was ten times worse. With time zones to consider, ludicrous power plant build times and twenty-four-hour-seven-days-a-week operations, it was amazing anyone managed to sleep at all. But perhaps he exaggerated.

Jim Fosse.

I finished my cigarette and lit another one.

It was a while since I'd spoken to the American. I saw him briefly at the last Chamber of Commerce meeting, but he was deep in discussion with a rather depressed-looking Mat Hoggard of Leicester Wheels Auto Limited, and I did not feel inclined to interrupt.

The real truth was that I was avoiding Jim.

Since I'd received the vindictive phone call and anonymous letter, and with the universe sending me coded messages about murder conspiracies, the last thing I needed was a conversation with Jim – especially one about killing his wife, even if it was in jest.

When midnight struck I had a whisky and went to bed.

I double-checked the address that Harry had given me before ringing the doorbell.

The house was in Hillfields, an area of Coventry redeveloped after the bombing of World War II had flattened much of the city. It is one of the most disadvantaged places in England, and this house had certainly seen better days. Grubby net curtains hung at the windows and the roof looked like it needed serious repairs. Tracksuit-clad teenagers wandered the street and gave me curious glances. Barely serviceable cars rusted at the curb. I was glad I was visiting during daylight hours.

One of the downstairs curtains twitched and a few moments later the peeling front door opened a few inches. Mark peered at me.

"David? What do you want?"

"Just to talk. Can I come in?"

"How did you get my address?"

"From Harry."

With reluctance, he stood aside to let me enter and I followed him into the living room. There was little furniture and the room was dusty and smelled of male sweat. A television muttered and a half-eaten carton of Chinese takeaway sat on the floor beside an old armchair whose stuffing was spilling out. Mark slumped into the chair and picked up the carton.

"Excuse me while I finish lunch," he said. Then, remembering his manners, he asked me if I'd like a cup of tea. I declined, and sat down on a straight-backed wooden chair next to the non-functioning fireplace.

Mark shovelled the noodles into his mouth with a pair of plastic chopsticks and waited for me to say something. He looked unkempt and I doubted he'd shaved that morning.

"How are you, Mark?"

He made a wry face and indicated the room with his chopsticks. "As you can see, I'm doing OK."

"Are you working?"

"What do you think?"

"Harry told me you and Janine are no longer together. He was concerned about you."

"Then why are you here and not him?"

"I'm here because I can offer you a job and Harry can't," I replied.

He leaned back in the chair.

"Yes, Janine and I have split up. Women, eh? Can't live with 'em and can't kill 'em."

"What happened?"

"I don't want to talk about it." He recommenced eating.

"We need someone at the Northampton showroom. I thought of you. It could be a bit of a new start for you."

"*Northampton?*" he said, dripping sarcasm. "Ah, the Venice of the Midlands. Culture, nightlife and all the tedium you can stomach."

"It's got to be better than *this*."

"And what makes you think I'd want to work for you, David? You're the one who sacked me in the first place. Without you I wouldn't be here."

"I'm not the one who broke up your marriage, Mark," I said. "*That's* why you're here. Pull yourself together, and stop this self-destructive behaviour."

"Well, pardon me, *Mister* Braddock, if we can't all have perfect marriages like yours. Although I doubt yours is exactly perfect."

"What do you mean by that?"

He dropped his eyes and put more food into his mouth. "Nothing," he mumbled.

I stood up and put one of my business cards on the mantelpiece.

"Call me when you're in a more receptive frame of mind, Mark."

"That might be some time," he responded. "Let yourself out, would you? I'd like to watch the end of the news."

My cell phone rang and I answered it without checking the caller.

"David Braddock."

"Hello, David," said a robotic voice. "Have you checked on Claire yet? You should, you know."

"I'm sorry, you must have the wrong number."

I switched the phone off.

"Who was that?" asked Claire, setting the dinner table.

"Another wrong number. I keep getting them. Damn phone company."

Without question, I should have just told Claire I'd been getting malicious calls. Then perhaps the whole thing would have been over. We could have had a laugh about it and put it to bed. But something held me back. I think it was a conversation we'd had a few years ago when we were on one of our regular holidays in Bali. It was the sort of exchange you have when you are in love and you know you have nothing to worry about.

We were standing on a hillside admiring the green rice terraces and some local girl had given me a flirty look. Claire had punched me when I'd waved back.

"If you ever decide to have an affair, David, just don't tell me about it, OK?"

"OK," I replied hugging her, "and if you ever have one don't tell me either."

"Deal," she said and kissed me.

"Oh, yuck," grimaced our daughter. "You two should get a room."

"We have one, sweetheart. And what is more we'll be making full use of it when we get back to our hotel."

"Too much information, Dad. Way, way too much. You know, I will have to have therapy for this later. It's not natural having parents this lovey-dovey."

"Oh, shut up, Katie," laughed Claire. "Now, let's have a family photograph."

Of course we don't really know anything for certain, do we?

Do we?

A POISON TREE

I don't know what it was that made me look through Claire's handbag that evening. Maybe it was that second phone call, although that seems a rather lame explanation. There was no logic for why I should give credence to the words of some malice-inspired coward who disguises his voice; for why I should mistrust my partner of twenty years.

But I did.

And let's face it, when it comes to matters of trust, logic has no part to play. We are at the mercy of our rawest emotions. Some creature decided to pour poison in my ear; invited me to act upon my vaguest and most ill-founded suspicions; then rubbed its hands in glee as I obeyed. And so, while Claire took a shower upstairs, I found myself rifling through her bag for evidence of culpability – since evidence of innocence is impossible to find. With alternate sensations of embarrassment and slyness, I examined the clutter that she carted around with her.

And then I found something.

It was a small piece of paper tucked into her purse. On it, in Claire's handwriting, were the words, *23-25 August, Imperial Hotel, Kensington*

The sensible Braddock said this was a discovery of no consequence, that I should be ashamed of myself for my shabby actions. Like Macbeth's conclusion on life, my imagining about Claire was a tale told by an idiot, full of sound and fury yet signifying nothing. The other Braddock, however, copied the words and filed them away for future reference.

Then I opened my Conan Doyle and read *The Adventure of the Red-Headed League.*

8

JAMES

The Thai Airways flight to Bangkok out of Heathrow was almost full and Jim Fosse was one of the last passengers to board.

He took his seat in business class next to a smartly-dressed Japanese man who was engrossed in some World Bank report.

"Can I get you a drink, Mr. Fosse?" asked the purple-clad stewardess. "I am afraid there will be a slight delay before we take off. Heathrow is very busy this evening."

"A scotch on the rocks, please."

"And anything else, sir?"

"Only your phone number."

Jim checked his watch. It was coming up to twenty past nine. The night flight was scheduled to arrive in Bangkok a little before four o'clock in the afternoon. He still had plenty of time, even allowing for a flight delay and queuing at immigration. His meeting in the restaurant was not until eight. He had two days in Bangkok before flying on to Manila for negotiations on acquiring a stake in a power plant – so even if the restaurant meeting did not resolve matters, there would be the opportunity for a further meeting.

The stewardess returned with the scotch and gave him a shy smile.

He took a scuffed black pocketbook from his briefcase and flipped through it until he found an entry for 'Khemkhaeng' beside which was a cell number. A shady business acquaintance in the Philippines had supplied him with the contact and a third party had arranged the introduction. That was how things operated in Thailand, and for that matter in most other places in the world where 'grey' transactions were involved.

A POISON TREE

Khemkhaeng worked for the Sangukhon family as a senior lieutenant who – at least allegedly – looked after the operational side of the family's drugs and prostitution business. He was a man who knew people. People who could get things done. Jim needed to talk to one of those people and he was hoping the Thai would be able to give him a name.

Jim flipped through the dog-eared book. Throughout it were scattered arcane lists, names, phone numbers, email addresses and sundry oblique snippets which would cause any casual reader to conclude the book's owner was a disorganised hoarder of random data. But Jim Fosse was anything but disorganised. He was a methodical concealer of information which might prove incriminating. Distributed over the pages – could anyone but find the trail of guilty breadcrumbs – was a coded record of signposts, checklists and activities dear to the heart of the illicit businessman.

He paused his page-turning at a scribbled margin entry which read *250k LIFW#2*, and beneath it a date in February 1998. Only the writer would know the note related to the taking out of a life insurance policy on his second wife. The rest of the page was covered in doodles, fictitious flight schedules and phone numbers taken from the pages of telephone directories. Furthermore, Jim Fosse was the only person who would be able to tell this was merely one item of an agenda which he was working his way through.

He picked up his scotch and turned to a page near the back of the book where in the top left-hand corner was written *David Braddock W#2*, and underneath it *Feb 99*. He took out a pen and wrote *Aug 99* beside the other date. Jim's brow furrowed for a few seconds as he looked at the entry, then a smirk crept over his face. He put away the book and checked what was showing on the in-flight films.

Tough choice: *Kiss Me Deadly* or *Double Indemnity*.

A POISON TREE

Maybe he would watch both. It was around twelve hours to Bangkok and Jim Fosse never slept more than six hours. It was all he needed to recharge. Besides, being awake was just too much fun.

9

ADELE

The girl was of elfin shape, her dark brown hair cut short. Her skin was pale, highlighting hazel eyes already enhanced by black mascara. She wore a greatcoat that was several sizes too big for her, making her look distinctively gamine.

She shook out her sodden umbrella on the steps of the apartment block before proceeding into the lobby. A small Indian man, who occupied one of the second floor flats, wished her a good afternoon before buttoning up his coat against the unseasonably cold weather and proceeding out into the rain. She had no idea what his name was. Indeed she didn't know the names of anyone in the block, nor did she want to. The bank of apartment buzzers was anonymous. It only showed the flat numbers. The tenants here changed often, and no one seemed interested enough to announce their presence. The girl surmised many of her fellow residents were either illegals or living on benefits. For all she knew she was the only one in the building who had a job.

She unlocked her mailbox in the dingy hallway and took out two envelopes, both bills, addressed to *Ms. Adele Darrow*. She pushed them into her shoulder bag and walked up the three flights of stairs to her floor. The lift had been broken for a few weeks and the landlord showed little concern with effecting repairs.

Once in the apartment, she hung up her coat, dumped her bag on the kitchen table and switched on the kettle. Through the window she could see the rain was now falling heavily, scourging the streets and the grey houses. A youth in a hoodie ran along the pavement and took shelter in a doorway.

He shivered, lit a cigarette and squinted up at the sky. He looked soaked through.

While she waited for the kettle to boil, Adele spooned instant coffee into a mug and checked the fridge.

"No fucking milk," she said in a voice that carried a slight Scottish burr. "It'll have to be black then."

On the fridge door, attached with small round magnets, was a photograph of a boy, aged around three years. The boy was sitting on a see-saw in a park and was laughing at the camera. Adele touched the photograph with the fingertips of her right hand and said, "Sorry for the swear word, Jamie. Your mummy is a wee bad girl."

She poured the boiling water into the mug, and managed to get rid of most of the floating lumps with a teaspoon. The two envelopes were retrieved from her bag and snorted at. She tossed them into a drawer.

Adele checked her watch while she sipped the bitter coffee. There was about an hour before the appointment.

She stripped off her clothes and stepped into the shower, relaxing while the hot water ran over her small breasts and slim body. She leaned forward and felt the soothing flow down her back to the Celtic tattoo symbolising a tree that spread out at the base of her spine. Her mind drifted.

Two years. It had been two years since she boarded the train in Glasgow and ended up in this unexceptional Midlands city. An old school friend had offered her a bed on her sofa until she got herself 'sorted out'. But in reality, it was her friend, Nicola, who needed sorting out. She was high on drugs most of the time – cocaine when she could afford it – and after Adele found a checkout job at a discount store she had moved into her own place at the earliest opportunity. Nicola for her part had disappeared off to London with her layabout boyfriend shortly afterwards and Adele hadn't heard from her since.

A POISON TREE

The job at the discount store paid the rent and utility bills, and her earnings from prostitution paid for everything else, with a little bit over for a rainy day. And there were plenty of rainy days in Leicester.

Adele had performed the occasional trick in Glasgow, and now that she had anonymity and no chance of bumping into anyone she knew, she decided to augment her income by joining the staff of the Gold Club where she worked two long weekend shifts.

The Gold Club was situated in an uncared-for Victorian house in the Frog Island area of Leicester. It was equipped with a dungeon – which Adele declined to frequent – and five bedrooms each containing a Jacuzzi and a corner shower. The Jacuzzis were hardly ever switched on, since most clients only wanted a one-hour 'quickie'. This was just as well as only two of them worked. The walls of each room were painted dark purple, the floors were uncarpeted and the whole building reeked of sweat and stale beer. Miss Connie, who owned and managed the place, sold booze as well as sex.

Adele found a degree of camaraderie among the ladies of the Gold Club, although she didn't want to become too friendly. It was better that way.

Most of the women who worked there were local housewives picking up a little cash on the side although Leona, a blonde girl from Wolverhampton, was working her way through Law School. When Adele had expressed surprise at this, her colleague had pointed out 'lots' of female students did it. Furthermore, according to Leona, many of the female lawyers in Cuba were also on the game. "Law practice just doesn't pay enough there," Leona announced. "Besides, there are plenty of men who would like to screw a lawyer after all the lawyers who have screwed them."

Because she could still pass for a teenager – at least in the club's low lighting and the twilight world of the male mind – Adele often attracted the sort of client who liked his women to dress up in a school uniform. She couldn't have cared less. The uniform attracted an extra payment. She didn't even bother to have a pseudonym, although everyone else who worked there did.

What the fuck, she thought. *Nobody knows me anyway.*

Adele soaped herself in the shower and reflected on just how creepy most men were when not bound by the chains of convention and everyday appearance. And the existence of the Gold Club's dungeon testified to how many men preferred to be bound by real chains. Nina (real name Daphne), the house dominatrix, had difficulty hiding her contempt for many of her clients. She took especial pleasure in inflicting beatings on some of them. It just seemed to make them eager for more.

"Civilization is a thin veneer over something really dark," Nina had observed to Adele one day. "I can't wait to save up enough money to get out of this business."

"What is it you want to do instead?" Adele had asked.

"I want to open an art gallery in Hull," was the enthusiastic reply, "and maybe offer painting classes for children. Now, would you be a darling look after my beer for me? I have to go and pee on a customer."

Adele switched off the water and stepped out of the shower. She wrapped herself in a thick white towel and padded into her small bedroom.

The walls were covered in an off-white pebbledash, which she deduced the landlord had chosen because a slop with a paintbrush would quickly conceal any nasty stains left there by less caring tenants.

She had made efforts to make the room more welcoming. Cheap prints of watercolours hung on the walls and a tapestry was positioned over the bedhead. Bright patterned cushions were piled on the bed itself and a large teddy bear sat on a cabinet.

Adele opened the bedside drawer to check she had a supply of massage oil. She had. Two half-empty bottles snuggled in the drawer among packs of tissues, tampons, condoms and a tube of lubricant.

A POISON TREE

While she dried herself, she selected an outfit from the wardrobe; a black lacy bra and panties, a short grey pleated skirt and a white blouse which she tied below her cleavage to expose her midriff. Then she returned to the bathroom to apply her makeup. Not too much. Her client didn't like her to appear too tarty and she wanted to please him.

There were only two men Adele allowed back to her apartment. She had almost increased the number to three a few weeks ago: a tubby American she had met at the Gold Club who was charming and generous with his tip. But something about his eyes made her pause. There was coldness and a ruthlessness lurking there, and it made her feel a little threatened. He was one of those men whose smile stopped at his mouth.

No. Two is enough anyway. And I don't want the neighbours seeing a procession of men in and out of the flat. That's a recipe for trouble.

She was fond of her two regular clients. Neither of them had any propensity for shows of temper or violence, and safety was a key consideration in Adele's line of work.

The first man was a fellow Scot who had taken early retirement from working in a coal mine not far from Glasgow, and later moved south to live with his widowed sister. Adele suspected from his occasional bouts of coughing that his retirement was on medical grounds, but he never proffered any information on this and she was too discreet to ask. She had met him at the club shortly after arriving in the city. He was a gentle individual – given to occasional bouts of melancholy – who would recite Burns' poetry any time the opportunity presented itself. He called himself Robbie, and Adele was inclined to believe that was his real name.

The second client was an Englishman, of athletic build, who had started seeing her eighteen months before. It had been, he said, his first ever visit to a brothel. More to the point, it would be his last, but would it be possible to see Adele again? She had given him her number without a second thought.

A POISON TREE

They had never met at the Gold Club again, and she knew he had never been back. It was just not his style.

Adele examined herself one final time in the mirror before consulting her watch. She had half-intended to call her mother, but was relieved to see there wasn't time now before her guest was due to arrive.

David was always punctual.

10

DAVID

I rang twice before I heard any movement inside the apartment. Then the door swung open and I was greeted by a sheepish grin.

"Is this outfit too schoolgirlish, do you think?"

"Not at all. You look delightful."

"I don't want anyone to think I dress up in a school uniform when my brother-in-law calls round for coffee."

"Listen, Anna, no man in his right mind is ever going to object to the way you look."

"Aww. You are sweet."

She kissed me on the cheek and I followed her through to the kitchen.

"You're prompt," she said. "Cappuccinos coming right up."

"I'm returning your copy of *Crime and Punishment*."

"Did you enjoy it?"

"Well, it's not exactly a laugh a minute, but yes, I did." I deposited the book on the kitchen table.

Anna set down the coffees in front of us. Beneath her makeup, her eyes looked slightly puffy and red.

"Are you OK?"

"I'm fine, David. Why do you ask?"

"You look like you've been crying."

She turned her eyes away from me. "Shit," she said.

I put my hand on hers. "What's the matter? What's happened?"

"Nothing, I'm fine."

"You're not fine."

She dropped her head. "I almost called you to ask you not to come. Then I thought I'd look all right with the make-up."

"You look beautiful."

I put my hand under her chin and raised it.

"I can't talk about it," she whispered.

"Yes, you can. You can talk to me about anything."

Anna looked at me for a moment before shaking her head.

"Is it Max? Have you had a row or something?"

I held both her hands in mine. "I'm not going to stop asking until you talk to me. Have you and Max had a row?"

"No."

I continued to look at her until she swallowed. Then she squeezed my fingers.

"Max is playing around again."

"Are you sure?"

She nodded.

"Max is a fucking idiot. If you were my wife, I'd never play around."

Anna began to cry and I passed her my handkerchief. "Oh, David," she said, "you don't want to hear all this."

"Yes, I do. Do you know who it is?"

"No, I don't. But I'm sure I'll find out soon enough. Max is hardly the careful type."

"I'm sorry."

Anna looked at me anxiously. "Promise me you won't say anything to Claire."

"Of course I won't. Not if you don't want me to."

She wiped her eyes. "God, I'm pathetic. And now I must look a mess."

"Not at all. Haven't I told you before I have a thing about runny mascara?"

A POISON TREE

She laughed.

"Would you like a hug, Anna?"

"Yes, please. That would be much better than coffee."

"Good. You make lousy coffee anyway."

Whatever happened to the old David Braddock?

I used to be something of a comedian; a man who didn't take life too seriously; a man who was going to have adventures. An optimist. A dreamer.

The person who first met Anna Holland all those years ago wouldn't recognise the serious, middle-aged family man that currently inhabits his body.

Is that former man still around somewhere, buried beneath the layers of responsibility and quotidian existence?

Life has an annoying habit of forcing you take stock from time to time. It makes you look around at the people you love, to see how the effluxion of time and the scars of experience have altered them. You gaze into their eyes hoping to catch a glimpse of that spark of youth and hope you once knew. You want to see the corners of their mouth turn upwards in a smile and hear the sound of childish giggling. You want them to punch you on the shoulder as you tell them a funny story.

Has our love for each other consigned both Claire and me to a life of comfortable compromise and the gradual erosion of the individuality that first attracted us? Is it a release from this stifling normality that she now seeks?

I have no answers to these questions.

But as I sit at the breakfast table holding Anna, I realise that something precious has been lost in the waterfall of years. That love takes a toll on everyone.

11

JAMES

Korean food was not Jim Fosse's favourite fare, but he was not in a position to object to the choice of venue.

The restaurant was off Bangkok's Sukhumvit Road, a short walk from the Metro station, and it had private dining rooms at the rear of the building. A bodyguard had frisked him before allowing entry.

The screen door was then slid back to reveal his companion for the evening. The bodyguard closed the door behind him.

Khemkhaeng was seated at the low table, but stood to shake hands. The Thai was dressed in a well-tailored grey suit and a blood-red shirt, open at the neck. His demeanour was relaxed but there was no missing the steely glint in the eyes. Jim felt the sweat forming under his armpits and resolved not to remove his jacket, however hot he might become. He needed to be calm and respectful. The man seated opposite had the power to make him disappear on a whim.

"You must excuse my English, Mr. Fosse. I don't get to use it as often as I would like."

"Your English is fine, sir. I am afraid my Thai is only good enough for ordering food or for asking directions."

A serving woman appeared and began gliding around the room.

"I thought we'd start with some kimchi, if that is all right with you?"

"Fine," replied Jim, although a side dish of fermented vegetables was not what his stomach told him it wanted.

Khemkhaeng sat back in his seat, as if to study the American for a moment. "I hope you understand, Mr. Fosse, I would not normally involve myself in intermediary work of this nature. However, our mutual Filipino acquaintance is an old friend of mine, so I am doing this as a favour to him."

"I am very grateful. I know you are a busy man."

There was a silence and Khemkhaeng continued to look at him.

"This meal is on me, by the way," Jim added nervously.

The Thai smiled. "Yes, I think it is," he said.

Food appeared on the table along with bottles of cheongju.

Jim sipped at the clear liquid.

"Do you approve?" The Thai raised an eyebrow.

"I do indeed."

"Good. The most popular brand of rice wine in Korea is *Chung Ha*, but I prefer this *Beopju* which is brewed in the old city of Gyeongju. Did you know, by the way, it is designated by the Government of South Korea as an 'Important Intangible Cultural Property'? We shouldn't even be drinking it."

Jim thought that was a cue for him to laugh, so he did.

"Most of our Thai wine tastes like piss, unfortunately. At least to the Western palate."

Jim laughed at this too, before realising he shouldn't have. "But your beer brands are excellent," he added.

"Anyway," said his host, "I am afraid I don't have much time this evening, so let us proceed to business. Lopez tells me you have a pest problem you need some help with."

"A pest problem – yes."

"There is a man who does some work for us in that line. He is not part of our family, more of a freelance operator, but he has performed satisfactory services for us over the years."

"Is he Thai, may I ask?"

"No, he is not. He was born in Scotland, but these days you might say he is a citizen of the world."

A POISON TREE

"I see."

"We have international investments and concerns where it is sometimes helpful to show a white face. Some things are best handled by outsiders. I am sure you understand."

Jim nodded and took a bite of the kimchi. It was every bit as sour as he remembered it. "So how do I get in contact with this man?"

"You don't. He gets in contact with you."

Khemkhaeng took a small notebook and pen from his pocket. "Give me your private cell phone number." The Thai wrote it in the book. "And where exactly is this pest infestation?"

"In England."

Khemkhaeng wiped his mouth on a tissue and rose to his feet. "Would you excuse me for a few minutes, Mr. Fosse?"

"Of course."

After his companion left the room, Jim sat and wondered what the hell he was doing sitting in a Bangkok restaurant with a Thai gangster. *Surely there was an easier way to do this?* Jim Fosse was used to dealing with shady politicians and fixers, but perhaps this time he had wandered into a transaction whose asking price would be more than hard currency. He wiped his wet palms on his handkerchief. His shirt was sticking to him and his heart was beating fast. He forced himself to inhale deeply a few times and gulped down some more of the rice wine.

The serving woman reappeared unbidden and placed another bottle of *Beopju* in front of him. She began cooking beef ribs on the metal plate positioned in the centre of the table. Jim wondered whether he should say something, but as the woman seemed disinclined to make eye contact he refilled his glass instead.

"My apologies."

A POISON TREE

The American jumped as Khemkhaeng slid back the door. He sat down without ceremony and said a few words to the woman. She bowed.

"Is your phone switched on?"

"Yes," answered Jim.

"You will shortly receive a call from a man called Andrews."

"Is he –?"

"Yes. You can talk freely in front of the serving girl, by the way. She speaks no English."

Jim's phone rang and Khemkhaeng grinned. The American wondered if he sensed his discomfort. Jim removed the phone from his jacket pocket and pressed the answer button.

"Hello. This is Jim Fosse."

"Mr. Fosse, good evening. My name is Andrews. I gather you have an infestation problem and require some help." The voice was low and measured. Jim had an ear for accents and dialects, and the man was definitely Scottish. Not from Edinburgh. A Glaswegian, maybe?

"Yes, Mr. Andrews. That is correct."

"And the problem is situated in the UK?"

"It is."

"Where exactly?"

"Near Leicester."

There was a beat before the Scotsman continued. "My fee for eradicating the problem is one hundred thousand dollars, payment to be made in cash. In advance. If it is more convenient for you, I will accept payment in sterling."

Jim took a deep breath.

"I will call you again in two weeks. If you are still minded to employ my services we will discuss it in more detail then."

"Can I call you on this number?"

"No. This number will be out of service once this call is ended. I will contact *you*. Goodbye, Mr. Fosse."

Andrews cut the line before Jim could respond.

Khemkhaeng put down his glass. "I am afraid I will have to leave you now," said the Thai. "I have things to do. Enjoy your meal. Do you want to take this woman back to your hotel with you later?"

"Er ... no. No, thank you."

The American looked at his phone. "Mr. Andrews called me from a Thai number," he said.

"Yes?"

"Is he in Bangkok?"

"That doesn't concern you," responded Khemkhaeng. "But as it happens, he is not. Andrews is in the north of the country doing some work for us at present which will keep him busy for a few weeks. I have no control over his schedule after that, so you will have to sort out the arrangements with him directly."

The Thai got up and offered his hand.

"Thank you for your assistance, sir. Do I ... um ... owe you anything for this introduction?" Jim asked. He hoped his moist palm didn't betray the extent of his apprehension.

"No. Andrews will take care of that with me when the job is done."

"Until we meet again, then."

"I don't think we will meet again, Mr. Fosse. Give my regards to Lopez when you next see him. In the meantime, I wish you a pleasant stay in Bangkok. Goodbye."

Jim pulled off his tie and jacket, loosened two shirt buttons and wiped his damp neck with a handkerchief. The woman put some galbi on his plate.

He wondered how much the meal was going to cost him.

12

DAVID

Yggdrasil.

It is the name given to the monstrous ash tree of Norse mythology.

"We should review all of our branches."

According to the collection of old Icelandic poems known as the *Elder Edda*, the tree's upper trunk supports the home of the gods, Asgard, while beneath its roots lie the three worlds of men, Frost Giants and Niflheim – the place of the dead. The old texts, only a few of which still survive thanks to the destructive zeal of Christian priests, paint a picture of a fatalistic religion. Courage and self-sacrifice are paramount. All heroes perish. Darkness abounds.

"I'm hoping this year they will all be in the black."

Furthermore, unlike in other religions, the austere Norsemen foretell the ultimate defeat of the gods at the hands of the brutal Giants, and the end of the universe. Serpents gnaw at one of Yggdrasil's roots and will eventually destroy the tree, since like the gods it is doomed to die. At this point reality collapses into the void.

"You think so?"

These gloomy thoughts in my head have not been triggered so much by my recent emotional conflicts, but rather by the experience of sitting in the brooding presence of Odin, aka Edward Braddock, reviewing yet more sales projections. True, he does not enjoy the actual attributes of divinity – except perhaps eternal life – neither does he have only one eye, wolves crouching at his feet, or ravens perched on his shoulders. He does, though, possess an aloofness and solemnity that would not be out of place in the Teutonic pantheon.

"I think so."

Where is Thor's hammer when you need it, eh? That's what I'd like to know.

Trees.

I see them everywhere. I see too many trees and not enough wood, if my father is to be believed. The way those with a sixth sense see dead people.

Maybe that's not so surprising. After all, according to the Norse poets, the first man was fashioned from an ash and the first woman from an elm. After that, I guess humanity sort of branched out ...

"Are you listening, David?"

"Sorry, what?"

Edward Braddock sighed.

I needed a drink. And a cigarette.

"Harry seems to be getting to grips with the Coventry business," observed Braddock Senior.

"Yes, he's doing all right."

"Are you going to make him permanent?"

"I haven't decided yet."

"You should decide. You don't want to piss him off any more than you have done already. It doesn't pay to make enemies, David."

I know that.

Enemies send you anonymous letters.

Enemies hate you.

Over dinner, Claire said, "Oh, David, before I forget."

"Yes?"

"I'll be staying away in London for two nights in August. There's a finance conference I need to go to."

"Sounds like fun."

"I have every confidence it won't be."

"Is anyone else going?"

"No, just me and the credit card. I might indulge in a bit of retail therapy while I'm there."

"Not even Jack?"

"Darling, this is a *finance* conference. Way too boring and detailed for Jack. That's what he employs me for."

"Presumably this is after we've been to Bali?"

"Of course, silly. It's from the twenty-third to the twenty-fifth. I'm not going to mess up our holiday, am I?"

Jack. Crusty and rather grizzled. Unsophisticated. Not Claire's type at all.

And yet over the last few months, as the demons of jealousy and suspicion had been drilling in my brain with their dirty little jackhammers, his was the name that kept cropping up.

Claire saw him every day. They were relaxed together. I could visualise him touching her arm, leaning over her desk, making some jokey remark.

The day after my dinner conversation with Claire, I checked the details I'd copied from the scrap of paper in her purse. The dates matched.

I sat in my office and looked at the ceiling for a while. Then I went on the web to find the phone number for the Imperial Hotel, Kensington. I pressed the relevant buttons on my desk phone.

When a young woman answered, I gave my name as Mr. Irving and said I was checking that my secretary had made a reservation for me in August.

"Could I have your Christian name, sir?"

"Jack."

I heard the tap, tap, tap of fingers on a computer keyboard.

"Yes, sir, two nights from the twenty-third, checking out on the twenty-fifth."

"Good. Could you confirm the rate and details, please?"

"One hundred and seventy pounds per night, executive bedroom for two adults with a king-size bed."

"That's fine. Thank you."

"Thank you, sir. We look forward to seeing you."

I sat in a daze for several minutes. I suppose I should have felt anger, but that would not come, not yet. There was only a cold hole in my chest.

I heard muffled voices from outside the office, saw people moving about. Time slowed down and unreality took possession of the room. The front page of the *Times* stared up at me from my desk; Prince Edward and Sophie Rhys-Jones' wedding, police clashing with protesters in London at an anti-capitalism demonstration, concerns about the Millennium Dome.

I looked at my hands. They were trembling and I had the sensation that they did not belong to me.

One of the serpents had taken a large bite from Yggdrasil's root.

"Do you want another beer? Or are you going to sit on that barstool all night taking up valuable space while I bleed cash?"

"Yes, give me another beer, Ian."

"Thank Christ for that. Maybe now I'll be able to afford something to eat this week."

He pulled me a pint, muttering to himself. "That will be a thousand pounds, please."

"Yeah, right. If you want to charge those sort of prices you better start serving your beer in clean glasses."

The Bell was empty apart from Ian, myself and a couple of old codgers in the corner reminiscing about their salad days. It was early evening. Katie was at home revising while listening to some horrible drone that passed for music, and Claire was working late. Something to do with the Kettering project. Or so she said.

"You've never been married, Ian, have you?"

"Nope."

"And I'm assuming you're not a closet gay?"

He narrowed his eyes. "Are you looking to get yourself barred?"

"So the question is: why would a man not want to get married?"

Ian sniffed and wiped some spilled beer with a bar towel.

"That's not the question," he replied. "The question is: why the fuck would any man in his right mind want to get married? To save on all that divorce crap, why not just find a woman you don't like and give her your house?"

"You bloody cynic, Ian. There *are* happily married couples, you know."

"Well, I don't know any," he said. "Do you?"

That weekend I did something I thought I'd never do. I read Claire's diary.

She had kept one for years, going back to before we'd met. There must have been a couple of dozen volumes at least, stacked under my old saxophone case in the wardrobe. I'd never been tempted to read her diary before. Why would I have been? Hadn't we always been happy? Hadn't we always shared all our experiences and thoughts with each other?

At least I thought we had.

But now all my certainties were mired in doubt.

I waited until Claire was out shopping and Katie was out doing whatever it is teenagers do when they're not with their parents. Sitting on our bed, feeling like a burglar, I flicked through the pages.

Most of it was mundane stuff, but an entry in November of last year caught my eye.

A POISON TREE

Remember this day, the twenty-eighth of November 1998. This was the day my life started again.

I tried to think where I was on that day. And then it came to me. I was in Derby, visiting my great aunt at her retirement home. I knew this because it was her birthday. Claire couldn't come because of business commitments. She and Jack had a meeting about the Kettering project. Did anything else happen on that day between Claire and me? No, it didn't.

This was the day my life started again.

I felt a tightening across my chest and a wave of nausea.

What could there be that Claire couldn't write down in her diary, that required this obscurity, this note to herself where the event would be remembered but the date may not? What else but *that?* What *happened?* The silence between the words screamed at me.

I read on, noting that from there the references to me became less while the dates and times relating to Jack Irving grew more numerous. Even the most trivial items were recorded: the day he bought a new suit, a call from him while he was in Portugal with Eleanor, coffee together in a motorway service area, the date of his anniversary in March (against the margin of which was scribbled, *Yuh!*).

After March there were only a few entries. They restarted on the fourteenth of April in a desultory fashion, then stopped altogether at the beginning of May. She hadn't written a word since.

Why had she stopped writing after all those years? Had she realised how often she was making references to Jack and thought it safer to stop? Could she no longer bear to fill the pages with trivia, given the nontrivial nature of a secret life?

I put the diary down and rubbed my hand across my eyes.

We were happy once. Was it so long ago? I needed to remind myself that we were happy, that there was a real life before this one.

I went to the wardrobe and pulled out an earlier diary from 1995. The tone was glad, gushing. There, in her neat hand, were the details of our love-making, passages of longing when I was away on business trips. Sadness when we quarrelled. Joy when we made up. The thousand particulars of Katie's achievements and tribulations. Gossip and humour. The sacred and the profane. This was the writing of a woman who was content, who had peace of mind, who had no need to conceal anything from her husband or from the world.

I put the diaries back where I'd found them and opened the bedroom window to take in some fresh air. The fluttering in my stomach subsided a little.

Should I confront her?

And if so, with what?

What did her diaries *say* after all? That her life had restarted on a day when I wasn't around – whatever that meant. That she'd met Jack on a number of occasions.

So what?

And so what if she's stopped keeping a diary?

Perhaps my inferences were nothing more than those of an unreasonable, untrusting husband. Perhaps the anonymous phone calls and letters had poisoned my mind. Perhaps there was another explanation for the hotel booking in London.

I forced myself to calm down.

I needed proof of infidelity. Real proof.

A POISON TREE

And for that I would need the services of a detective.

At the top end of London Road, as it approaches Victoria Park, there are a number of solicitors' offices, clustered together for mutual comfort. There are also two private investigator firms in this area, one of which, Cumberbatch Surveillance Limited, describes itself with pride as the 'Number One Infidelity Investigator'.

I parked my car in a nearby side road, walked the short distance to their rather run-down office, and made it inside just as the rain started.

A scrawny girl with too many piercings, eccentric makeup and spiky purple hair sat behind a reception desk, tapping her black fingernails on the desk phone in time to the heavy metal music playing through her headset. An old couch, a dusty photocopier and a calendar on the wall were the only other things in the room.

As I entered and closed the ill-fitting door behind me, she removed one of her earphones with reluctance and said, "Yeah?"

"This is Cumberbatch Surveillance?"

"Yeah. Do you have an appointment?"

"Whoever he is, he doesn't need an appointment, Dolores," came a voice from a side-room. "We need the business, for Christ's sake. And turn that music down. I can hear it from here."

"You can go through," said Dolores, reinserting the earphone.

The business office was as sparsely furnished as reception.

A portly man with a florid face and a shock of white hair greeted me. He was dressed in a brown suit and a wide green tie with some kind of acorn motif.

"Lucien Cumberbatch," he said, shaking my hand.

"David Braddock."

91

"Please take a seat, Mr. Braddock. I apologise for my receptionist. She's still learning the job."

I must have been wearing a bemused expression because he went on, "We're having the place decorated soon."

"Ah."

"Well, not *that* soon. This business pays peanuts. If I didn't have a daughter to support I'd have chucked it in ages ago and I'd be full-time painting narrow boats now. That's my real passion. But that doesn't pay much either."

"*Narrow boats?*"

"Yes, you know, canal art?"

"I'm afraid I'm not familiar with it."

"Too few people are," he sighed. "It's a dying tradition. Only that and the Morris dancing keeps me going since my dear wife passed away."

"I'm sorry," I muttered, for want of anything better to say.

"Oh, that was ten years ago now. I think I'm over the worst. Remarkable woman, my wife. Enormous bottom but a heart of gold. She used to be a Morris dancer too, bless her."

"Mr. Cumberbatch, this *is* a private investigations firm, correct?"

He assumed a serious expression.

"Of course," he replied. "Best in the city. Don't be put off by appearances. Excuse my waffling, Mr. Braddock. I don't see many people during the day so I tend to talk a lot when I eventually get a client. I'm afraid I suffer a bit from verbal diarrhoea. It's been like that since school, where I was always trying to think of something to say to stop myself getting beaten up. With a name like Lucien Cumberbatch at a comprehensive school, well, you can imagine. Mind you, the bullying wasn't half as bad for me as it was for my brother, Shirley."

"Mr. Cumberbatch –"

A POISON TREE

"Did I mention that Dolores, whom you met in reception, is my daughter? Skinny little thing, I can't think where she gets it from. I've thought it could be from her great-uncle Silas' side of the family. He was a human skeleton in a carnival freak show, until he started to put on weight. Dolores has hopes of being a makeup artist, but between you and me, I don't think there's much chance. I'm pinning my faith on her boyfriend, Sid. He's a carpenter. Good, steady work. The world will always need chippies, in my opinion. Would you like a drink?"

"A coffee would be good," I said, hoping the tirade was over. "Black. And strong."

"I do have something a bit stronger than coffee," he grinned, reaching into a drawer of his desk and producing a bottle of whisky and two glasses.

"It's a bit early for that, isn't it?"

"Every private detective, no matter how humble, should have a bottle of Bells in his office," he replied, splashing whisky in the two glasses. "It makes me feel a *little* like Humphrey Bogart. No ice, I'm afraid. The fridge has packed up. Cheers."

He grimaced as he swallowed, then looked at me.

"Confidentially, Mr. Braddock, I hate the stuff, but it's good for the image. I once tried filling a bottle with Lipton Iced Tea, but it's not the same. The client needs to smell the alcohol. Don't you want yours?"

I raised the glass and downed it in one.

"I know what you're thinking," he said.

"I rather doubt that, Mr. Cumberbatch."

"Don't worry, I'm always dry when I work. And I do get results, trust me. Hard not to. This is an easy job, really. Following folks, taking pictures, making a few notes. A trained monkey could do it. Even you could do it. Whoops, that didn't come out right. No offence."

"None taken."

A POISON TREE

He put the whisky and the two glasses back in the drawer and picked up a pen.

"So, Mr. Braddock. What can I do for you?"

I considered getting up and leaving. My marriage was going down the tubes and I was thinking of entrusting my problems to this clown.

"Maybe this was a mistake, my coming here," I said.

Cumberbatch held up a hand and took a deep breath.

"It's the nerves, you see. I'm sorry, Mr. Braddock, it's the nerves."

His boisterous demeanour evaporated. His voice became quiet and slow.

"I've been in this business for over thirty years. It's a long time. I've seen so many clients with failing marriages. It gets to you after a while. So I try to keep things upbeat, at least at the start. It's a self-protection thing."

"I see."

"So now that I've taken a deep breath, why don't you take one, then tell me why you're here?"

I followed his advice.

I told him about my suspicions, about the phone calls and the anonymous notes. He listened with patience, enquired diplomatically why I had not contacted the police about the poison pen, and looked understanding when I explained. I gave him photographs of Claire and of Jack taken from our family scrapbook and he jotted down details, addresses and dates.

Cumberbatch would perform some discreet surveillance over the next few weeks. Then he would take a train to London and see what transpired at the Imperial Hotel.

I felt strangely reassured. God alone knew why.

I shook hands with the odd little man and signalled goodbye to his daughter.

A POISON TREE

As I left Cumberbatch's office, I saw the rain had stopped and a bright grey light was filtering through the clouds. Over the skyline of the city, a rainbow shimmered.

My fanciful mind, tripping for a moment on mythology, thought that maybe it was Bifröst, the rainbow bridge between Asgard and the world of men. The more logical Braddock, however, asserted that it was a meteorological phenomenon, the result of light hitting water droplets in the atmosphere: a much more mundane and less romantic notion.

The rational Braddock also insisted this was no time for misplaced sentiment and, moreover, dreams were for fools and madmen.

I stood in a doorway and smoked a Marlboro. Then I smoked another.

When I next looked, the rainbow had gone.

Perhaps there comes a point in everyone's life when we have to shoulder aside our nobler feelings and face an unkinder truth; when our romantic ideals wither and, like the Norse gods, discover it is time to die.

13

ADELE

Adele sat in the back room of the Gold Club, drinking tea from a chipped mug while Leona lit a cigarette from the stub of her last one.

Nina was off work with flu. The new girl, Samantha, was the only one with a customer. It was a slow day.

Samantha was half-Italian, nineteen and dumb as a stone but she had long black hair and great legs. She was therefore the natural first choice for most of the club's patrons. Intelligent conversation wasn't that high up their list of desirable attributes. It fell well below enthusiasm and physical flexibility.

Leona readjusted her skirt and said, "Did Nina tell you she once had a client drop dead on her of a heart attack?"

"Christ, no."

"The good news was that she was on top at the time, but the bad news was they were in the back of his car. She's not been able to look at a silver BMW since without having flashbacks."

Adele giggled and almost spat out a mouthful of tea. "Is that a true story?"

"As true as they come. She said they were parked up behind the big TESCO store in Nottingham. It's a rather popular location after midnight."

"What did she do?"

"She called a taxi. What else? She couldn't very well drive his car home with a stiff in the back seat, could she? There are sodding CCTV cameras all over the place in Nottingham.

"When they found him the next morning it caused a bit of a stir. It was all over the local papers. I told Nina she could at least have put the poor man's cock away."

The women heard the thud of feet on wooden floorboards above them.

"Sounds like Sam's finished," said Adele.

"Uh-huh," muttered Leona, blowing smoke towards the ceiling. "So," she went on, "what do you do when you're not working, Adele?"

"Work some more elsewhere."

"I know that feeling. I was studying property law last night. I fucking hate it. I'm never going to pass these exams."

Miss Connie put her head around the door.

"Leona, you have a customer. It's the Irish gentleman."

"Right," she replied, stubbing out her cigarette. "Mick's a non-smoker. Better give my teeth a scrub and gargle with some mouthwash. Back to the grind. See you in an hour, unless you get lucky."

The wall clock showed it was coming up to three twenty in the afternoon.

Adele told Miss Connie she was going out into the back yard for a smoke, then took one of Leona's cigarettes and her lighter. She didn't normally smoke, but she needed *something* before she phoned her mother.

She'd been putting off calling for days. The conversations always depressed her.

The back yard was high-walled and half-full of rusting junk. It hadn't been swept in months. Adele found a rickety stool, sat down, lit up and felt the burn in her throat. She shivered a little despite the afternoon sunshine. Then she pressed the buttons on her cell phone.

"I was wondering when you were finally going to call." The Glaswegian accent was slurred, as usual. By this time in the afternoon her mother would have got through at least half a bottle of spirits. Rum, vodka, whisky. It didn't matter much to her what it was. Whatever was selling cheapest at the off-licence on the corner.

"Hello, Mam. How are you?"

Adele knew the answer to that question. It was always the same, a litany of complaints about the neighbours, about her health, about anything and everything and everybody. She could see her mother in her chair, an overflowing ashtray perched on the arm and a glass of spirits within easy reach. She could visualise the dusty council flat, the damp seeping through the wallpaper, the stained carpet and the grey net curtains hanging, lopsided, at the window.

Flora Darrow was a bitter and disappointed woman.

Her first husband, Declan Gallagher, a merchant seaman, had been killed in a bar fight in Port Swettenham, in Malaysia – or the Federation of Malaya, as it was then. Years of financial struggle trying to bring up their son, Ross, followed. The bad days appeared to have ended when Flora met and married Malcolm Darrow.

At first the marriage had been happy. Darrow was a welder at the Govan shipyard, rarely drank and was sensible with money. What was more, he took his duties as stepfather to the boy seriously. Within two years, Flora was pregnant with Adele (or *Adaira*, as she was christened).

But when Adele was twelve years old, everything changed again for Flora. Darrow started seeing another woman. He moved to Aberdeen to work on the oil rigs and took his new love with him. Although he continued to send money to the family in Glasgow, and there was no divorce, neither Flora nor Adele ever saw or spoke to him again.

It was then that Flora Darrow began her slow decline into alcoholism.

Adele's half-brother Ross was by this time in the army and the money he sent home supplemented Darrow's remittances. It kept the family with a roof over their heads and food on the table, just about.

A POISON TREE

Despite being a bright girl, Adele left school at sixteen and worked at a number of menial, badly-paying jobs until she discovered she was pregnant by a casual boyfriend. Then her world started to fall apart in earnest.

"Did you hear what I said, Adele?"

"Yes, Mam. You want me to send you some money."

"You know I don't like to ask, pet, but that good-for-nothing brother of yours never sends me anything."

Adele knew that wasn't true, but she couldn't be bothered to argue. She was desensitised after years of her mother trying to play off her children against one another, and usually found it convenient to bite her tongue. What the older woman did not realise was that Adele and Ross did communicate about her and compared notes. They had agreed to keep their mother in the dark about this so as not to fuel Flora Darrow's inclination to play the victim card.

Once she had listened to more complaints about the state of her mother's knees, Adele could finally hang up. She felt drained of energy and wished she'd taken two of Leona's cigarettes, instead of just one.

She hoped she wouldn't get any weirdo customers today. She wasn't up to it.

The week passed quietly for Adele.

As usual for the English summer, the weather was changeable. The customers at the discount store for the most part presented faces of habituated disillusionment and grumbled that prices were going up. It was a treat when she received a smile or a thank you. She was usually invisible: it was the lot of the check-out girl.

Adele wondered what, if any, changes the Millennium would bring. None, in all probability. Life just went on until the day it didn't.

A POISON TREE

On the Saturday morning she found herself doing shopping in the city centre. It was her normal routine before her afternoon shift at the Gold Club.

"Good morning."

The friendly greeting took Adele by surprise. She turned to see a young man with sandy-coloured hair dressed as a vicar and holding out a cupcake.

"Can I give you something to ruin your teeth?" he said.

Recovering herself, Adele saw the man was standing at a church stall, along with three middle-aged ladies. She had never noticed the stall before. A red and gold banner was strung overhead announcing 'Christ Has Risen'.

"Is this new?" she said, before realising how stupid that must sound.

"Yes," replied the man. "Our church attendances have been falling recently, so we're trying a new approach, luring people in with the promise of cupcakes. If that fails, we're going to resort to kidnapping."

"So you're a real vicar?"

"It seems that way. Don't I look like a vicar? I've got the collar and everything." He grinned.

"I'm sorry, I didn't mean that. It's just that you look so –"

"Young?" he sighed. "Yes, I get a lot of that."

"I was going to say, *sexy*."

It was the vicar's turn to look flustered. Adele noticed one of the women throw a disapproving look in her direction.

"Well, in that case perhaps you should have two cupcakes. They are delicious. Eleanor here made them. She's a whiz in the kitchen." He indicated the sour-faced woman who was still glowering at Adele.

"I'm sure they are. But I'll just take one. I'm watching my weight. Thank you, vicar."

"It's 'Simon', not 'vicar'. 'Vicar' sounds so ... unsexy."

They both laughed, and he handed her a leaflet.

"Come and join us on Sunday," he said. "I need some constructive feedback on my sermons. Maybe that's what's driving folks away by the busload. We don't bite and you get free tea. You'll find us at St. Mark's, just off Northgate Street. You can't miss it. It's the sullied monstrosity of a building that looks like it should be in some creepy vampire movie."

"You make it sound very appealing, but I'm not a churchgoer, Simon."

"You're Scottish, right?"

"A good guess." She laughed.

"Well, we're not exactly a Scottish kirk, but at least you won't have to listen to any fire-and-brimstone stuff."

"You must be way down on your quota for saving souls this month to be resorting to these tactics."

"I am. I'm desperate. Come."

He has nice eyes.

She pushed the leaflet into her bag. "I'll think about it."

"Promise?"

"Cross my heart. I'm Adele, by the way."

"I'm delighted to meet you, Adele."

He shook her hand.

That night Adele tossed and turned.

Something in Simon's kind manner had triggered a realisation that she was in deep isolation. How else could a few polite words from a stranger have touched her so? The chance encounter had unsettled her, infiltrating her carefully-constructed emotional armour. The human contact she had assiduously avoided for the past two years all at once presented itself in an unexpected fashion.

Adele was used to being alone, indeed she regarded it as her natural state. She was not, by temperament, outgoing. Solitude was comforting, it fitted her like an old shoe. Her own company was safe: nothing could hurt her.

What Adele was not used to, was feeling *lonely*.

She had gone through her Saturday shift at the Gold Club on automatic. On several occasions Leona had asked her, "Are you with us today, love?" Adele responded by making some general reference to it being a tiring week.

When the glow of dawn began to filter through the curtains, she gave up the futile attempt at sleep. She showered and made breakfast.

Sunday morning.

Adele chewed without enthusiasm on a slice of toast and looked at the clock. It was only just after seven.

She rummaged in her bag until she found the pamphlet Simon had given her the previous day.

"Fuck it," she said out loud. "Why not?"

St. Mark's was easy to find, within ten minutes' walk of her apartment. It was more or less on the way to the Gold Club, as fate would have it.

As Adele approached the begrimed exterior of the church, she felt her courage ebbing away with each step.

This is insane. What the hell am I doing?

Yet she kept walking until she reached the door where Simon was greeting the faithful. She took a deep breath and, hoping her dress was demure enough and her makeup aptly discreet, stepped forward.

"Adele! How wonderful to see you!" Simon sounded genuinely happy.

"Well, I couldn't face vacuuming my flat this morning, so here I am."

"Dust gives a place character, anyway," he responded with a twinkle. "As you will see inside."

The interior of St. Mark's was indeed gloomy. The day's light struggled to penetrate the stained glass windows, and the lighted candles and suspended bulbs made little difference. A large statue of the crucified Christ drew the girl's eyes. He looked sad, hanging from the tree, and infinitely desolate. Above his head was nailed the sign 'INRI' – *Iēsus Nazarēnus, Rēx Iūdaeōrum* – 'Jesus the Nazarene, King of the Jews'.

Even God is alone.

Adele sat down at one of the dark wood pews towards the back. She estimated there were about fifty people in the church, mainly old or middle-aged, although she spotted three young families with fidgeting children. She could see the profile of the sour-faced Eleanor a few rows in front of her. She was sitting about half-way back with two other women.

The husband, if she has one, is not a churchgoer.

Eleanor caught sight of her and gave a brief, loveless glance before turning her face away.

Adele tried to remember the last time she had been anywhere near a place of worship. About seven years before, at her uncle's funeral. She didn't exactly come from a religious family.

The service began and Adele bluffed her way through it, copying the other members of the congregation. She moved her lips as the hymns were sung, but was too self-conscious to make any sound. When it came to the sermon, Simon chose forgiveness as his theme, citing Isiah.

"Though your sins are like scarlet, they shall be as white as snow."

He spoke with passion, but without artifice, on occasion throwing in a joke or a humorous remark. It was not what she had expected.

As the service finished, Adele tried to slip away but was accosted by a jolly-looking man with an Edwardian moustache and sideburns who insisted she stay for tea and biscuits.

"We don't see many new faces," he said, "so you'll have to excuse us if we seem a bit overwhelming."

Others said hello and hands were shaken. Eleanor declared it was nice to see her, although her eyes spoke otherwise. Adele felt self-conscious and willed the ordeal to end.

"I have better tea at the vicarage," Simon whispered in her ear. "Lady Grey."

"Oh, um, I need to go," Adele stammered.

"Ten minutes. Come on," he insisted. "It's kind of a 'thank you'. You've reduced the average age of the congregation by about a quarter this morning."

With reluctance, Adele accompanied him to the vicarage, which sat behind the churchyard. The other worshippers had dispersed, although Eleanor seemed loath to leave the two of them alone.

"So, what did you think of the sermon?" said Simon, after they had settled themselves and he was pouring tea. "Milk, sugar?"

"Just a splash of milk, thanks."

He handed her the cup.

"There wasn't a lot about God in your sermon, since you ask."

"No. Well, I save Him for special occasions. Some would like me to preach a bit more about damnation too."

"Like Eleanor, for instance?" The words were out before she had time to think. "I'm sorry, that's rude. She makes excellent cupcakes," she added.

"She does indeed." He looked amused before adding seriously, "And she does a lot for the church."

"I'm sure she does. You need to have some believers around."

"Aren't you one, then? A believer, I mean."

"No. That must be a disappointment. I'm drinking your tea under false pretences."

"Yet you came to the service."

"Yes. I'm not sure why I did that."

"Maybe it was the free cupcakes. You felt guilty."

There was a silence. Adele felt the need to break it. She wasn't equipped to handle a religious discussion. Time to move to firmer ground.

"I have to say, you don't look like a vicar."

"Do you know many vicars, then?"

"Actually, I don't know any. I seem to be making a habit of saying stupid things to you. I should have said, you don't look like my *idea* of a vicar."

"Bald or grey-haired, you mean?"

Adele nodded, embarrassed.

"Give me time," said Simon. "I'll get there."

She sipped the tea and decided to change the subject.

"This is a nice room, very cosy. Your wife has good taste."

"I don't have a wife."

"Oh, I'm sorry. I wasn't fishing."

Simon raised an eyebrow. "Really?"

Adele blushed. "Well, maybe a bit."

"It's OK. People get curious about vicars' private lives. Some of the older ladies in my congregation are forever trying to marry me off. Maybe they're worried that I might be gay."

He looked at her for a moment.

"Are you married, if you don't mind my asking?"

"No, I don't mind, and no, I'm not. I'm not sure I even believe in marriage."

"So," he said, crinkling his brow, "you don't know whether you believe in God or marriage. What gets you through the day? Your career, perhaps?"

"Hardly that. I work on a checkout at the Bargain Mart. It's not exactly a professional occupation."

"Hey, that's an important job, don't knock it."

"Please don't patronise me, Simon. It's *not* an important job," she said, "but it pays the bills. And as for beliefs, I'm too busy trying to make ends meet to worry about what I believe in." The strength of her words surprised her.

"I'm sorry," Simon said. "I wasn't trying to be patronising."

Adele put down her cup. "No, *I'm* sorry. I guess it's been a while since I sat down and talked to anyone."

"Perhaps you should talk more."

Adele looked at her watch. "I have to go. Thank you for the tea."

They both stood up.

"Will you come again next week, Adele?"

"Well, we'll see."

"I'd be grateful, if you could spare the time."

"If you're thinking of saving my soul, Simon, I'm afraid you'll have your work cut out."

"I'm up for a challenge."

Adele left the vicarage and hurried home to change. She was going to be late arriving at the Gold Club and Miss Connie would not be pleased. She did not want to explain that she was delayed because she had been having tea with the vicar.

She felt flustered by the unforeseen intimacy, and had a sense that a section of the ice wall around her heart had cracked a little. She knew from past experience that was a dangerous sign. The priest was disarming and open, too much so. Hostility, she was used to, but kindness unsettled her. Her indifference was her protection. It was what stopped her from falling apart.

Adele walked more quickly, so she could get to the club, to smoke one of Leona's cigarettes.

A POISON TREE

She needed to gather her scattered thoughts, and to lie with strangers who would neither know nor care who or what she really was.

14

ANNA

"Max?"

"Yes?"

"Your tie's crooked."

"Oh, we can't have that."

Anna adjusted her husband's Windsor knot and brushed his lapels with her hands.

"Thank you, my darling."

Max picked up his briefcase. "By the way, I'll be late home this evening. Don't bother cooking. I'll grab something while I'm out."

"What time will you be back?"

"I'm not sure."

"Max?"

"Yes?" he said with impatience. "Listen, Anna, I have to go. I have a meeting at nine. What is it? Can't it wait?"

Anna looked at him for a moment, then dropped her eyes.

"It's not important. I was just wondering if you're playing golf with David this weekend."

"I shouldn't think so. I have to play a round with some clients on Saturday, so that would be too much golf. Call him and let him know for me, would you?"

"You never said anything about playing golf on Saturday."

"Christ, Anna, do I have to tell you *everything?* You make me feel like I should be wearing an electronic tag."

"I'm sorry, I –"

"Just ring your brother-in-law and tell him I'm busy, OK? If you're that worried about it, *you* play golf with him."

"Well, maybe I *will*." She replied with a pout.

"Well, good for you."

Max slammed the door behind him and Anna had to fight back the urge to throw something against it.

She sat at the dining table. On it were two manuscripts she needed to go through and there was a deadline looming.

But instead of attacking the paperwork, Anna picked up her cell phone and looked at it. She wondered if David would be at his desk yet. She knew she was calling him a lot lately, and on one level it made her feel pathetic and helpless. The fact was, however, that she was always calmer and more optimistic after talking to him. But sooner or later his sympathy and patience might run out. The more often she pestered him, the earlier that day might arrive. Then what would she do?

Damn it, I have an excuse to ring him. I have to tell him Max is not available for golf.

Anna pulled herself up.

An excuse. An excuse to ring him.

The term worried her. Was she *looking* for reasons to call him?

"Don't be so bloody stupid, Anna," she said aloud. "This is *David* we're talking about." She pressed the buttons on her phone.

"Hi, Anna."

"Hi, David. I'm not interrupting you, am I?"

"No, I've got a few minutes. What can I do for you, my dear?" The voice was relaxed, reassuring.

"Max asked me to tell you he's not available for golf this weekend. He has to play golf with a client."

"It's no problem."

"Yes, it is. It's inconsiderate of him not to have told you. Maybe I should play with you instead."

Shit, I shouldn't have said that.

David laughed. "Since when do you play golf?"

"I could learn. It can't be that difficult if a man can do it."

"True."

"Listen, David," Anna said, choosing her words. "I have to come into town. I don't suppose you're free for lunch?"

"I can't today. I'm supposed to be meeting Claire for lunch."

"Oh, OK."

There was a pause on the line. Then David said, "Are you all right?"

"Yes, I'm fine."

"No you're not."

"I am, honestly."

"No, you're not. I can tell. Look, I'll meet you for lunch. As it's a nice day, how about we have baguettes in the Town Hall Square? I'll bring the baguettes. We can have a little picnic."

"What about Claire?"

"I'll tell her something came up. We can have lunch another day. It's only a little white lie. It's not like we're having an affair or anything."

"No."

She heard David sigh. "Oh, I'm sorry, Anna. That was a stupid thing to say."

"You don't need to tiptoe around the subject, David. And I don't want you lying to Claire on my behalf."

"Now you're just being silly. I'll meet you on a park bench at one o'clock. Don't argue."

"All right. I'll bring wine. Just enough for two glasses."

"Good. It's a date."

A POISON TREE

She picked up a manuscript and worked on it for two hours before she started fretting about what to wear.

Anna parked her car near the mock-Tudor houses tucked behind Leicester's small cathedral, and walked the short distance to the Square. It was a pretty spot, on two sides of which were well-preserved civic buildings and an impressive clock tower. In the centre of the square was a large fountain of dark brown marble, guarded by four gryphons. People were milling around, tempted outdoors by the bright sunshine.

She spotted David sitting on one of the park benches. He had taken off his jacket and laid it over the back of the bench. His tie and the top button of his shirt were loosened, and he had rolled up his sleeves. He waved to her.

"Hello, sister-in-law," he said.

"Hello, brother-in-law. I brought wine and two plastic glasses." She pulled them out of her shoulder bag.

"Ah, what decadence. I have baguettes." He unwrapped them. "Oh, bollocks. They've given me two ham and cheese. I specifically ordered –"

"Never mind," Anna replied. "Pass it over."

"But you're a *vegetarian*. You can't eat ham."

"Let's say I'm re-evaluating some of my life choices." She took a bite. "Mmn. It's good."

David looked at her aghast. "You haven't eaten meat in two decades. And now you just casually bite into a ham sandwich?"

"You know what they say about change? It either happens in an instant or not at all. Shall I pour the wine?"

"Yes." He continued to look at her. "Shit, I feel like the devil or something."

"The horns suit you."

"Cuckolds have horns too."

"What?"

"Oh, nothing," He looked for a moment as if he wanted to say something serious, but then added, "I was just thinking about that manuscript you gave me to look at a few months back."

"Ah."

They sat in silence for a while, eating and staring at the fountain.

"Will you tell Claire we met for lunch?"

"No."

"Why not?"

"It's not important she knows."

"I'm so lucky to have you as my brother-in-law, you know, David. I hope we will always be friends."

"You said that to me once before. A long time ago."

"You remember that?" she said, surprised.

"Of course. I remember everything. I have a memory like an elephant. For some things, anyway."

A couple walked in front of them. David leaned closer to Anna and lowered his voice. "How are things with you and Max?"

"Not so good." She finished the baguette and brushed the crumbs from her lap. "I'm wondering whether I should be hiring a private detective. Maybe it's time I did something about the situation."

"Hiring a private detective is the beginning of the end," said David, and Anna thought she saw a shadow of sadness cross his face.

"I know. Now finish your wine. I've monopolised you long enough."

"Do you have any idea yet who it is?"

"No."

"Max needs his head examined."

"Yes," Anna replied quietly. "But maybe I do too."

15

CLAIRE

Every time Claire visited her family's farm it filled her with nostalgia and a sense of loss.

She had believed that after her father's fatal heart attack five years ago, her mother would sell the farm and move somewhere more appropriate for a lady of advancing years. But Natalie Holland was made of stern substance and was adamant that she would stay in her home until it was her turn to 'go underground'. She had hired the necessary additional labour and soldiered on.

While on the outside Natalie presented a cheerful face to the world, Claire was aware of how deeply her husband's death had affected her. Their marriage had sometimes resembled a comedy double act, with Frank playing the straight guy to Natalie's hippy butterfly. Like all couples, they had rowed, but the disagreements had never lasted long. They were too committed to each other and shared too much love for that.

Claire knew her mother would have liked more grandchildren, but her daughters' marriage choices and other happenings had denied her the consolations of an extended family. Consequently, Natalie Holland focused her considerable affections on Katie.

Claire looked around the dining table in the Holland's large farmhouse kitchen. It was, as always, piled high with more food than could be eaten at a single sitting. Katie and her grandmother were in deep conversation about university matters. The lunch was a delayed celebration to commemorate the end of Katy's exams. School was over. Adulthood beckoned. The nest would soon be empty.

A POISON TREE

Anna was chatting to David about some manuscript she was reading. Anna's husband Max had not turned up, detained by some unavoidable business matter. Claire doubted that was the real explanation, but the subject of her sister's marriage was no longer something to be discussed over a meal, or indeed anywhere. Anna refused to talk about it.

A gap had opened up between the sisters recently that was only in part to do with Anna's domestic situation. Claire suspected the rest was to do with her and Jack – that seeing him had in some way changed all her relationships. None of them knew about Jack, of course, but *she* did.

A subtle alchemy had begun to erect a barrier between her and her loved ones, and was inexorably altering the way they saw each other, like a slow onset of blindness.

It brought to Claire's mind the anecdote about the frog in the saucepan of water. Bit by bit the water heats and the frog doesn't move until it is too late and it is boiled to death.

It was the minute changes that cumulated and destroyed. The little things you didn't notice until the day you woke up and everything was strange – even yourself.

If only she were stronger... but she was not.

Claire sat eating robotically. She felt isolated. Around her on the walls were framed photographs of what seemed like a distant past. Her father was dead. One of her bulwarks against mortality had been removed. What would her father have thought of the woman she was today? She felt vulnerable and alien. Above all, she felt ashamed.

"Are you all right, Claire?" It was David's voice.

Four anxious faces turned towards her and she blushed.

"Mum?" said Katie. "You look a bit odd."

"I'm – um – feeling a bit dizzy. I think I need some fresh air."

"Well, luckily we have plenty of that here, dear," said her mother.

A POISON TREE

"I'll take her outside," announced David, rising from his chair.

Claire held David's arm and they walked out into the yard where one of the farm workers was bent over a piece of machinery.

"Working on a Sunday?" asked David.

The man wiped the sweat from his face with a crumpled handkerchief. "It's either that or go with the missus to church," he replied. "This is the lesser of the two evils."

Claire tried a smile.

They rounded the corner of the buildings and leaned against a wooden fence. The landscape looked peaceful. A lazy tractor moved across a distant hillside, and the white smoke of a bonfire rose upwards. Two ramblers disappeared into a wood, their laughter floating in the still air. High above their heads the vapour trails of aircraft cut gashes in the blue sky.

Claire took a few deep breaths and squeezed her husband's arm.

"Is that better?"

"Yes. Sorry. I was just a bit light-headed."

"It's OK. I'm quite glad to get away from the food for a few minutes."

"And from Anna's talking about books, eh?" She nudged him with an elbow.

"I quite enjoy talking about books." There was a slight edge to his voice. He turned his face away from her to gaze across the fields.

"Maybe you married the wrong sister."

"I don't think so," he muttered.

"I'm just kidding. No need to be so grumpy." She could hear her own forced cheerfulness.

"I'm over-full with Yorkshire pudding and meat. Your mother put half a cow on my plate."

He seemed at once wistful and self-absorbed, quite different from how he appeared while talking to Anna only a few minutes earlier.

A POISON TREE

"Sorry, if I've been on edge lately," he said. "I feel a bit burned-out, work-wise. But our holiday in Bali will fix that, I'm sure." He took a pack of Marlboros from his pocket and lit one. "Just the one, OK?"

"OK."

I need to cancel the trip to London. I'm hurting this man. He doesn't know it, but I am.

But even as the idea formed, she knew she wouldn't.

She couldn't.

She hugged David and kissed his cheek.

Life is always telling lies to us.

Katie appeared and threw her arms around them both. "You feeling better now, Mum? Gran is worried she might have poisoned you."

"I'm fine, sweetheart."

"Gran also thinks you should buy me a car for university."

"In your dreams," said David Braddock. "In. Your. Dreams."

16

JAMES

Jim Fosse slid back the glass door of his room and stepped out onto the veranda. He was wearing nothing but his underpants, but he was not concerned about being seen.

The sky was just beginning to lighten and the dawn chorus was in fine voice. From his vantage point he could see miles and miles of tropical greenery, punctuated by the occasional corrugated iron roof. Morning mist floated between the trees.

He was glad to have escaped from Manila for a couple of nights. When his business associate had offered him the use of his palatial house on the hillside, Jim had not needed to be asked twice. The American appreciated the finer things in life, and Lopez had an impressive wine cellar he had put at Jim's disposal, along with the expensive escort still sleeping in the bedroom behind him.

Maybe my next wife will be Asian. I think I'm ready for a change.

He replayed in his head the tasks that needed to be achieved over the next few months, mind-mapping the intertwining branches of possibility and contingency to check whether he had overlooked anything.

"I need to buy a new black tie," he said to nobody in particular.

The girl on the bed stirred.

But not today.

He slapped at an insect on his arm and went back inside.

17

DAVID

Dotted along Monkey Forest Road in Ubud, Bali, are Internet cafés. They are frequented for the most part by backpackers trying to organise transport or accommodation. Sometimes these low-budget tourists are there to check in with the folks back home to give reassurance that they have not been kidnapped and are not out of their head on drugs or *arak*. Money, or the lack of it, usually features in this category of emails and messages. All around the world some parent somewhere is sighing at the fecklessness of their offspring.

Claire and I collected Katie from Funky Monkey Internet. It was her favourite hangout that served fruit shakes 'to die for, and so cheap', as my daughter informed me.

"Come on, pumpkin, time to go," I said.

She settled up with the pretty Balinese girl at the desk.

"Anyway, Dad, good news," she announced as we started walking up the road.

"Good. I could do with some of that."

"I've just had an email from a Nigerian prince who wants to share two million dollars with me. I only have to send him my bank account details. It looks like you won't have to buy me a car."

"Are there people so stupid as to fall for these scams?" said Claire.

"Wherever there is a credibility gap, there is a gullibility fill," Katie replied. "Anyway, there was a great scam our business studies teacher told us about.

"Imagine you receive an email from an unknown person representing a financial advisory company that specialises in currency movements. He

118

doesn't ask you to invest anything he just gives you their company's prediction that, say, the dollar will strengthen against the pound by the end of the month. Are you with me so far?"

"Yes. But is this going to be a complicated story?"

Katie sighed. "Just pay attention, Dad, OK? Anyway, it gets to the end of the month and you see the dollar did indeed strengthen against the pound – in fact, you get another email pointing it out, and telling you that, say, by the end of the next month the dollar will weaken against the pound.

"This goes on in total for three months and each time the prediction is right. Then you get an invitation to invest in that month's movement – but they don't tell you in advance this time which way the exchange rate will move. If you saw they had a *pukka* website, and based on their track record, you might be tempted, right?"

"If they'd got all three months' predictions correct, I guess you might be," responded Claire. "But only if they got them *all* right."

"Well, at that point you could kiss goodbye to all the money you invested with them. And by the way, they didn't get *any* predictions right, for the simple reason that they didn't make any."

"I thought you said –"

"No, wait. Here's the beauty of it. A few months before, a group of scammers set up a good-looking website for a bogus investment company. Then they searched the Internet – using sophisticated software – to find the email addresses of a half a million possible investors.

"To half of these they sent the email predicting the dollar would strengthen and to the other half they sent an email predicting it would weaken. It's a fifty-fifty bet, right?

"The next month, they only email the people they had told the dollar would strengthen – since with the others they will have no credibility. That's a quarter of a million people. They divide these into two again and tell half the dollar will strengthen and half it will weaken.

"They repeat this process once more in the next month, and by that stage the 'lucky' ones have received three correct predictions. They now number one hundred and twenty-five thousand.

"If the scammers can only get *five per cent* of those people to invest twenty thousand dollars, that's over a one hundred and twenty thousand dollar profit, give or take. For no outlay. Then they vanish. Portfolio theory for the criminal mind."

"That's cool," I said.

"And do you know what makes it work? It's that you *assume* you're looking at a prediction. It's never going to occur to you that the same person would also make exactly the opposite prediction too. Or that he's not even making a prediction at all. Your brain tells you – like in the *Highlander* films – 'There can be only one'. And even though we *know* it's a random mailshot, we still think it's aimed uniquely at us."

I scratched my head. "Shouldn't you be, like, interested in boys by now, Katie? Or girls, I don't mind. Why aren't you out getting drunk like normal people of your age?"

Katie sighed again. "I'm going to be a lawyer, Dad. Lawyers are not normal. That's why they make so much money. If I was a high-functioning sociopath, I could be a millionaire by the time I hit thirty. But, hey ho. You have to play with the cards you're dealt. I'm not responsible for my genetics."

We arrived at the Royal Palace and took our seats for the Ramayana Ballet. We sat together under the stars while the gamelan orchestra played, and the brightly-costumed dancers reminded us there was yet grace and beauty in the world.

A POISON TREE

Bali has always cast a spell on me.

In spite of the melancholy about Claire that sucked at my insides, the island exerted a healing effect on me. Not for nothing does the word 'Ubud' come from the old Balinese term for medicine. At home, pretending that everything was as before came hard. I had had the odd outburst of temper, which was so unusual for me, that it resulted in shocked looks from those around me. I always cited work stress, and even my father declared I needed a vacation. *That* was a first.

An informed and impartial observer might have questioned why I did not just raise the issue with my wife, get it into the open to stop the wound from festering. The more cynical members of humanity would applaud my silence. They would whisper that knowledge was power and that by keeping quiet I was preserving my alternative courses of action without alerting anyone beforehand. But what alternative courses of action? It wasn't as though I was going to kill my wife, was it? It's not like I was Jim Fosse.

And even Jim Fosse wasn't *really* going to kill his wife. That was just his strange idea of humour.

The unvarnished truth was that, despite my earlier reflections on the subject, I was reluctant to let a dream die. I clung to the hope that the private detective would furnish me with a rational explanation for Claire's behaviour. One that did not involve disloyalty.

So for the duration of our time on Bali, I sought to keep these thoughts at a distance, and instead to reflect in the quiet moments on who had made the anonymous phone calls and sent me the toxic letter.

The most likely candidate was Mark Standish. Embittered by his failure at our company and with a collapsed marriage, he fitted the profile of someone who would be tempted into malice.

Then again, perhaps it wasn't the case that I had an enemy. It could be someone bent on stirring up trouble for Claire. Like Jack's wife, Eleanor, for instance.

I knew Eleanor slightly. Although I had put her into the 'god botherer' box, she struck me as a cold woman who might well be given to spiteful actions if provoked.

But could a voice synthesiser disguise a woman's voice to sound like a man's? Maybe, although I was sure my mysterious caller was a man. Did Eleanor have a brother who might do the dirty work for her? I knew she didn't have a son, only a daughter, Ruth, who was about Katie's age.

Also, the lack of contact in recent weeks was puzzling. The unknown caller had just stopped, and no more letters had arrived.

Maybe like the scammers in Katie's story, the poison pen had moved on to his next mark.

Since we'd already visited Bali several times before, we felt no need to rush around doing touristy things. So aside from a trip to the waters at Danau Bratan in the great volcanic crater to the north, and a tramp through some lime green rice terraces outside Ubud, we spent our time pottering around. We watched the ladies in their traditional dress, making offerings to the gods by the roadside, swam in the hotel swimming pool, and enjoyed the various organic dishes served at our favourite restaurants.

Every day I went to the same spa for a massage with Wayan, the gentle, pretty and inexplicably-unmarried Balinese woman whom we'd befriended many years before.

"If anything ever happens to me," said Claire, after Wayan had given her a pedicure and manicure, "you have my permission to let Wayan take care of you. She is just the type of woman you'd need."

"Don't you ever say that sort of thing in front of Wayan," I chided. "It will embarrass her. Anyway," I added, "Nothing is going to happen to you. We're going to grow old and crabby together."

Claire put her arms around me. "You just don't know. I've never thought I'll make old bones. And if you do take up with Wayan, I promise I won't haunt you."

"How about if I take up with a young Thai woman instead?"

"Then I *will* haunt you."

"Racist."

Towards the end of the holiday, Katie found me alone in the hotel gardens. I was puffing on a Marlboro and reading a paperback.

"What's the book, Dad?"

"It's called *The Kommandant's Mistress*. Auntie Anna recommended it to me."

"What's it about?"

"It's a novel about how a Jewish girl was enslaved and made into a sex toy of the Kommandant of one of the Nazi death camps during World War Two."

"And you read this for fun?"

Katie sat down beside me. "I have weird parents," she said, "and on that basis, a weird aunt too. I hope it's not going to affect my legal career."

"Oh, shut up, you." I put my arm around her and tickled her ribs.

After a pause, she said, "You seem much happier than you've been recently."

"I'm always happy when I'm in Bali," I replied, in a non-committal fashion.

"I was a bit worried. I've detected some tension between you and Mum."

A POISON TREE

"That's just teenage over-sensitivity. Your mum and I are fine. We're always fine." I put down my cigarette so I could hug her. "We're in this for the long term, sweetheart. We'll be together until the Grim Reaper comes calling. And even then, I'll make a fight of it. I promise."

"OK," she said, reassured. "I'll let you get back to your romance."

"You're a little smart-arse, do you know that, Katie Braddock? You'll no doubt make a fine lawyer. And for your information," I said, waving the book, "this is *literature*."

18

DAVID

I put my elbows on the bar of the Bell as Ian pulled me a pint.

"So tell me," I said. "Where does all this wisdom of yours come from, O Guru?"

"I've been studying Buddhism."

"You mean you've been reading books? Familiarising yourself with sacred texts like *The Dhammapada*? I find that hard to imagine."

"The Damn of What?"

"*Dhammapada*. The sayings of the Buddha."

"Who's got the time to read all that shit? I've got a pub to run. No, I picked up a copy *of Enlightenment in 15 Minutes* from a car boot sale."

"Profound."

"I skimmed some of it, mind you."

"Of course you did. It would be too much to ask for you to concentrate on anything for a whole fifteen minutes."

Ian set the pint in front of me.

"Want me to summarise Buddhist philosophy for you?"

"I can't wait."

"OK." He concentrated hard. "*No birth, no death, not coming, not going, not existing, not non-existing, not the same, not different.*" He looked pleased with himself.

"Thanks. I feel a lot better now. None the wiser, but much better informed."

"It just means that everything you see is an illusion."

"So this beer is an illusion?"

"Exactly."

"So I don't need to pay you for it, because you're not really selling me anything?"

Ian shook his head vigorously. "Ah, no. You pay me but with imaginary money."

"Imaginary money?"

"Yes, but it has to be *real* imaginary money."

I took a five pound note from my wallet and handed it to him.

"I thought I read something about Buddhists believing in compassion, not imaginary money."

"That too. It's about making people happy."

"So how do you make people happy? You're a miserable bastard."

"Beer makes people happy. I sell beer."

"But it's imaginary beer? So presumably it's imaginary happiness?"

"Now you're getting it."

Imaginary happiness.

Is that what we all have?

We act. We share. We strive for purpose in a world without permanence. We create our own realities. But it is all inside our head.

All is illusion.

All is cant.

All is vanity.

Katie got the results she needed for Oxford.

We had a few anxious days after returning from Bali, and then the dark clouds dispersed and our daughter's career hopes took a mighty step forward.

A POISON TREE

We had a celebration dinner with the whole family at the most expensive restaurant in the city. Even Max came along and did his best to fit in and show appropriate enthusiasm.

Claire's trip to London was approaching. As the date edged closer I found myself growing anxious. On a couple of occasions I almost asked her not to go, but I held back. There were other times when I considered telling her of my suspicions and asking for an explanation. But the moments passed, and we continued to trundle along the path of unknowing.

I had handed the torch to the private detective, Cumberbatch.

I would wait.

Meantime, I endeavoured to act as normal as possible. It was a busy time at work and this served as a partial distraction. But another surprise lay in wait.

The day before Claire was due to leave for London, I had an emotional phone call from Harry.

"David, have you heard?"

"Heard what?"

"About Mark."

"No."

"He's killed himself."

I drove over to the Coventry showroom straight away, trying to process this information. On arrival, I found the staff in a state of shock. Some of them had known Mark for several years and it hit them hard.

Harry sat in his office. His face was ashen. "I went round to Janine's last night, after I'd heard," he said. "The woman was in a terrible way."

"What happened, Harry?"

He scratched at his brow and looked down at the desk before replying.

"You remember earlier this year when Mark said he might have a medical problem?"

127

"He was having blood tests. Yes, I remember. But the tests came back OK. He told me."

"That's what he told everyone. But they weren't OK. And they weren't ordinary blood tests. They were for HIV."

"Oh, Christ. He tested positive?"

"Yes. Of course, he had to tell Janine. He might have infected her too. That's when everything blew up and he moved out."

"She's not –?"

"No, thank God. He confessed he'd been seeing this hooker for a couple of years, and apparently they hadn't always used protection. That's presumably how he got it."

Confethed he'd been *theeing*. Even now I couldn't help noticing Harry's lisp.

You cold bastard, Braddock.

I took out my cigarettes and lit one. "Sorry, Harry, I think I need one of these."

"It's OK, David," he said, and handed me a mug to use as an ashtray.

"How did Mark –?" I couldn't finish the question.

"He drove out to a wood and hanged himself. Two ramblers found him."

Harry got up and opened a window.

"He left a note for Janine on the mantelpiece of that hovel he lived in. Said he was sorry, but he couldn't face the shame. You know, that kind of thing."

Mantelpieth.

Thaid.

Thorry.

Fayth.

"The poor bugger."

If my anonymous caller was Mark Standish, I'd never know now.

128

But then, we can't know everything.

Can we?

I spoke to Claire a couple of times on the phone while she was away in London. She didn't sound happy, but neither did she sound miserable. She just sounded like Claire. I listened to the rhythm of her voice, dismantled later her choice of words, fixated on the length of the call. And I came up empty.

Mark's death had only served to accentuate the numbness that had taken possession of me. I felt lost, disoriented, glued to the spot while a sinkhole opened beneath my feet. I lacked the will to act, to speak even.

When Claire returned, I met her at the station, hugged her and told her I'd missed her. She hugged me back and told me she'd missed me too. Then she kissed me.

That was the first time I felt the bite of anger.

We all indulge in magical thinking.

We cross our fingers and decline to walk under ladders. We scream at the television during football matches as if that will somehow alter the result. We ascribe events to fate or destiny. The mother comforts the child with the grazed knee by 'kissing it better'. We wish for things.

It is all illogical and irrational, and we do it all the time. It is the consequence of being equipped with a brain that constructs reality around a premise of *usefulness* rather than *truthfulness*.

We love wizards and warlocks. Human characteristics are routinely ascribed to family pets, as though they think and feel the same way we do. The magic amulet that wards off evil assumes many shapes and forms, but its essence remains the same – an attempt to exercise control over those things which we cannot control. It is a charm to provide a protective barrier against the vagaries of the world and the unfairness of life.

And the lure of the magical is at its strongest at those times we experience cognitive dissonance; that unpleasant, grinding sensation when our deepest-held beliefs are exposed as fallacies. We fight against facts and bend logic until we can explain away the hard evidence that contradicts our world view or threatens our fragile peace of mind. Either that or we ignore the evidence altogether where the consequences of paying attention would be too painful to bear.

The belief that ultimately there is meaning to our existence, is our last redoubt. Without meaning, it is problematical to hold onto the delusion of our eternal existence. The pillars that support our idea of self, and our own unique place in the universe, collapse, and the rubble that remains is incomprehensible.

We can live without happiness. But we cannot live without meaning.

The day of reckoning eventually dawns. The bitter time when we will have to stare at the sun, even if it blinds us.

That day for me was the occasion I went to see Cumberbatch for the second time, on the first of September 1999. It was the Wednesday – Odin's Day – following Claire's trip to London. Not a date I would forget any time soon, if ever.

Driving to his office, I felt hollowed out, like the aftermath of a neutron bomb explosion where the buildings remain but the people who occupied them have perished. I had become a pseudomorph, a creature of structure but without essence. My recent happy time with Claire had been nothing but a sham, the lovemaking of actors playing a part. My thoughts teetered on the edge of the void.

A POISON TREE

Yet even then, I entertained a residue of hope. So much of my life's purpose, I realised, was invested in my marriage. If I could have prayed, I would have.

I had to park several streets away from Cumberbatch Surveillance, thanks to some oaf in a sports car who sneaked in to take my parking spot while I was waiting to reverse. It didn't improve my mood.

Dolores was reading some style magazine when I arrived. She got up with reluctance and knocked on the door to the inner office. There was a muttered voice from inside and I was shown through.

I knew immediately the news was going to be bad.

Cumberbatch's bearing as he greeted me was that of a funeral director comforting a bereaved relative. He was far removed from the rambunctious individual I had encountered some weeks before.

He opened a khaki wallet file and began reading in a dull monotone. He told me that on two occasions Claire had met Jack during the day at a teashop in Market Harborough, and he had followed them three times to Kettering where they had visited the site of Jael Construction's new development. The only untoward behaviour he had witnessed was that once Jack had put his arm around Claire.

"That's not conclusive of anything," I said. "So I didn't know about them meeting for tea or coffee or whatever, but that isn't a crime."

"No," Cumberbatch said carefully. "It isn't."

"Tell me about London."

He consulted the file. "They both stayed at the Imperial Hotel. Your wife had a room on the first floor and Mr. Irving was in a suite on the top floor."

He put down his papers and looked at me. "It's difficult to track movements inside a hotel without being obvious, and my appearance is rather, um, shall we say, memorable?" He pointed to his white hair. "I've tried wearing wigs but –"

"Can you just get to the point, please, Mr. Cumberbatch?" I sounded testy.

"Of course. Yes. Well, I figured if they were staying in the same room, it would likely be Mr. Irving's, given that it was a suite. However, as I didn't see them both go into it, I couldn't be sure. I'd just be speculating."

"I see."

He paused. "I do know they spent the night together, though."

"How?"

He took a sip from the whisky glass on his desk and pulled a face. "I thought I needed some hard evidence for you, so at one o'clock in the morning I set off the hotel fire alarm." He seemed embarrassed. "Yes, I know. It was a bit naughty of me. I'm afraid I've had to resort to this sort of thing before. But I couldn't hang around the hotel all night. It would have been too suspicious."

"So you saw them both come out of Irving's room?"

"A few minutes later, yes. Then when the all-clear was sounded, I followed them back upstairs."

"And they went back to his room?"

"Yes."

I looked down at the floor.

"I'm sorry," he said.

"I want you to go on following my wife."

Cumberbatch looked pained, as if he were the one who had received the bulletin of betrayal.

"Mr. Braddock," he began, choosing his words with care, "I could take your money. God knows, I need it. But you have all the evidence you need. I will provide you with a full, written report, and I have photographs of your wife and Mr. Irving together, should you want them.

"But I must tell you, I have seen this sort of reaction before. I had one female client whose husband I trailed for eighteen months after she learned of his affair with another woman. She couldn't confront him, you see, and just went on hoping the liaison would stop. She wanted me to tell her it had stopped. It never did.

"What happens now is up to you, Mr. Braddock. I've seen enough heartbreak to want to drag out the agony further."

He reached into the drawer of his desk and pushed some advertising blurb and leaflets at me. "Here is all sorts of information on surveillance devices, if you want to continue with this. I get a lot of this sort of stuff in the mail every week, and you're welcome to it. There are other private detective agencies here who will pick up where I left off. I know of reputable ones I can recommend, if necessary."

"You are a rather sentimental private detective, Mr. Cumberbatch," I observed.

"Yes. Yes, I am," he said. "And a rather tired one. Do you want me to send the full report to you, or will you collect it in person? I'd advise the latter."

"I'll drop by next week and pick it up. Can I settle your bill now? I've brought cash with me."

"No problem. Dolores has your itemised invoice with all the receipts attached."

I stood up, but Cumberbatch forestalled me.

"Discovering something like this is rather like a bereavement," he said. "I suggest you take some time to think about what you are going to do. And like a bereavement, you will go through the four stages of grief: shock, anger, depression and, finally, acceptance. The sequence of emotions is inevitable and, I'm afraid, unavoidable."

"I'm not shocked, Mr. Cumberbatch. I was expecting this."

He looked concerned. "I know you're not shocked, Mr. Braddock. I can see that. What worries me is that you are angry. Anger is a dangerous thing."

"I am not angry."

"People do stupid things when they are angry."

"I am not angry," I repeated. "I haven't even raised my voice, have I?"

"Often the anger of the quiet, reasonable man is the worst," he said.

I went to the street where the Maserati that had taken my space was parked, and ran my car key all the way along the bodywork on the passenger side.

Then I took out my cell phone and called Jim Fosse.

19

ADELE

Adele did not go often to the Internet café for two sound reasons.

The first was that there were only two people who sent her emails, her old school friend, Moira, and her half-brother, Ross.

In the case of Moira, she would email once a month as a sort of digest of what was going on in her life in Aberdeen. These missives usually comprised a blow-by-blow account of what her kids were doing, along with the occasional complaint about her husband or in-laws. Adele didn't mind what Moira chose to burble about. She was the sole friend from her past with whom she stayed in touch. Adele felt obliged to make things up in her own monthly report, just to sound interesting, and of course her employment at the Gold Club did not feature.

Ross' communications were more infrequent and less predictable. His usual method of contacting Adele was by phone, but sometimes he would send an email from whichever exotic part of the globe he was currently based. These locations changed often, but recently he seemed to be spending a lot of time in Asia.

What Ross did for a living was a mystery to Adele. When she asked him about his work – as she did from time to time – his answer was always vague and technical to do with 'security'. She had gathered, however, that whatever it was he did, he was freelance. He was not employed by conventional companies, or at least not overtly. Whenever he did mention names, which was rare, they were foreign-sounding and unfamiliar. Adele imagined it was his army experience that made him valuable in the security business: she couldn't think what else it could be.

A POISON TREE

Whatever it was he was being paid for, it paid well. Ross regularly sent both her and their mother money; money that Adele, at least, was reluctant to take.

The second reason Adele was apprehensive of frequenting the Internet café was its less-than-salubrious location. She never went there after dark. There were often winos and other undesirables hanging around in the street outside, and some of the clientele did not look particularly reputable either. Sometimes the manager had hit on her, although that had stopped after her last visit when she gave him a piece of her mind, an experience he did not enjoy. The Glasgow brogue lends itself to cursing and amoral discouragement. When coupled with a finger poked in the chest, it usually makes any further assertion of rights unnecessary and the point clear.

On that Saturday morning, the lecherous manager was nowhere to be seen. His balding, combed-over head was elsewhere. In his place was an overweight, pasty-faced individual in an Iron Maiden vest, who looked like he wished he were elsewhere. The only other customer was another male who, Adele thought, had the aspect of a basement-dweller. He was engrossed in some online game involving swords and monsters.

Adele logged on to find she had two emails.

Ross' email announced in his usual dry style that he had suffered one of his recurring bouts of malaria while in northern Thailand, but that he had since recovered. He hoped to be back in the UK for a visit in the next few weeks and would call her when his travel plans were fixed. It was dated eight days before. Adele replied by saying she would love to see him. It was true. In spite of the fact that her half-brother was taciturn, difficult and secretive, he was the closest thing she had known to a father for some years. Plus, he did look out for her in his own gruff way. Just so long as she didn't ask too many questions, he was fine.

A POISON TREE

The message from Moira was about her son Jack's wisdom teeth, sleepless nights, and the fact that she was considering a boob job to reinvigorate her husband's interest in afternoon delight. For want of anything better to write in response, Adele reported that she had been to church. That would surprise Moira. She disliked religion more than she disliked the English. And she disliked the English *a lot*.

Adele sat back on the uncomfortable metal chair, her work done.

It was three weeks since her morning at St. Mark's, and she had not been back.

"Hello."

Adele was daydreaming on the checkout – a not unusual state for her, as the ennui of repetition tended to block out conscious thought after a few hours – but the unexpectedness of the friendly greeting made her look up.

It was Simon. He grinned at her. "Sorry, did I wake you?"

"What are you doing here?"

"It's good to see you too."

Adele felt her cheeks colour. "I'm sorry. I was just a bit surprised."

She started to process the purchases.

"What *are* you doing here, though?" she said, still a little flustered.

"Even a vicar has to eat."

"Yes, but I've never seen you in here before."

He looked thoughtful. "Well, I wondered whether I'd said something to upset you, since you haven't been back to St. Mark's."

The elderly woman behind Simon in the queue seemed to be enjoying their conversation.

"I remembered you saying you worked here, so ... um." His voice tailed off.

"So I'm being stalked by a vicar?" She thought she may as well give the woman something to talk about with her friends.

Adele finished putting Simon's groceries into bags and indicated the amount owed on the display.

Simon produced two twenty pound notes and handed them over.

"Listen," he said. "What time do you finish your shift?"

"Why?"

"I wondered whether you would agree to let me buy you a coffee."

Adele handed him his change. "I don't know whether that's a good idea," she said. She wasn't sure she wanted to be seen in public with Simon. Something about the idea made her feel uncomfortable.

"Please," he said.

"Oh, go on, dear," chimed in the old lady. "Say yes. He seems like a nice young man. And if you don't, I will."

"Do you have a car?" said Adele.

"Yes. It's a bit of a banger, but yes. Why?"

"We can have a drink at my flat if you don't mind instant coffee. I'll meet you beside the central clock tower in about an hour and a half, OK? You can drive me home. That way I can get some shopping done too."

"That sounds eminently practical, dear," said the old lady.

"Yes, it does." Simon bowed to the woman. "Thank you for your help."

"My pleasure, vicar."

Simon was standing beside the mock-medieval clock tower as Adele approached. The stationary vicar attracted glances from passers-by – just the sort of attention Adele liked to avoid. Her spirits sunk a little. Simon's carrier bags were by his feet and he was reading some flyer, so he did not notice her at first. She regretted her hasty offer of coffee, but it was too late to back out now. Besides, it was easier than walking home with her own shopping bags, she told herself. She remembered that Simon had bought a few frozen items and felt guilty they might have started defrosting while he was hanging around waiting for her.

He looked up, and saw her. "Oh, hi. Right on time. It's about a five-minute walk to where I've parked the car. Here, let me help you with your bags."

The journey to Adele's apartment block was spent in non-contentious small talk. Simon's car sounded as though it needed a service. She hoped it wouldn't break down, and fortunately it didn't. Perhaps that represented some kind of divine intervention.

To Adele's relief they did not meet anyone in the lobby or on the stairs, the lift still being out of commission. She cast an anxious glance around her flat, and was relieved to see it was tidy, with no dirty crockery in the sink.

While the kettle boiled, she put away her shopping

"So, what shall we talk about now?" asked the young clergyman. "We seem to have exhausted the trivia."

"Ah, I suppose this is where I get the God-sell," said Adele. "I knew there was no such thing as a free lunch, or a free lift."

"I'd rather get to know a little about you, if that's all right."

"About my beliefs, you mean?"

"No, about you. We don't have to talk about God. I'm off-duty, even if I'm still wearing a dog-collar."

"Is a vicar ever off-duty?"

"Well, this one is. I can even take my dog-collar off if it'll make you feel better."

"How do you take your coffee?"

Adele handed him a coffee, hoping it wasn't too lumpy for his tastes.

Simon took a sip. "Delicious," he announced.

"I thought vicars were supposed to be truthful."

"OK, then. It's bitter and it has bits floating on the top. But other than that, it's perfect."

A silence descended while Adele tried to think of something to say.

"All right," said Simon. "If you don't want to talk about yourself –"

"There's not much to tell. I grew up in Glasgow. I have one tattoo. I also have a half-brother who is a lot older than me, and a mother who lives alone and drinks too much. I work on a check-out. That's it."

"No boyfriend?"

"No time. No inclination either."

"Why did you leave Glasgow?"

"I had enough of cleaning up my mother's sick and trying to police her drinking. Which, by the way, is impossible."

"I have an uncle who's an alcoholic, so I know how that goes."

Adele lifted her coffee mug. "Your turn," she said.

"I've had life pretty easy, to be honest."

"How so?"

"Well, I have no tattoos, but one sister. My family owns an estate in Warwickshire." He paused. "I'm not bragging, you understand?" He looked concerned.

"It's all right. I'm not judging you."

"My family expected I would take over the running of the estate. So it came as a shock to them when I announced I wanted to become a priest. At least my family is Church of England. If I'd converted to Catholicism, I'm sure they would have washed their hands of me. As it is they tolerate what they refer to as my 'temporary insanity'."

"But it's not temporary, is it?"

Simon tilted his head. "I don't think so."

"So your sister runs the estate with your parents?"

"No, for the moment my mother and father run it with the help of an estate manager. As for my sister, Rosie, well, I guess you'd call her a free spirit. She spends as much time as she can travelling. She thinks I'm an idiot too, by the way."

"I like her already."

Simon put down his mug and gazed at her for a moment. Then he said, "Can I ask you something?"

Adele felt herself stiffen. "What?"

"I'm not going to ask you why you didn't come back to church, don't worry. I just wanted to know whether there is any chance that I – I mean 'we' – will see you there again."

Adele studied Simon. There was something of the little boy about him. Something charming. Something earnest and ingenuous. Something that made her want to say, "Yes."

She fought the urge.

"Simon, you're a nice man. But I'm not a believer. Not really. My going to church would be a bit hypocritical. I know I went once but –"

"No one is a hypocrite in their pleasures," Simon interjected.

"Is that from the Bible?" Adele asked with suspicion.

"No, it's Albert Camus, the French philosopher. He was an atheist too. You'd be surprised how many of us priests have nonbeliever friends."

"Still."

"Supposing I were to say I'd like a friend, not a convert?"

The tart and the vicar. It was a sad old cliché. And Adele did not want to be half of a cliché. She suddenly became conscious of the hour.

"Oh God," she exclaimed. "Look at the time. You must be hungry. I should have made you a sandwich or something."

Adele pressed her palms to her cheeks.

"Oh, Christ. I shouldn't have said, 'Oh God'." She thought this over. "Or, 'Oh Christ', either. Shit," she concluded.

"Listen," he said. "We passed a fish and chip shop on our way here. How about I pick us up two portions and bring them back here? You need to eat too. But only if I'm not imposing."

"Well," Adele sounded doubtful. "To be honest, it feels a little weird to be having fish and chips with an off-duty vicar. Maybe not appropriate. For you, I mean."

"If it will make you feel any better, I can talk about the parable of the loaves and the fishes while we eat," he said with a twinkle in his eye. "Or alternatively, you can think of it as the piece of cod which passeth all understanding."

Adele had just finished straightening up the bedcovers when David emerged from her bathroom. He was wearing nothing but a towel around his waist, and drops of moisture glistened on his body.

"Do you mind if I have a glass of water?" he asked.

"Sure. Help yourself. The glasses are in the cupboard over the kitchen sink. If you don't fancy tap water, there is some bottled in the fridge. I don't trust the stuff out of the tap, despite what the water companies say."

He padded through to her kitchen.

"Is this your little boy?" He pointed at the picture on the refrigerator door.

"Yes. That's Jamie."

"He's a handsome chap. He's going to break a few hearts when he's older."

Adele made no comment and went through to the living room.

David followed. After a moment he said, "I'm sorry. Have I said something wrong?"

"No. It's just that I prefer to keep my family life separate from what I do here."

"I understand," he replied. "Insensitive of me." He drank from the glass and put it down. "Well, I'd better get dressed." He kissed her lightly on the forehead.

Outside there was the rumble of autumnal thunder and seconds afterwards the rain began. It cascaded out of the broken drainpipe from the roof of the apartment building where it flecked and streaked the windows of Adele's flat like bitter tears of loss.

20

DAVID

The day after I saw Adele was a Saturday. It was also Daniel's birthday.

After the rain of the previous day, the air felt washed clean. Summer was over, yet the trees still clutched their leaves, as a parent might hang onto a departing child. The green was succumbing in silence to the red – a subtle and melancholic tribute to the universality of decay.

I asked Claire if she wanted to come with me, but she refused, shaking her head tersely. She had things to do. Unspecified, but important. My wife was not in a talkative vein.

I drove the twelve miles to the small village church in a sombre mood, stopping en route to pick up some flowers.

There was no one in the churchyard when I arrived. That suited me. I was pleased to see the graves and grounds were being well-maintained.

I walked slowly to a plot near the west wall, where a small grey headstone bore the inscription:

Forever in our Thoughts and Prayers
Daniel Braddock
1997
Beloved Son of David and Claire

We had not known what to put on the headstone. Neither Claire nor I was religious, and my father had had to pull some strings so that Daniel could be buried in this alien churchyard. So we ended up with this half-hearted, clumsy expression of grief and helplessness. Our son was dead. Or rather he had never been. Stillborn. Nothing anyone could have done. Move on.

Claire's reaction had been to go into denial, although her version of it was couched in fatalistic pragmatism. It was something we needed to put behind us. What was the point in mourning Daniel? He had never drawn breath. He had never suffered. He was just some 'thing' that had happened.

A month afterwards, Claire and I went on holiday to the Greek island of Skiathos to 'get away' for a while. We left Katie with Claire's mother. I thought it would be an opportunity for us to grieve together, but that never happened. Instead, we pretended we were coping, even though we both knew it was a lie.

I have a photograph of Claire, taken without her knowledge, of her sitting with her back to me on a wooden jetty and gazing down at the water. It is the saddest thing I own. A picture of desolation. My lost wife.

There is a term for someone whose spouse dies. A widow or widower, we call them. A child whose parents die is an orphan. Yet there is no word – at least not in the English language – for a parent who loses a child. It is as if the blow is too awful to bear, too much against nature, too painful to grant recognition, to give it a name.

The Zen Buddhist's definition of good luck – at least according to the monk Bodhidharma – is, 'Father dies, son dies.' The motif has the ring of profundity to it. We should not outlive our children. It is not the natural order of things.

Claire and I should have taken up the offer of counselling. But we did not. We thought we were strong enough. Therein lies the folly of the weak.

Such research as exists on the marriages of bereaved parents, indicates they are especially vulnerable to failure owing to the feelings and pressures associated with the child's death. One study suggests that divorce rates may be as much as eight times the norm. Guilt, painful associations, and loss of purpose and cohesion are among the reasons cited for it becoming impossible for the couple to stay together.

With Claire and me, I reflected, it was a minor miracle we had survived the last two years. The unpalatable fact was that, in spite of the love between us, we had been unable to help each other through the trauma of Daniel's death, at least in any meaningful way. Claire began to close down, while superficially remaining unchanged. I baulked at the idea of seeking a psychiatrist, preferring instead a do-it-yourself route to healing. I took courses on hypnotherapy and neuro-linguistic programming. Along the way, I learned a lot about myself. But it didn't change anything.

Six months after Daniel's death, I found myself unaccountably outside a brothel in Leicester, and I went in. That's where I met Adele.

I had no idea how Claire coped. I tried to get her to open up to me but she wouldn't. Perhaps she was worried that if the dam burst she would be washed away, forever. Whatever the truth of the matter, I didn't help her. I didn't know how to. And neither did she know how to reach out to me.

Perhaps that was why she had reached out to Jack.

I knelt in front of Daniel's grave and arranged the flowers. I wanted to talk to him, but in my mind there was no image of my son I could attach myself to, no conversation we could ever have. The picture of his pale, helpless body filled my vision. He had never existed. He had never so much as cried.

So I cried for him. I cried for Daniel and for all the things that would never be. Neither for him, nor for me.

21

DAVID

About two weeks after I had called Jim Fosse, Claire and I received an invitation to dinner at his house. Of course, by that time, the surge of anger following my meeting with the detective, Cumberbatch, had abated. It was replaced with feelings of sheepishness and regret that I had phoned Jim.

His request to dine with him and his wife was couched in the most polite, innocuous terms. Two other couples would be joining us for the dinner party, and he would be most honoured if we could attend. It was high time Monique met some of his business associates in a convivial atmosphere.

I hesitated to accept. Yet a voice inside me told me Jim had been joking about the whole 'let's-murder-our-wives' scenario, and he was looking to set the record straight, to put an end to an inappropriate levity that had gone too far. In addition, I reasoned a dinner party might help rebuild some – unacknowledged – broken fences between myself and my wife, and dissipate recent tensions. I must confess I also had a prickle of curiosity about Jim's wife, Monique. I wanted to see what sort of woman would want to be married to that perplexing American whose intentions crouched behind a wall of enigma. So we said, "Yes."

Claire and I were the first to arrive. We had to park on the road because the Fosses' drive was piled high with paving slabs.

"Sorry about the builder's yard," said Jim, ushering us inside. "That's all for my new patio out back."

"That stone has been lying around there for weeks," called out a female voice from the kitchen. "My husband won't pay anyone to sort out the patio. He has to do it himself. In his own sweet time, of course."

Jim winked at me. "You can't rush perfection. I need to be in the right frame of mind before I start digging. Plus the weather forecast needs to be right. Which, of course, it never is. Do you know, by the way," he went on, "the people of Bolivia bury a llama foetus under the foundations of new buildings to ward off evil spirits? If it's a particularly grand house, they bury an adult llama."

"Jim has threatened to put me under there if I don't behave with his credit card," the disembodied voice added.

The party started with a setback. One of the couples – identity unspecified – had called off at the last minute, so that left Claire and me, Jim and Monique, and our mutual acquaintance Mat Hoggard and his wife Rebecca, to make up the table. The six of us sat in his large living room drinking wine from Jim's extensive cellar while we waited for the declaration that dinner was ready. The room was furnished with taste, and when Claire commented on this, our host was at pains to praise his wife's good eye for interior décor. He squeezed her hand and she gave him a peck on the cheek.

Monique was an attractive woman with the pneumatically-enhanced breasts to which Jim had previously alluded. Her brown hair was cut in a bob, and she had dark eyes and a sensuous mouth. Her accent had a slight twang of the capital about it, and I gathered during the course of the evening that the two of them had met in London. She worked as a management consultant and seemed sparky and intelligent, if a little lacking in the sense of humour department. Were Jim indeed planning her imminent demise, she was patently unaware of it. They *looked* happy together.

For certain, they were more contented than Mat and Rebecca. The Hoggards hardly spoke to each other, and the rest of us had to work hard to maintain an atmosphere of jollity. I wondered what Mat and his wife were doing there. The prospect of a row between them hung over the room like the promise of winter. You knew it was coming sooner or later, you just didn't know when.

"This classical music is depressing, James," said Monique.

"We have cultured guests, my darling," her husband responded. "They appreciate Mahler."

"Well, I'm putting on something a little more upbeat. Otherwise you'll turn this dinner party into a wake. And not an Irish one." She went to the music system and ejected Jim's CD.

"So what are you doing to celebrate the Millennium, Jim?" asked Rebecca.

"I'm taking Monique to New York as a surprise." Jim laughed. "Oh, whoops, she heard. Scrub that. Now I'll have to take her somewhere else. Perhaps Coventry. What about you?"

"Maybe we'll go down to London," Mat said, stirring from his lethargy. "See a show at the Millennium Dome, now that we know the damn thing is finished. We might as well get something back from all our taxes that have been thrown at the ruddy eyesore."

"That's the spirit, darling," Rebecca said. "Start the next thousand years in the same generous spirit that you're ending this year."

Bryan Ferry's 'Slave to Love' started playing on the sound system.

To need a woman
You've got to know
How the strong get weak
And the rich get poor

Once we had taken our places at the dinner table, the Hoggards decided to make more of an effort at getting along. With Jim playing the cheery host, it was difficult not to wring some enjoyment from the evening. Monique's nouvelle cuisine was delicious. Fresh bottles of wine kept appearing on the table, and in the end I had to put my hand over my glass, otherwise our drive home might have become perilous.

The conversation lingered on the Millennium theme. Would life be any different on the first of January 2000? Would the world's computers crash? Was anyone making any special resolutions? Had we stocked up on tinned food for the Apocalypse?

"Well," said Jim, "if Jesus is coming, we'd better look busy. And send that Oxfam donation we've been promising."

"In the last two months we've had a total solar eclipse, earthquakes in Athens and Taiwan and an F2 tornado in Salt Lake City," piped in Mat. "Sounds to me like we're warming up for the End of Days. What do you say, David?"

"Just so long as no idiot cancels the Rugby World Cup next month," I replied. "I've already bought my tickets."

The Hoggards left just after ten, citing the need to relieve their babysitter. It felt more like they wanted to get out of each other's company and the best way to achieve that was to go home and retire to their – presumably – separate bedrooms. But perhaps I had read them wrong. For some couples, squabbling is as natural as breathing. One of these fine days, spouse baiting may become an Olympic sport. To my mind, synchronised swimming's admission has opened the flood gates to all sorts of weirdness.

"Let's leave the ladies for a few minutes," said Jim. "I have a couple of special cigars I've been saving. Monique won't let me smoke indoors, so let's go out back."

"Yes, take those filthy cheroots outside," chimed his wife, before returning to her conversation with Claire.

I was glad to puff on a quality cigar. I hadn't had a Marlboro in over three hours.

A POISON TREE

The night air was cool, but not enough to make us shiver. No breeze stirred the trees and, beyond the end of Jim's garden, the fields were black. The headlights of a car poked over a rise in the distance, then disappeared. Nearby, a barn owl hooted. A sense of stillness prevailed.

Jim closed the patio doors behind us. We sat down on large wooden chairs with deep cushions, and lit the cigars. They were huge. It would take some enthusiastic puffing to keep them burning.

"What's wrong with this patio you already have here, Jim? It looks fine to me."

"There's a problem with the foundations."

"Really?"

"Yes. Monique isn't under them."

In the darkness I couldn't read his expression, but as his cigar glowed I could see his eyes watching me.

"Very funny."

He reached into a trouser pocket and handed me a folded sheet of paper.

"What's this? I can't read it. It's too dark."

"Oh, wait. I've given you the wrong paper." He grabbed it back from me and passed me a small white envelope in its place. "Don't open it now, David. Just put it away. Read it when you're alone."

"What is it?"

"It's my schedule for when I'll be out of the country over the next couple of months. Also some information about Monique. Where she works, the places she goes to, and some other snippets you may find useful."

My mouth felt dry. And it wasn't just the effect of the cigar. "Why would I need to know these things?"

Jim didn't answer. He just dangled his arms over the side of the chair. After a few moments he said, "Why did you call me, David?"

"I just considered it had been a while since we'd had a drink." I chose my words with care. "We are friends, after all."

The smoke from his cigar curled upwards. Through the glass I could see Claire and Monique in a smiling tête-à-tête.

"I don't have any friends," Jim said. "I don't need them. Friends are an unnecessary burden. I only have accomplices."

"I think we've taken this joke far enough, Jim." Even to my ears, my voice sounded stiff and priggish.

He took a puff on his cigar.

"What did you make of Mat and Rebecca tonight?"

"How do you mean?"

"Well, would you say they were happy together, for instance?"

"Obviously not. But what's your point?"

"Mat is the sort of guy who would like his wife dead. But he lacks the will. You would also like rid of your wife. The only question is whether you have the will."

"What makes you think I want rid of my wife? That's absurd."

Jim gave a deep sigh. "I am a student of human nature, David. I make my living from observing people. Finding the chinks in their armour. Sniffing out their weaknesses, their desires, their fears. That's why I am in such demand in negotiations. You might describe me as a connoisseur of corruption. I know for a fact that you and Claire are not happy. I can read you like a book."

"That's ridiculous."

"You see?" He waved his cigar. "The extent of your indignation is itself revealing. If I hadn't touched a nerve, you would have simply laughed at the absurdity of my assertion." He paused. "But you didn't."

I stood up. "Well, Jim, it's been an entertaining evening. But I think it's time we were going."

"I see you have pocketed the envelope I gave you, nonetheless."

"That's just –"

"Never mind. We don't need to discuss this now. Think it over. You know the terms of my offer. An 'aye' for an 'aye'. A wife for a wife." He chuckled. "We don't even need to speak again. In fact, it's better if we don't. The details are up to you. Just make sure it happens when I'm out of the country. After that, I'll do the same for you."

"Just like that, huh?"

"Just like that. We often overcomplicate life, don't you think? Death, on the other hand, is best kept simple."

I stubbed out my cigar. "You are insane, Jim."

He laughed. "It has been said. I blame the Millennium. It neutralises our sense of right and wrong, gives us permission to contemplate all sorts of unspeakable actions. That's my take on it, anyway." He stood up and clapped me on the shoulder. "Now, how about a nightcap for you and the lovely Claire before you go?"

22

ADELE

Sometimes, you have to do the right thing.

So Adele went back to St. Mark's. She felt obligated, despite the fact she found her situation absurd. She knew that if Simon was aware of how she spent the bulk of her weekends, he would be horrified. At the very least, his interactions with her would take on a more formal character. He would mutate from a friend into a priest who was trying to save a fallen woman. She didn't want that. For one thing, she didn't want to be saved. She liked Simon, and found him easy to be with, but she valued her independence.

Adele put aside her nascent concern that his interest in her might go beyond friendship. A fish and chip supper did not a romance make.

He is a nice man, whose company I enjoy. Period.

For her second trip to the church, she carried with her a holdall containing clothes to change into for her Sunday shift at the club. She was acutely aware there was something downright sacrilegious about bringing skimpy lace underwear, condoms and sex toys into a church, but she couldn't risk being late to work again if Simon invited her back to the vicarage for tea.

In spite of the vicar's enthusiasm and charm, the service had a sluggish quality about it. Adele put this down to a lack of energy on the part of the congregation. It was like wading through porridge, trying to stir this lot. Other than one little boy who was either hyperactive or had an infestation of ants in his trousers, the worshippers were lethargic.

Perhaps it was the pre-Millennium blues, or trepidation that the Second Coming was still some way off. For many of them, their own funeral service would likely precede the destruction of the planet. As they filed out of St.

Mark's through the churchyard, Adele could not banish the idea that for the more doddery attendees, the Grim Reaper may well be hovering nearby and checking his watch.

Hardly worth their while going home.

An invitation to tea followed the service, but this time it was not for Adele alone. Two of the blue rinse brigade were invited, along with the Edwardian-looking gentleman – who, Adele had learned, was called Ambrose - and the ice-faced Eleanor.

The gathering was inhibited, to say the least. Curiosity about Adele was evident. If the good parishioners of St. Mark's had been aware of the contents of Adele's bag, they would no doubt have been even more fascinated. However, only Eleanor was interested or nosey enough to ask questions, which she did with the subtlety of a blood-covered assassin wielding a broadsword.

"So do you have any children?" she said, with a sideways glance at Simon.

"Yes, a boy. Jamie."

"That's nice," observed Ambrose, helping himself to a biscuit.

"And Darrow is your husband's name, presumably?" Eleanor pressed. "It doesn't sound Scottish."

"Well, it is Scottish. My family is originally from Darroch, in Stirlingshire. The name comes from the Gaelic, *darach*, meaning 'oak tree'. And it's *my* family name, by the way. Not my husband's. In fact," she said, bending forward to pick up her cup, "I don't have a husband."

"Are you a widow?" said Eleanor. "Or divorced?" The older woman's top lip curled in undisguised distaste.

"No. I've never been married," Adele replied, enjoying the uncomfortable silence.

"So your boy is –"

"Illegitimate, yes. And where I come from in Glasgow, people are a lot less mealy-mouthed about it. They would say he was a bastard. In much the same way as they would refer to a certain type of woman as a bitch."

Ambrose stifled a laugh.

"More tea, anyone?" said Simon.

Adele applied the massage oil to David's shoulders.

She sat astride him as he lay face down on her bed, a small towel draped across his buttocks. She worked her way down his back and pressed her thumbs on the line of his spine.

"Can I ask you a question, David?"

"Is it a personal one?"

"Yes. Yes, it is. You don't have to answer."

"All right."

"Well, I know you're married and you told me a while back you have a daughter." She stopped massaging and rested her hands on his lower back.

"That's not a question."

There was a beat before she spoke again. "Why do you come to see me?"

"Don't you want me to come and see you?" He sounded tired.

"It's not that."

"What, then?"

"That first time we met – at the Gold Club – it was obvious you felt uncomfortable, and had come to the club on a whim or something. You were embarrassed and quite sweet. I liked you straightaway. And I knew we weren't going to have sex. It was evident you weren't the sort of man to pay for sex. Yet there you were."

She stopped to let him speak, but he continued to lie still, listening.

"I was surprised when you asked me for my number. And since then, of course, you've been here many times, yet every time ... uh, this is none of my business." Adele paused, unsure how to continue.

David turned so he was resting on his right elbow.

"Do you want to know why I come here to see you and every time just have a massage? You want to know why I don't make love to you?"

"Yes."

He swivelled further so that he could look at her.

"Maybe I can't get it up, but I'm too proud to admit it." He smiled, but she detected a sadness behind his eyes.

Adele moved her head to one side. "No, that's not it. You've had some sorrow in your life that you come here to escape. Something you can't talk about with your wife and family. You want some quiet, I think. And maybe some non-judgemental physical contact."

"Have you ever considered taking up psychiatry?"

"I'm not trying to get rid of you, David. I am putting this clumsily, I know. I'm sorry."

He reached out and squeezed her hand.

"I'm conscious that you're paying me a lot of money just for a massage. I feel like I'm taking advantage of you. And I like you, so it makes me feel bad."

"Do you want us to have sex? Would that make you feel better about our arrangement?"

She slapped him playfully on the back. "That's a trick question. You and I both know that's never going to happen. If my feminine wiles haven't worked on you in the last eighteen months, they're not going to start working now."

Adele kissed him on the shoulder. "I've had customers who only want to talk. All the girls have. They usually see us once or twice then disappear, because they move on. Maybe it's time for you to move on. Anyway, supposing your wife were to find out you come to see me. She will find out sooner or later, you know. Do you think she'll believe you only have a massage? Would any wife believe that? Seriously?"

"You think I'm taking a big risk for nothing." David sighed. "Do you know you're the second person in the last few weeks who has refused to take my money? And on the same grounds. That it's not good for me."

"Are you annoyed with me?"

"No."

"Do you think I'm crazy turning away business?"

"No. I think you're a good woman. And there aren't too many of those around."

"The tart with a heart, right?"

He studied her for a moment. "You're not a tart. Not at all. And what is more, you're right. I do need to move on."

Adele climbed off the bed and David sat up, wrapping the towel around himself. "And by the way," he said, "I guess I owe it to you to tell you why I have needed to get away."

"No, you don't."

"I lost my son,"

"Your son?"

David spoke slowly, his voice low. "Or to be more accurate, I never had a son to lose. He was stillborn, you see. Two years ago. A few months before we met. I've had difficulty coming to terms, getting over it. But at some stage, I realise I have to. We can't mourn forever, can we?"

"No. We can't."

"I'd better go."

At that moment, she wanted to embrace him, to pour out her heart and her own loss. She knew he would understand. Of all people, he would understand. But she couldn't. She had held back too long. And now she would never see him again.

In our end we find our beginning.

"I'll miss you, David. I hope you know that."

"I'll miss you too, Adele. And I hope you know *that*."

After David left, Adele straightened up the apartment and made herself tea.

She had surprised herself, talking like that to him. It hadn't been planned, but on reflection it felt right. Yet there was a price. She had lost a friend. A friend who, unknowing, shared with her a common sorrow.

Sometimes, you have to do the right thing.

23

DAVID

We can rail against the storms and injustices of the world.

But the world won't care.

We can exhaust ourselves attempting to retrofit reality so it makes sense to us.

But it still won't. We can pretend it does, but it won't.

The universe remains obdurate to our cries. Mulish deafness is its natural state.

And so, in the absence of a caring sentience, we are left to make the best of things.

We manage.

We adjust our expectations, pare down our dreams.

We carry on, because the only alternative is not to carry on. Whereupon we allow ourselves to tumble into the void.

So I gave myself a stiff talking-to. I pronounced that there were many people worse off than me – most of the six point billion something humans on the planet, to be almost-precise.

Everything is changed, yet everything is the same. How pernicious is knowledge. How comforting is ignorance. It is our refuge. I wished I had never gone to see Cumberbatch. If I could have put my hands around the throat of the poison pen writer, I surely would have done.

For that was the only killing to which I would have been a willing party.

I was not Jim Fosse.

Whatever twisted mind games it was that aroused him – whether he derived his sick pleasures from screwing with my mind, or from contemplating his wife's death, was of no interest to me. I may have been a man sinned against, but I had done my own share of sinning too.

The resolution formed never to see Fosse again. The American's appearance may have been unremarkable, but his mind went to places where it was dangerous to follow. There would be no Faustian pact between us.

I decided to wait out the end of Claire's affair with Jack. I would hold my tongue, rein in the proud part of me that felt the sting of humiliation. Claire had always been faithful before. Of that I was certain. I had not fallen prey to a complete collapse of reason. She was a loyal person. This current aberration aside, I knew her. And because I knew her, I also realised how her infidelity would tear at her too. Deception came at a cost. Claire was worth the wait. Our marriage could survive this, I told myself.

I recalled those words she had said to me long ago.

You will always give someone a second chance, David. And we all need that at some time.

It became a mantra for me, a charm to stop the embers of resentment from catching alight. I repeated it when Claire told me she would be making another trip to London in November.

"If a tree falls in the forest, and there is nobody there to hear it, does it make a sound?" I asked Ian.

"What?"

"It's a Zen riddle, isn't it?"

"Is it?"

"Yes. I assumed with your accumulated Buddhist wisdom, you'd be able to solve it for me."

"The ants would hear it."

"Come again?"

"Or the tree sloths. They'd hear it."

"What tree sloths?"

"Or the spiders."

"Do spiders have ears?"

"Or they'd fucking feel it come down. Especially if it fell on them."

He went back to stacking bottles. It was quiet in the Bell. Two customers, including me. I wasn't even sure whether the old guy in the corner was still alive.

"Are you going to have another beer?" he said. "If you want to take advantage of my transcendental knowledge, you have to expect to pay for it."

"Go on, then."

"Anyway," he continued, pulling the pint, "I've got a question for you."

"I'm all ears. Like the spiders."

"If a woman cuts down a tree in the forest, and there is no man to help her, how long will it take?"

"Do you know what sexism is, Ian?"

"Isn't that a company that specialises in making bikinis for girls with big butts?"

"Oh, Jesus."

"I think they also manufacture tents."

Jim Fosse did not attend the next Chamber of Commerce meeting. Lots of bored, miserable-looking people did, though. I know because I was one of them.

The guest motivational speaker lectured us on what business in the twenty-first century might be like. Robots and the Internet took prominence in his nasal diatribe.

A POISON TREE

"Seven billion people on the planet by the end of the next decade." His voice rose like that of a ham actor in a Shakespearean tragedy. "Imagine all those new customers!"

I imagined them. Most of them would be in emerging nations, born into poverty where the vast majority would remain as slaves to the triple deities of capitalism, religious bigotry and predatory politics. The new Hindu pantheon for the Information Age. Or the Disinformation Age, perhaps. We are born, we buy stuff, then some more stuff, and finally we die. The Hymn of the Market.

Some days I wonder what the hell I am doing in business, accumulating wealth the same way clogged arteries accumulate more fat. We need to question what it's all for, how much is enough. It's easier, however, just to keep going, to stay with the trajectory. It's hard to turn around a super tanker.

Poor indeed is the man who just has money. Though not as poor as those as-yet-unborn souls in Africa. We in the West are complaining bastards.

Chief moaner of the evening, and front-runner for Grumpy Git of the Millennium Award (Leicester Area), was Mat Hoggard.

"I hate futurists," he muttered, as the speaker turned his attention to the topic of genetically-modified crops. "They always make me feel like a dinosaur."

"That's probably because you are a dinosaur," I said. "Perhaps you should be genetically-modified too."

Mat grunted.

"What's eating you today?"

"Ebola."

"That's almost funny."

The voice from the podium had segued into the human genome project and the prospect of a much-extended lifespan.

"Consider the implications for evolutionary progress and for population size."

We had circled back to customers. It sounded like most of them would be ancient and in need of high-quality medical services. I sneaked a look at my watch. I hoped the talk would be over soon. Going by the glazed sets of eyes around me, there wouldn't be many questions.

"What do you make of Jim Fosse?" Mat whispered to me.

"He's a bit –" I grappled for the right word, and settled for *unusual*.

"He is that. Do you know why he invited us all round to dinner like that, out of the blue?" Mat was studying me.

"No. No idea. Why do you ask?"

Mat's eyes became evasive. "No reason. I just wondered."

After the lecture ended, I made a fast getaway. I had a headache and needed some fresh air, so I took a stroll through the evening streets of the city. It gave me the opportunity to call Katie to see how she was settling in at Oxford. She sounded bubbly and full of an enthusiasm I could only envy. I was in no hurry to get home. Claire was working on year end accounts and would be locked away in the study for a while yet.

I wandered into the Town Hall Square where I'd last had lunch with Anna. It was deserted apart from a courting couple on one of the benches.

It had been a while since Anna and I had talked. I had played golf with her unreliable spouse since then and done my best to be amicable, for my sister-in-law's sake, but I found it hard to disguise the fact that I found him a superficial and slippery customer.

Then, as I left the Square, I saw Max.

He was headed towards the clock tower and appeared to be in a hurry. To see him on foot was unusual. The only time I ever saw him walking was on a golf course. He was one of those people who parked right next to wherever he was going. He liked to be seen arriving in his flashy sports car.

A very noticeable, easily-identifiable sports car.

Some impulse made me follow him. Whether it was concern for Anna or idle curiosity, I couldn't say. But there was something about his movement that looked furtive, and every few yards he would look around as if he were somewhere he shouldn't be.

I trailed him from what I considered to be a safe distance, staying close to the shop frontages. He walked briskly past the clock tower and took a left turn into the High Street.

Even a trained monkey can be a private detective, Cumberbatch had said. I would put that hypothesis to the test. I switched my cell phone to silent. Just in case.

There were a lot of people milling around restaurants and watering-holes, which made my task of remaining invisible easier. A couple of skateboarders zipped around and a weary-looking tramp held out his hand as I passed. It was just coming up to nine o'clock.

Almost at the end of the street, Max headed right. I paused at the corner to make sure he hadn't stopped. About fifty yards ahead of me was a hotel, of the type frequented by travelling businessmen or families on a budget. The sign proclaimed the Lodge. As Max reached the entrance, he scanned the street and I dodged behind a parked car. He hadn't seen me.

Approaching from the other direction was an attractive woman in a business suit, who waved to him. I recognised her immediately.

It was Jim Fosse's wife, Monique.

They embraced and went into the hotel.

I rested my back against the wall of a shuttered shop and lit a Marlboro while I considered what to do next.

It was then I received my second surprise of the evening.

A POISON TREE

Concealed in a doorway across from the Lodge, his face lit by the glow of a cigar, was a tubby man of middle height. His eyes were focused on the front of the hotel. I watched him take out a small book and make some notes.

So now I knew why Jim Fosse had not been at the lecture. He had more pressing matters to attend to.

24

JAMES

At the south edge of Leicester's Victoria Park, near the concert venue of De Montford Hall, stands a tall, imposing memorial to the dead of the two World Wars.

On this particular afternoon, the grotesquely oversized edifice looked bleaker than usual, more inhuman. The sky was weighed down with grey clouds and a cold wind whipped across the park. The trees were shedding their leaves, capitulating to the gusts that invaded their branches. Only a few people braved the threatening weather. They scuttled across the expanse of grass, hands in pockets, heads down.

Jim Fosse hunched his shoulders and shivered as he walked towards the symmetrical stone construction. He disliked the English autumn and winter. Spring was little better and the summer was too short and unpredictable. He much preferred the tropics.

I will be glad to be off this shabby little island. It's so fucking pleased with itself. I've been here too long.

The towering memorial encapsulated for the American everything that was wrong with England. Forever chained to its glorious past, it had no meaningful focus on the present or the future. The country was like some old dowager who demanded respect, yet was no longer capable of wiping her own bottom.

A man waited for him. He was tall and clad in a long black coat with the collar turned up. In spite of the opaque light, he wore mirrored sunglasses. His hair and full beard were bright ginger, the only splash of colour in an otherwise dreary landscape. If the sunglasses were meant to be some form of disguise, it seemed like a waste of time. The red facial hair drew immediate attention.

"Mr. Andrews?"

"Mr. Fosse."

They shook hands. Andrews' grip was firm and dry.

"Let's walk while we talk," said the Scotsman. "It's too cold to stand around."

"Agreed. I wish you'd picked somewhere warmer to meet. Can't we find a café or somewhere more hospitable?"

"A public park is better. There's less chance of being overheard. And on an afternoon like this, nobody will take any notice of us. Everyone just wants to get somewhere warm."

Jim looked up at the sky.

"If it starts raining we'll get soaked and there's nowhere to shelter. I should have brought an umbrella."

"How very English of you." Andrews gave him a humourless look. "This will only take a few minutes."

Three students from the university sprinted past them, heading for the pub on the corner of London Road.

"When we last spoke," said Andrews, "I had the impression that you might be having second thoughts about our arrangement."

"No," Jim responded quickly. "Not at all. I emailed you the information you requested, didn't I?"

"You did. That email account is now closed, by the way."

"You're a cautious man, Mr. Andrews."

"I still require your travel schedule."

Jim reached into his coat pocket and handed the Scotsman an envelope. Andrews removed the paper from inside and looked over it. "So you're leaving for the Philippines the day after tomorrow?"

"Yes."

Andrews grunted. "Good. And you have the cash? I gave you enough time to get it together."

"I have the cash."

"Sterling?"

"Yes."

"Denominations no larger than ten pounds?"

"Yes. As you specified."

"And you are sure you just want the one person taken care of?"

Jim tried to swallow but found his throat was dry. The man's matter-of-fact manner unnerved him. "How much would it cost to take care of the two?"

"Double the price of one."

"No discount? As you're here anyway?"

"I am not a wholesaler, Mr. Fosse. I don't negotiate on these matters."

"Everyone negotiates."

"I assure you, you are mistaken." The voice was cold.

"Just the one problem to be taken care of," responded the American. "That's enough for me."

They walked in silence for a while. Then Andrews said, "Here is what you will do. Tomorrow morning at around eight o'clock you will deposit an attaché case containing the money at the front desk of the Grand Hotel. You will say it is for me to collect. The case will have a combination lock. You will set the combination on each lock dial to six. Is that clear? I don't want to have to break it open."

"Perfectly clear. Are you staying at the Grand, then?"

"That is not your concern. But the hotel staff will be expecting it."

"I see."

"If the case is not at the hotel by eight-thirty at the latest, I will consider our arrangement null and void."

"It will be there."

"I hope so. If it is not, you and I will have a problem." Andrews stopped walking and looked at him.

"There will be no problem, Mr. Andrews."

"Good. Then our business is concluded."

"What happens if I need to contact you again? Can I call you?"

"That won't be necessary."

The Scotsman turned and walked away, his feet crushing dead leaves.

25

ADELE

While she waited for her brother's arrival, Adele busied herself tidying her apartment. Ross had phoned her earlier. He was already in Leicester, enjoying the miserable weather, as he put it. She plumped cushions and dusted surfaces.

Idle, random themes meandered through her head. She reflected back on the Sunday of her second visit to St. Mark's. That had been a surreal day. After crossing swords with Eleanor at the vicarage, she had gone to the club, where Nina had been in a sparkling mood.

"The other day, I had a customer that wanted me to dress up as a nun for him," she had announced.

"That sounds a bit of a passive role for you, sweetheart," Leona had responded. "Do you even have a nun's outfit?"

"Nope. But he'd brought one for me."

"What did you do?"

"I told him it was a filthy habit."

Adele laughed. "You are so outrageous."

"We agreed on a compromise with a religious theme. I put a dog collar on him."

"A vicar's dog collar?"

"No. One of my leather studded ones, with a lead attached."

"What was religious about that?"

"Well, he spent a lot of time on his knees."

The entrance buzzer interrupted Adele's reminiscences.

She gawped at the sight that greeted her when she opened the door. "What on earth have you done to yourself, Ross?"

"I needed to look different for a while." He took off his sunglasses and moved past her, dropping his coat and bag on the sofa.

"Ginger? You dyed your hair *ginger*? And what's with the beard? You're like something out of *The Lord of the Rings*."

"Yes, I need to get rid of this. Can I use your bathroom?" He took a box of brown hair dye from the bag.

"Give that to me. I'll do it for you. You'll make a mess and end up green. That would not be a good look."

"Thanks, Ad. Let me shave first though."

"Please do. That beard is disgusting. I'm surprised it hasn't got birds nesting in it."

Ross emerged from the bathroom a few minutes later and Adele stood on tiptoes to give him a peck on the cheek. "That's better. You're my handsome brother again. Now we just need to lose the red hair. Want a cup of tea first?"

Adele knew better than to ask the reason for the heavy disguise. Ross would only give her some vague answer which would stimulate her curiosity further. Whenever he turned up with an altered appearance, his explanations included 'bodyguard work', 'anonymity while in a Muslim country' and 'client instructions for security reasons'. It crossed her mind that perhaps he was involved in spying and bound by the Official Secrets Act. More likely, however, was that criminal activity was involved, and his silence was his way of protecting her.

Maybe someday he'd tell her.

Or maybe not.

Now and again, Adele had asked about his love life. He always replied that he travelled too much to have a regular girlfriend, so he had to 'make do' with whatever female company was to hand in whichever Third World country he was billeted. She had a dread that he would turn up at the Gold

Club during a visit, and discover other men were 'making do' with his sister. When he had been in Leicester previously, she had to make up late night stocktaking duties to explain her absence. It was fortunate he never stayed long.

She handed Ross a mug of tea. "Still one sugar, right?"

"Right."

"Where are your suitcases?"

"I've checked into a hotel."

"Why? Isn't my flat good enough for you?"

He hugged her. "Don't be silly. I didn't want to impose."

"You imposed last time without any problem."

"Well, I have a couple of business meetings at one of the hotels in town, so it seemed best to stay there. I might have a few drinks, and I don't want to drive afterwards."

"You've hired a car?"

"Yep. Stuff to do," he added without further explanation. "Plus I want to take you out to dinner at one of the nice little restaurants in Harborough tonight. Get out of the Leicester for the evening. What do you say?"

"Sounds good to me."

Adele watched Ross as he sipped his tea. He was a good-looking man and he kept himself fit. He appeared less stressed than the last time she had seen him, although his eyes were always alert, as if some unidentified danger might lurk close by. She put this down to his time in the army. Alertness meant survival in a combat situation, and Ross had been in several of those. Friends of his had died on active service. Those sort of experiences could have your eyes scouring rooftops for snipers for the rest of your life, if you couldn't find some way to make peace with yourself. She wondered whether he suffered from nightmares. There were many things she wondered about her half-brother. Most of her questions would remain unanswered. Of that, at least, she was sure.

"How long are you staying for?"

"A few days. Then I'll go up to see Mam before I fly out again."

"Ah."

"Have you spoken to her recently, Ad?"

"A few days ago."

"And?"

"Nothing changes, Ross. If you want to see her sober, you'd best arrive before breakfast."

He sighed. "And what about you, then, sis? What are you up to at the moment?"

Oh, you know, the usual thing, Ross. Fucking complete strangers for money every weekend and hoping the condom doesn't split.

"Same old, same old. Working on the till. Doing overtime when it's available. Watching TV and doing laundry."

"No man on the scene?"

Only an hour at a time.

"No. But I have started going to church recently."

Ross looked up in surprise. "You're kidding me."

"I'm not. And it's a Church of England one too."

"Sleeping with the enemy, Adele?" He laughed. "Does your friend Moira know about this? She'll bloody well kill you."

"No way am I telling Moira."

"So what's brought this on? Does this church have a cute vicar, or something?"

Adele felt herself blushing. "Don't be silly."

"Oh, my God," Ross said, feeding her embarrassment. "He *is* a cute vicar, isn't he? You've got the hots for a reverend."

"Shut up."

Ross smirked and swallowed another mouthful of tea.

"Oh," he said, looking animated, "before I forget. I brought you a present."

He went to his bag, pulled out a small blue box with a ribbon and handed it to her.

"What's this?"

"Open it."

The box contained an intricately-wrought silver bracelet. Adele put it on.

"Oh, Ross, you shouldn't have. It's beautiful." She kissed him.

"Who else am I going to buy things for, other than my little sister, eh? If I bought one for Mam she'd just pawn it to buy booze."

"I'd best dye your hair then, by way of a thank you."

"I'll take a shower first, OK? Then I'll let you know when I'm decent."

"There are towels in there."

"Right." He washed out his mug in the sink and disappeared into the bathroom, closing the door behind him and locking it.

Adele went to move Ross' bag off the sofa. As she did so, she caught sight of a passport poking out and tucked beside it, another passport. Curiosity got the better of her. The first passport was in Ross' name, but the second, which contained a different photograph of him, was in the name of Laughlan Andrews.

Either Ross was indeed working for the British Government, or the explanation as to why he needed a fake passport was altogether more sinister. Adele could hear the shower still running. She had a minute or two yet. She rummaged deeper into the holdall, being careful to make as little noise as possible. Most of the contents were unremarkable. But at the bottom, something heavy was wrapped in a hand-towel. She unwrapped the object and her hand touched metal. It was a gun. In another towel was an ammunition clip and what she took to be a silencer.

At that moment, the shower was turned off.

She arranged the contents of the bag as she had found them, and hurried back into the kitchen.

A few seconds later, Ross poked his head around the bathroom door and called, "I'm ready for you now, sis. Come and make me look beautiful."

"Coming."

"Then we'll go out. I'm starving, and I could kill for a pint."

26

DAVID

October had arrived.

Originally the eighth month, thanks to the conversion of the 10-month Latin calendar into a twelve-month one, it now found itself a misnomer, a throwback to the days when togas were fashionable.

Weather-wise, the month had started horribly. Gales off the Isles of Scilly resulted in the death of a fisherman when his boat sank. Swathes of England were flooded. In Herefordshire, a man was drowned trying to release flood waters through a sluice gate. Wales opened the Rugby World Cup with a 23-18 victory over Argentina in the new Millennium Stadium in Cardiff, and England thrashed Italy 67-7 at Twickenham – a game I watched from the comfort of my dry armchair. For England's next game against the All Blacks, I would be there at Twickenham in person, assuming civilisation hadn't come to an end in the meantime.

The portents weren't good. In the days that followed, thirty-one people died in the Ladbroke Grove train crash two miles from Paddington Station, and Dr. Harold Shipman went on trial for murdering fifteen female patients in the Greater Manchester area. In the end, up to two hundred and fifty deaths would be ascribed to him, making him one of the most prolific serial killers in recorded history. Hitler, Stalin and Mao Tse-tung aside, that is.

Elsewhere in the world, Japan was struggling to come to terms with its worst-ever nuclear accident – excluding Hiroshima and Nagasaki, if you classify those as 'accidents' – at a uranium reprocessing facility in Tōkai-mura, northeast of Tokyo. I had little time for world events. There was enough to worry about in Little England.

A POISON TREE

Work remained busy. Rover had launched the 25 and 45 models in the previous month, and it was announced that Nissan's facelifted Primera would be built at NMUK, Washington. My father continued to nag and fret about the state of our business, in spite of the fact that, as far as I could see, 1999 was going to be a record year for us. I confirmed Harry in post, to his obvious relief. After the shock of Mark's suicide, the Coventry staff needed some stability and a familiar face in charge.

At home, things were calm. I chatted every week to Katie on the phone. Oxford suited her. Claire seemed more like her old self, and whenever she said she had a late meeting, I said I understood and told her not to work too hard. I gathered from incidental remarks that Jack and Eleanor were having some problems with their teenage daughter, Ruth, who was around Katie's age but much less mature.

"Boys," said Claire. "And maybe older men too," she added darkly.

"I bet that doesn't go down too well with Eleanor. Embarrassing for her, particularly. Fornication is not exactly encouraged in church circles, is it?" I observed.

"Jack's not too thrilled either. If he has a temper outburst, I'd worry for any boyfriend of Ruth's on the end of it."

I didn't know how to broach with Anna the subject of my seeing Max at the hotel. She had been operating below the radar recently, snowed under with manuscripts, and I didn't feel I could just call her and tell her what I'd seen. That felt like a clumsy, insensitive thing to do. Yet I needed to talk to her.

Then an opportunity presented itself.

"Anna is going to be down in London at the same time as you're there for the New Zealand game," Claire told me one evening as she unpacked groceries. "You should meet up and have dinner."

"That's a good idea."

A POISON TREE

I called Anna from work the next day.

"Hello, stranger."

"Oh, hi, David. How are you?"

"I'm good. I hear you'll be in London on the ninth. I'll be down for the rugby. Want to meet up for dinner or will you be eating with boring, self-obsessed writers?"

"No. I'll get my full quota of writers and agents during the day. It would be lovely to have dinner with you."

"I might be a bit late getting back into central London from Twickenham."

"I don't mind if you're buying."

"Where will you be staying?"

"At the James Hotel, off Victoria Street. I can walk to the Bright Sparks offices from there. We've got some important meetings coming up. They're still trying to persuade me to join them instead of me being freelance."

"Of course they are. Why wouldn't they? OK. I'll see if they have any rooms or find a place nearby. I'll call you again nearer the time."

"You've left it late to book."

"I know. I like to make things difficult for myself."

The day before the rugby, I worked late and grabbed a coffee and a sandwich at Leicester railway station. I couldn't face the driving and parking hassle in London, so the train was the sensible option. I had no intention of rushing around. This was going to be a relaxing and civilised trip, culminating, I hoped, in an unlikely English victory over New Zealand.

On the platform, I struck up a conversation with an attractive Asian woman who, while petite, had legs that went on forever. In my mind, anyway.

A POISON TREE

What is it about black boots? They elicit a Pavlovian response in any libido in possession of a male. They should be outlawed. They stack the deck unfairly against stupid men. Which is to say, most men.

She introduced herself as Ellen, and told me she was touring the UK and had been misinformed about the Midlands being interesting. She was from Hong Kong, had black shoulder-length hair and a cuteness about her. Ellen was 'doing' Europe, and I had no doubt Europe would only be too happy to 'do' her.

I helped her with her luggage as the train came in, and we sat opposite one another. We almost had the carriage to ourselves, just a couple of weary backpackers and a grey-haired guy wearing nothing but purple who muttered to himself from time to time. The train needed a good clean, just as the girl who had made my sandwich needed a lesson in what constituted food.

"So how is the approaching Millennium being viewed in Hong Kong?" I asked.

"We've already had our Apocalypse in 1997."

"Ah, yes, the handover of the colony back to China. With our Mr. Patton making things difficult, I understand."

"There has been some tension. Things will change, but so far nothing too fundamental for the ordinary person."

"Are you sure it's OK for you to talk to me? I am one of the Running Dogs of Imperialism, you know."

"I'm an English major, so everyone thinks I work for the enemy anyway," was her response. A collection of Charles Bukowski's poems rested on the table. I wished I'd brought something more highbrow to read than Nick Hornby. Ah, well.

As it turned out, neither of us opened our books. We passed the journey chatting about nothing in particular, while the English countryside sped past us in the dark. It was almost midnight when we pulled into St. Pancras, and I bade goodbye to my black-booted companion.

"If you're ever in Hong Kong," she said, "Call me. I can tell you where all the best restaurants are." She scribbled her number on a scrap of paper and handed it to me.

"Thank you. I can't see me visiting Hong Kong, to be honest, but you never know."

"You never do. Lots of Western people end up living in Asia, though admittedly Thailand is a more popular destination, especially Phuket and Samui."

"I'm sorry I don't have the time to show you around London."

"Don't worry. I'm used to finding my way in strange cities. Anyway, your wife might not be too happy about it." She grinned as I touched my wedding ring.

"You could be right."

"Nice to meet you, David. Thank you for your company."

"Likewise. See you in Kowloon."

I took a taxi to the James Hotel, where I had secured a room.

Anna would be fast asleep by now.

I checked in, had a shower then crashed.

"That looks like a healthy breakfast."

I kissed Anna and sat down. The dining room was busy. I ordered coffee and tucked into bacon, eggs, sausages, fried bread, beans, mushrooms, the lot. There is nothing to beat a Full English breakfast on a cold morning.

"What time are you off to Twickenham?"

"After breakfast, I think. Kick-off isn't until half past four, so I'll have time for a couple of drinks beforehand."

"I hope you're not going to get rowdy and turn up pissed to take me to dinner." My sister-in-law fixed me with a stern eye.

"That's football supporters you're thinking of. We rugby types are much better behaved."

"I hope so."

"I'll get back into town as fast as I can, OK?"

"No problem."

"So what's happening with you today?"

"Author culling. That always happens on a Saturday, so the authors don't expect it."

"Sounds nasty."

"It is."

An expensive taxi ride got me to Twickenham, where I watched a rampant Jonah Lomu power the All Blacks to a 30-18 victory over England. We were behind after eleven minutes and the raucous home support in the end counted for nothing. A second-half fight back got us to 16-16, but then we ran out of steam. In spite of the defeat, it was difficult not to feel exhilarated by some terrific rugby. Never mind, a win over Tonga would still see us through to the next stage.

Finding a taxi after the game was hell, and the drive back into central London slow and frustrating. I arrived at the hotel around twenty to nine. I'd called ahead to Anna, so I leapt into the shower, changed and met her in the lobby ten minutes later.

We agreed to walk down Victoria Street where Anna knew there was a reasonable Italian restaurant. They managed to find us a table and we ordered some pasta and a good bottle of wine.

"This is going to ruin my diet, David."

"You don't need to diet."

"I do."

"Shut up and have some more wine."

"OK." She giggled.

"Are you still eating meat?"

"Yes."

"I'm shocked."

By the time we'd had Irish coffees, it was approaching half past ten. I still hadn't brought up the subject of my seeing Max.

When we stepped outside it was cold, but the hot food and alcohol served to keep us warm. Although the sky was overcast and we couldn't see the stars, rain seemed unlikely.

"Do you fancy a stroll down to the river?" I said.

"Why not?" Anna put her arm through mine.

We walked at a slow pace, huddling together against the chill. We passed the Collegiate Church of St Peter and the Houses of Parliament. Big Ben chimed eleven. We stopped at the centre of Westminster Bridge, and leaned against the iron fascia. On the South Bank, preparations were under way to lift the great wheel of the London Eye into place. The sluggish river flowed below us and a slight breeze blew through Anna's hair. I put my arm around her shoulders.

"There is something I need to tell you," I said.

"What?"

"There hasn't seemed an appropriate time before –"

"Never mind that. What is it?"

"I saw Max. In Leicester. He was meeting a woman outside a hotel."

She looked away from me. "I don't want to know."

"I'm sorry."

A POISON TREE

Anna was silent for a few moments. Then she turned her face back to me. "I'm thinking of leaving him, David. I'm considering taking the job with Bright Sparks and moving to London."

I looked down at the black river. "I see."

She put a hand on my arm. "What do you think?"

"What does it matter what I think? It's your life, Anna."

"It matters to me what you think."

"Claire is having an affair." The words were out before I could stop them.

She took my head in her hands and held her face close to mine. "Are you sure?" She sounded more concerned than shocked.

"The detective I hired is sure."

"Oh, David. I don't know what to say."

"You don't have to say anything. I shouldn't have spoken. I'm sorry."

Anna pulled me away from the parapet and wrapped her arms around me.

"Shall I tell you what we are going to do now?" she asked.

"Yes, tell me."

"We are going to go back to our hotel and raid the mini-bars. We'll never have a better excuse than this for getting drunk."

"Are you serious?"

"I absolutely am." She gave me a peck on the cheek.

We retraced our steps and in spite of everything, we joked. It felt like some great weight had been lifted off both of us.

When we arrived back at the James, Anna went to her room to collect bottles. Within five minutes she was knocking on my door. She arranged the miniatures on my bedside table and sat down on the bed next to me.

"Are you sure this is a good idea, Anna?"

"Do you have a better one?" Her eyes suddenly seemed very big.

I bent forward and kissed her on the lips.

A POISON TREE

We looked at each other.

"Would you mind doing that again?" she said.

She pulled my mouth to hers, then looked at me anxiously. "This is not a revenge fuck, is it, David?"

"You never use the word, 'fuck'."

"I might use it tonight. Several times, if you like."

"No it's not a revenge fuck, I promise."

"For me neither. Now stop talking, David, and undress me."

Desire is a chameleon.

He blends into the brickwork and the rocks of those lanes and pathways down which we walk. He lurks like a highwayman at the crossroads of our lives, waiting to rob us of our reason.

And he does so for sport.

He lies on the rooftops of our imagination, armed with a high-powered rifle.

Desire is a tireless hunter.

He plants seeds of mephitic longing in our minds; seeds that germinate, take root and put out branches of madness to infect and torment us.

He is a poison tree.

His words whisper to us in that place between sleep and waking, when we are at our most vulnerable. He chases ambulances, frequents emotional train-wrecks. He sits in the empty chair and attends lovingly to his business.

Having cast off his cherubic shape, he appears in a new Bacchanalian form, pouring the wine of lust down our all-too-eager throats.

He can walk through walls, travel down cables and reach out from the phrases of a letter or the bright glow of a computer screen.

A POISON TREE

His arguments carry neither sense nor logic, and they do not need to. They speak to something primeval within us, transform us into animals baying at the moon. We have no defence.

He is the unexpected guest, the friend we once knew, the stranger, the casual acquaintance.

He is all this and more.

He never rests.

And, under his remorseless gaze, neither do we.

27

ADELE

Adele had taken an instant liking to Rosie Fletcher.

The pair of them stood outside the back porch of the vicarage, puffing cigarettes like a couple of naughty schoolgirls, while Simon amused the churchgoers inside with tea and Biblical anecdotes. The day was grey and cold and more rain was expected.

Simon's sister, who was in Leicester for a few days, wore an eccentric outfit that put Adele in mind of a loopy psychic she had seen on television. Her sweater looked like it had been knitted by someone with their mind only half on the job. Her wrists were covered in beads and bangles and her curly hair had a life of its own. No makeup, no bra and no concern with what anyone thought of her. Adele had seen Eleanor struggling to find the right things to say to the vicar's sibling.

Eleanor was accompanied that morning by her daughter, Ruth, who, in Adele's opinion, looked like trouble. Ruth's sensible attire did little to counter the impression that there was something slutty about her, although Adele could appreciate the irony of her view on that subject.

She hoped nobody in the vicar's front room would demonstrate the same level of curiosity that she had with her brother. If a parishioner opened the bag she had left beside the coffee table, the contents for sure would convince them that sin had assumed human form and was attending services at St. Mark's.

When Rosie suggested a smoke outside – after announcing she had been 'good enough' for one Sunday – Adele had grabbed the opportunity to escape the stifling atmosphere for a few minutes. Half the attendees at that morning's ceremony had joined them for tea, and Adele had the uncomfortable feeling it was because they wanted to see how Simon and she behaved with each other. She had witnessed knowing looks exchanged. Paradoxically, Adele felt more relaxed in the company of Rosie, in spite of the fact that they had only just met, although Rosie's first words on the porch discomfited her somewhat.

"I think my brother's a little in love with you."

Adele coughed.

"Whoops," Rosie laughed. "Sorry, I didn't mean to choke you."

"I need prior warning if you're going to make statements like that."

"Apologies." Rosie took a deep drag on her cigarette and blew out the smoke. "He does talk about you rather a lot, though."

"Oh?" Adele had no idea how to respond.

"It's all right. I'm not here to check you out."

"That's a relief."

Rosie removed a flake of tobacco from her tongue before saying, "Did Simon tell you I'm an atheist?"

"He did mention it, yes. Did he tell you I'm one too?"

"Not in as many words. It was good to see someone else in church this morning that looked as out of place as me. I assume as you didn't take communion you haven't been confirmed either?"

"You assume right. I only go to church in the hope I'll get a glimpse of Simon's butt."

"Simon does have a nice butt."

The two women caught each other's eye and giggled.

"So what do you do, Rosie?"

"Anything that enables me to save money to indulge in my real love, which is travelling. I'd rather have a plane ticket than a man any day. I don't want kids and I'm too young to be a cat lady. I also sponge off my parents quite a bit, if I'm being truthful."

A POISON TREE

They smoked for a while in silence. Then Rosie said, "Simon told me you work at one of the supermarkets in the city centre, I think?"

"That's correct. For this week, anyway. I'm looking for a new job."

"Oh?"

"Yes, but not by choice. On Friday the supermarket manager told me he was going to have to let me go. They are 'redoing the rotas', and employing less full-timers, more part-timers. What they are really doing is taking on students. They can pay them shit hourly rates. The manager offered to keep me on part-time, but of course there would be a reduction in my hourly take-home pay. I told him to stuff it. I'm currently on four weeks' notice."

"Can they do that?"

"They've done it."

"What will you do?"

"God knows."

"You should ask Simon to have a word with the Almighty, and get Him to reveal His greater purpose for you."

"I'd rather Simon asked Him to smite the supermarket manager. God used to be big on smiting, but He doesn't seem to do it much these days."

"Do you want another cigarette?"

"We shouldn't, should we?"

"No. But I'm having one anyway."

"Go on, then."

They lit up.

"What do you think they're talking about in there?" asked Adele, with a glance behind her.

"I know what they'd like to be talking about."

"What?"

"You, my dear."

"Can we change the subject, Rosie?"

Rosie winked. "Of course. Listen, would you like to meet up in town for a bite to eat later? Much as I love my brother, I can only stomach one portion of God per day."

"I can't, I'm afraid. I'm busy today. But tomorrow evening, maybe, if you're still here?"

"That would be nice."

They exchanged numbers.

"You know, it's a funny thing with brothers and sisters."

"What is?"

"Well, my brother came to visit me recently, and we spent very little time together. You come to stay with Simon and you can't wait to get away either."

Rosie chuckled. "I know. I love Simon, but we don't have a lot in common."

"Neither do Ross and I."

Except for the fact we both have secrets. We have that in common. In spades.

"I much prefer the company of women to men," Rosie said, before adding, "but not in *that* way. I won't come on to you, I promise. At least not on our first date."

Two of the rooms at the Gold Club had been redecorated. The whole building smelled of wet paint.

"It is part of our commitment to the ongoing upgrading of our establishment," Miss Connie informed everyone. She felt sure the regular clientele would understand and put up with the temporary inconvenience.

While Nina moaned that she had put on a few pounds ("A chubby dominatrix with cellulite is not the look I'm aiming for"), and Leona berated exam invigilators for no obvious reason, Adele speculated.

A POISON TREE

What did these other girls at the club think about while they were servicing their customers? What they were having for dinner? Where they would go on holiday this year? How long before this guy finishes and I can have a cup of tea?

She doubted whether matters of religion featured, even if they were wearing a nun's costume at the time. In spite of her best efforts she found herself wondering what Simon would be like in bed. Adele was not one given to either flights of romantic fancy or exotic sexual fantasies. She was too wise to the ways of the world for that. Her adolescent years had squashed any unrealistic notions about love or escaping the grind of daily life by swallowing the placebo of carnality. Indeed, she always had to wear her poker face whenever a client asked for anything unusual, lest she make them both feel ridiculous. Fortunately, that didn't happen too often.

Adele also fretted about a remark made by Rosie Fletcher – her suspicion that Simon might be regretting his choice of career. It was not that he had lost his faith, she explained, just that perhaps he wasn't cut out for the priesthood as a vocation. Adele was not sure how to deal with this information. She did not want to be a contributing factor in any decision on this point. That was not a responsibility she was ready for.

She told herself she was not that important to the vicar of St. Mark's. Surely not. He was looking for a friend with whom to assuage his obvious loneliness, someone as lonely as himself. Adele Darrow fitted that bill all right.

It was a source of some puzzlement to her why the members of his flock could not sense his underlying unhappiness. Perhaps they only saw what they wanted to see: a priest, a bedrock for their faith. What Adele saw was a man.

"Oh, Jamie," Adele said to the photograph on her fridge, "what's your mamma going to do, eh?"

Initial queries to shops around the city centre indicated jobs were in short supply. Adele could not afford to be out of work, and she recoiled at the idea of asking her half-brother for money. It was not that Ross would refuse her, or even make her feel bad about it. It was more that recent events had made her question just how 'dirty' his money was.

Ross' visit had been brief, a mere four days, and she had only seen him on two occasions. On his third day, he had called her late in the evening from what sounded like a motorway service area, judging from the background noise of cars travelling at speed. He had not said where he was, but cited an unavoidable business meeting as the reason for his standing her up for dinner. They did eat together at Adele's flat the following evening and then Ross was gone, heading north to Glasgow in his hire car. Or so he told her.

When Adele spoke to her mother on the phone a few days later, it seemed Ross had a 'missing' day between the time he left Leicester and the time he arrived in Glasgow. That did not necessarily imply anything untoward, and there was always the possibility that Flora Darrow's drink-addled memory was playing tricks on her.

Adele said nothing to Ross about the gun she had found in his belongings, even though it preyed on her mind. What was the point? He wouldn't tell her the truth about it anyway. And supposing he did confess to her the reason for carrying what she was convinced was an illegal firearm? It was unlikely to be a palatable revelation. Knowing might be worse than remaining ignorant.

Limited though it was, Adele's relationship with Ross was important to her, and she was fond of him. It wasn't as though she had an extensive support network to fall back on, either. Yet she was fearful of being drawn into any criminal sphere. It was bad enough that she was working in the sex industry. Adele had to attain a position of financial stability and, at least, apparent respectability, if she was ever to have any chance of wresting her son Jamie from the tenacious grip of the Social Services.

If her brother was a criminal, Adele could not afford the added burden of guilt by association.

Leona shook her shoulder. "Wake up, Sleeping Beauty," she said. "You've got a customer. And it isn't Prince Charming."

28

DAVID

I dreamed I was walking barefoot along an exotic beach, somewhere in the tropics. The sun was low in the sky and the coconut trees at the edge of the sand cast long shadows. The beach was deserted apart from a couple of dogs and a figure in the distance at the water's edge. As I made my way closer, I could discern the figure was a woman with long red hair. Claire. She was unmoving, gazing at the setting sun.

A slight wind blew in from the sea, masking the sound of my approach. I tapped her on the shoulder and she turned. It wasn't Claire.

It was Anna.

"Surprised to see me?" she said.

The sound of a kettle boiling woke me. Anna was spooning coffee into two cups. She was dressed in one of the hotel robes. Our clothes still lay scattered over the floor. She pushed back her hair and saw me watching her.

"Hello." Her voice was quiet. "I was just making you a drink."

"What time is it?"

"Around seven."

"It's early. Come back to bed."

She padded back and climbed under the covers. I undid the loosely-tied belt and slid the robe off her shoulders. She ran her tongue over her lips.

"I want you again," I said.

There was a sharp intake of breath and her cheeks coloured. "Are you sure?"

"Yes, I'm sure."

"I was worried perhaps this morning, you'd feel differently about me."

I kissed her breasts. "No."

I held her head, my fingers grasping her fiery hair, and pulled her mouth to mine. Anna moaned softly and swung herself over me.

"Oh, my God," she exclaimed, "you're hard already."

She touched my face with her palm and scrutinised me. "Tell me."

"Tell you what?"

"When we made love last night, did you make love to me or to Claire? In the dark, whose face did you see?"

"Yours. As I see your face now."

"Good. I'm happy about that."

Afterwards she lay with her head on my shoulder, her left hand stroking my chest. The intensity of our climaxes had surprised us both.

"I suppose we need to talk about this, David," she whispered.

"I suppose we do."

"I know you would never have slept with me if Claire wasn't having an affair. You're not that sort of man."

"I don't want you to think –"

She put her hand to my lips. "Ssshh. Just listen, OK? I need to say something to you."

I kissed her fingers. "OK."

"Last week, Max and I made love. If you can call it that. It was the first time for a while. I lay there while he grunted over me, wondering who it was he imagined himself with. Afterwards he said it was like fucking a dead fish."

"Jesus."

"No, he was right. I was beginning to suspect I'd become frigid. Maybe that's why he was going with other women." She propped herself up on one elbow and put her face close to mine.

"That's why I will never regret this. I feel like a person again, like someone can love me."

I started to speak, but she shook her head. "I know this is all wrong, making love to my sister's husband, but you see – from my side anyway – this has been coming for some time. Sorry, but there it is. I might as well be honest, even if it makes me a bad person."

"You're not a bad person."

"Well." She shrugged. "It's too late now, anyway."

"I had no idea, Anna."

"I've been thinking what it might have been like between us if you'd never met Claire. Am I scaring you?"

"No."

Anna ran her finger across my breastbone. "Maybe we should both get divorced and marry each other. It's legal, you know, to marry your sister-in-law."

"Is it?"

"Yes. Actually, it's been legal since 1907 to marry your dead wife's sister. In England, anyway."

"How do you know that?"

"Don't panic, I didn't look it up specially. It's in a manuscript I'm editing. Apparently, making it legal was a *cause célèbre* during the Victorian era. Lots of Bills introduced in Parliament. I wasn't suggesting you do away with Claire, by the way. Sorry, I'm rambling. I was trying to be funny, but this is most inappropriate and not funny at all. I didn't mean to make you uncomfortable."

"You don't. You've never made me uncomfortable."

"I'm not going to tell you I'm in love with you, or anything like that."

I grasped her hand. "Anna, it's all right. This is *me*, remember?"

"You know we can never do this again," Anna put her head back on my shoulder. "David?"

I didn't respond.

"It would all just be too messy and awful to imagine. That's the only reason. It's not because I don't want to. Because I do."

I tried to come up with something to say. Words that would reassure her. Words that might reassure me. But my mind was a blank. The actuality of our betrayal was too much to grasp. I couldn't take it in.

The worst part was, I didn't *feel* like I'd done anything wrong. That's when I knew I was in trouble. Shouldn't I be consumed with remorse, with self-loathing? Why was there no shame?

I was stretched out naked on that hotel bed with the sister-in-law I had known as a friend for twenty years, and I realised for the first time how much I felt for her. Not friendship. Not love. Something else. Something that had no label, but which was a big part of my life.

We lay in each other's arms, silent, for I don't know how long. Then Anna said, "Will we be able to meet for lunch like we did before?"

I turned my head towards her. Her eyes were wet and there were trails of tears on her face. She hadn't sobbed. Her despair had instead seeped noiselessly from her eyes. I wiped the tears away. "Of course," I said as gently as I could.

"It will never be the same, though, will it?"

"It will be how we want it to be."

"I should take the job in London. Then I won't be under your feet."

"You shouldn't take the job for that reason."

"Well, it also occurred to me that if I was here, and you came down for the rugby at Twickenham, you could stay with me. " She looked solemn. "Yes," she said with a catch in her voice, "that's how crazy I am, David."

A POISON TREE

Anna and I took the same train back to Leicester.

The carriage was almost full, in contrast to my journey down to London. I attempted to read my Nick Hornby novel while Anna worked her way through some author's draft, annotating it with a red pen. Now and then I detected a faraway look in her eyes, but for the most part she appeared calm, contented and focused on her editing.

Strange to tell, but I felt happy. Perhaps it reflected something lacking in my moral character, that I could make love to Anna and experience no embarrassment or unease about what had occurred. She was still just Anna. Except she wasn't. Whatever might come of this, our relationship was forever changed. Images of my undressing her and holding her floated through my head. When she put her pen in her mouth, a studious expression across her face, I had a strong urge to reach forward and grasp her arm. Underneath the table, my legs rested against hers, and neither of us felt the need to move them. We were comfortable together.

While pretending to read, I studied her. Anna's red hair lay soft against the whiteness of her neck. I had forgotten how graceful and angelic she could look at times. In some ways she was so much like Claire, and in other ways so different. If the carriage had been empty, I would have sat beside her and kissed her neck. I wouldn't have been able to help myself.

She caught me looking at her a few times, and each time she treated me to a bashful grin. On the third occasion, she moved her leg against mine before turning her attention back to her papers.

"Can we meet for lunch this week?" I said, as the train approached Leicester station.

"I'd like that."

"Maybe somewhere out of town?"

"Just tell me where and when."

"How about Friday? I have to drive over to Coventry. We could maybe meet at a country pub?"

"A quiet one?"

"Yes."

As we were leaving the station, my phone rang and I indicated for Anna to wait a moment.

"Hello, David." It was Jim Fosse.

"What do you want, Jim?" I turned away from Anna.

"I'm just calling to say thank you."

"For what?"

There was a laugh at the other end of the phone. "I must confess, I had my doubts whether you were my man, but I'm happy that you came through for me."

"I don't know what you're talking about." I glanced at Anna. She could see from my expression that something was wrong.

"Have it your own way," said the annoying voice. "I've just got home from the police station, where they questioned me about my wife's disappearance."

"Monique has disappeared?"

"As if you didn't know."

"I didn't."

"In any event, I just wanted to say don't worry. I won't forget my end of the bargain. I have to go away again this week, but as soon as I'm back, I'll take care of business. You'll be a free man soon enough." Jim cut the line.

I tried to ring him back, but he had switched off his phone.

Anna moved closer to me. "What's wrong? Is it Claire?"

"No. It's a stupid situation I've got myself into with a man called Fosse."

Anna looked puzzled. "Jim Fosse?"

I felt my heart racing. "You know him?"

"No, I don't know him personally, but Max works with his wife Monique. We were supposed to go to a dinner party at their house a couple of weeks ago, but at the last minute Max said he was too busy."

"A dinner party at the Fosses'?" I stared at her. "Anna, it's important you and I meet on Friday, if not before."

"It's something bad, isn't it, David? I can see by the look on your face."

"Yes. But we can't talk here."

"Call me."

We gave each other a hug and a chaste kiss on both cheeks before we parted.

I needed to think fast.

I had a couple of hours with Claire before I went out again to see the Italy vs Tonga match at Welford Road, and I needed to appear 'normal'. Or as normal as it is possible to be knowing your wife's life might be in danger and that you've just slept with her sister.

"How was the rugby?" asked Claire.

"Great match, even though we lost." I feigned enthusiasm.

"Did you meet Anna for dinner?"

"We just grabbed a pizza. It was a bit late by the time I got back into London."

"Did you talk about books?"

"We always talk about books."

"Just as well I wasn't there then."

I switched on the television and watched the local news. There was no mention of Monique Fosse.

Was Monique really dead? Did Jim seriously think I'd killed her while he was abroad and then hidden her body?

The whole thing was implausible, insane.

A POISON TREE

Why had Fosse invited Max and Anna to dinner? Just to torture Max and Monique a little? To let them know he knew?

None of this made any sense. Jim Fosse didn't make any sense. My mind was buzzing with questions.

I tried Jim's phone again, several times. It was still switched off.

If Claire was in danger, I had to *do* something.

Then something else occurred to me, quite aside from my concern for my wife.

I had apparent motive to kill Claire. She was having an affair, and so was I. At least that's how the police would see it if the facts ever came out.

I drove into the city and parked. While I walked to the ground, I smoked a cigarette and called my old school friend, cursing myself I hadn't done it months before. Leicester wasn't his patch, but he would have friends in the Leicester police force. I told him I needed his help, that it was urgent, but that I couldn't talk about it over the phone. He agreed to drive down from Sheffield and meet me the following evening.

Ian Kenney was waiting for me at Welford Road and we went into the match together. He had taken a rare evening off from depressing the customers at the Bell to depress me instead. In truth, I was glad it was Ian. He didn't talk much and I didn't want to talk. We watched Tonga beat Italy, then filed out.

I became aware he had been saying something to me.

"Sorry, Ian, what was that?"

"I was just completing your Buddhist education on karma in the context of the Rugby World Cup."

"Oh, yes?"

"Tonight's result will have consequences. All our actions have consequences. Everything we do affects somebody."

"I get that."

A POISON TREE

As I arrived back at my car, I saw I had a message on my phone. It was from Jim Fosse. It read:

I am going to start laying my new patio next weekend

I called his number. There was no answer.

29

DAVID

A certain amount of stress can invigorate our minds to higher levels of creativity and productivity. The gurus call this *eustress*. Once we pass a tipping point, however, our ability to think with clarity erodes fast, and we descend into a crevasse of emotional burn-out where unreason, inertia and indolence lie in wait.

At work the next day, concentration proved hard to come by.

I kept my office door closed and dealt with administrative matters, all of which could have waited, and under ordinary circumstances would have done exactly that. But these were not ordinary circumstances.

At lunchtime I phoned Anna.

"Are you OK to talk?"

"Yes."

"Good."

"You frightened me half to death yesterday at the railway station. If you hadn't called me, I was going to call you."

I opened a windows and lit a Marlboro. "I'm sorry, Anna. That wasn't my intention. And, by the way, this crisis – or whatever the hell it is – has nothing to do with you and me."

"All right." I could sense her relax a little. "So tell me, what *is* going on?"

"This man I mentioned to you, Jim Fosse, he's what's going on. This year, I've bumped into him a few times, and all our meetings have been, well, weird to say the least. You remember that dinner party you and Max were invited to? Claire and I were also invited." I flicked ash out of the window and tried to work out how to explain the situation to Anna without sounding completely mad.

"Go on."

"Fosse is one of those people who is difficult to read. You can't tell whether he's joking or not. He will say things which, if he's not kidding, mean he's a complete card-carrying psycho."

"Like what, David?" I could hear the anxiety in her voice again.

"He put a proposal to me. If I kill Monique for him, he'll kill Claire for me."

There was a shocked silence. Then Anna said, "He can't be serious. This has to be a bad taste prank."

"That was my first reaction. But while he was out of the country on business recently, Monique disappeared. His call yesterday was to thank me for ridding him of his troublesome spouse."

"Oh, my God. Have you said anything to Claire?"

"No."

"Why not, David?"

"Because for one thing, I don't know if Monique *has* disappeared. He may just be screwing with me. Tonight I'm meeting an old friend who's in the police to see if he can tell me anything about Monique. According to Fosse, the police have had him in for questioning already, so I can at least find out whether that's true."

"Have you called Fosse back?"

"He's not answering his phone." I wondered how to bring up the next point without panicking Anna. "You said that Max works with Monique Fosse?"

"Yes. They're at the same consulting firm. Do you want me to ask Max whether she's been at work lately?"

"No." My reply was a little too vehement. "Anna, there is no easy way to tell you this, so I'll just say it. The woman I saw Max meeting at the hotel? It was Monique."

There was a pause. "Are you sure?" She sounded doubtful.

"I'm sure."

"Because, you see ... Oh, God."

"What?"

"Only last week I saw Max with a young woman in his car. A very young woman. A *girl*, really. And I am not the only one who has seen him. It was not Monique Fosse. I know because I've met her. This girl looked like a student. Maybe about Katie's age." I heard Anna swallow hard.

Max could well have been seeing two women. I wouldn't have put it past the slimy git. That would feed his over-inflated ego. A married woman and a student simultaneously? I could see the smug leer now. But I couldn't very well say that to Anna.

"It's Monique I'm more concerned about now, Anna. If she has vanished, it could spell trouble for Max. And, sweetheart, it could spell trouble for you too."

"Yes, I can see that. So what happens next?"

"Let me find out whether Jim Fosse is feeding me a cock-and-bull story. In the meantime, I suggest you say nothing to Max. Or indeed, to anyone. I'll call you as soon as I know anything, OK?"

"OK."

"And we still have that lunch on Friday, right?"

"Right."

"I have to go, Anna. I'll be in touch soon."

"All right, David. I love you."

I cut the line before I realised what she had said.

Chief Superintendent Bill Munks of the South Yorkshire Police was not a man who suffered fools gladly. At the minor public school where we both found ourselves incarcerated for the duration of our rebellious years, Bill had acquired the nickname 'Mad Munks' for his over-enthusiastic playing style on the rugby field. His habit of leading with his head had resulted in his having his nose broken twice to my knowledge. He was a big man, and a brusque one, with a pronounced Yorkshire accent.

Bill came from a family of policemen. His father had risen to Assistant Chief Constable in the Derbyshire Constabulary, and his younger brother, Ron, had joined the Royal Hong Kong Police Force before becoming the head security advisor to a large corporate in the Far East.

Bill's career had been hampered by his reputation as a maverick. During the miners' strike of 1984, he was implicated in the police attack on striking miners in South Yorkshire, where it was shown that the South Yorkshire Police had fabricated evidence and carried out false arrests. No officer was ever disciplined over the incident, but it appeared to have cast a pall over some of those involved. The Hillsborough disaster five years later pushed the force even deeper into public opprobrium.

Bill sat opposite me at a discreet corner table in the country pub between Leicester and Coventry where I had planned to meet Anna on Friday. It was beyond my limited brain capacity that week to come up with two venues.

My companion was dressed informally so as not to draw attention. He had put on some weight, but his pugilistic air was still evident. His shoulders were even broader than I remembered them to be. That was just as well, given what I was about to tell him.

"Thanks for driving all the way down here, Bill. I appreciate it."

"By the tone of your voice, it sounded urgent. So, talk." Straight to the nub, as ever.

"Can I speak to you in confidence?"

"Up to a point, David. I am a police officer, and if there is a crime involved there is a limit as to what can be kept quiet. I may as well tell you that now before you say anything." Bill fixed his steel-grey eyes on me and I wondered what it would be like to be in an interrogation room with him.

"I'm not sure where to start."

He said nothing. Instead he took a drink of beer.

I had already decided not to tell Bill about the anonymous letter and phone calls. If I could keep Claire out of this, I would, even though that might cast me in a guilty light should he later learn about my wife's affair.

"There is an American I have come to know through the Chamber of Commerce. His name is James Fosse and he is some kind of consultant to the power industry. He spends a lot of time travelling in Asia, doing deals and fixing things. Some months ago, during an evening where we'd both been drinking, he raised the subject of my doing away with his wife in return for his disposing of mine. Sort of a tit-for-tat thing, where we would present each other with solid alibis."

"Go on."

"I wrote it off as a joke at the time. But he kept coming back to me about it."

"Why you?"

"I don't know."

"Did he think there was some reason you might want your wife dead?"

"No."

"*Is* there some reason you might want your wife dead?" The tone was casual, but Bill was watching my reaction.

"No. For goodness' sake, Bill, you've met Claire."

He scratched the back of his neck. "Relationships change, David. The divorce rate testifies to that. And do you know in nine out of ten murders, it's the spouse that did it? He or she always starts as the prime suspect, despite the many tears they shed. It's a sad fact of modern life." My companion gazed moodily at his beer. "Though, to be frank, I doubt it's a recent phenomenon. As soon as the first caveman learned how to use a club, I expect the next thing he did was to hit his woman over the head with it. Forget about serial killers and robberies gone wrong. The most insidious crime ring on the planet is the one you wear on the third finger of your left hand."

Bill stretched back in his chair and his gaze flicked over the horse brasses that were nailed to the pub's wooden beams. "Still," he said lightly, "it sounds like Mr. Fosse has a fertile, if somewhat febrile, imagination. 'You kill my wife and I'll kill yours.' You must admit, as a proposition, it has an alluring symmetry to it." He looked back at me. "I take it there is more to this story?"

"Yesterday he called me and told me his wife – Monique – had gone missing. He thanked me and said he would repay the favour."

"And has she indeed gone missing?"

"I don't know. There's been nothing in the news that I've seen."

Bill flexed his legs. "Fosse sounds like a Walter Mitty character to me, David. Someone who gets his kicks from winding people up."

"Maybe so. But he said he'd been questioned by the Leicester police."

"Well, that's easy to check. Give me five minutes to make a call and put your mind to rest."

Bill rose to his feet and lumbered out of the pub, leaving me with the distinct impression he regarded me as a hysterical idiot.

When he returned, his attitude was completely different.

"I've just spoken to DCI Banks at Leicester. A Monique Fosse has been reported missing and her husband has been questioned. Banks is sure she disappeared while her husband was out of the country. You'd better go through this with me in detail and I need to make some notes. I haven't mentioned your name to Banks yet, but you'll have to talk to him too."

"I understand. There is something else about Jim Fosse you should know. Monique is his second wife. His first wife, in Greensboro, Carolina, died of mushroom poisoning."

"Did she, now?" Bill paused for a moment. "I have a friend in the NYPD. Met him on an exchange programme. He might be able to dig out something for me on that, as a favour. Tell me everything you know, David. And I mean *everything*."

I told Bill *almost* everything. The anonymous letter, the phone calls and Cumberbatch did not feature in my narrative. Bill wrote a lot of notes.

"I can't promise to keep this quiet, David. You may end up as a material witness, depending how things go. Have you said anything to Claire?"

"No. I want to keep her out of this if I can."

"Have you mentioned it to anyone else?"

"No."

Anna doesn't count, right?

"Have you spoken to Fosse again?"

"No. He's not answering his phone."

"Don't ring him again. Not yet, anyway."

"Gotcha."

He tapped his fingers on the table.

"Let me see what I can find out about Fosse from the other side of the pond. But you must understand, this is Banks' baby, not mine."

"Understood. By the way, there is one other thing. The bastard sent me a text message that he is going to start laying a new patio next weekend when he gets back from his business trip."

"Fosse sounds like a right twat." He beamed at me. "That's a technical police term, by the way."

I felt drained when I finally arrived home.

A POISON TREE

"Work is just ridiculous at the moment," I told Claire.

"You'll cope, darling." She kissed me. "If not, you're not the man I married."

The creature who was evolving into a new, mendacious David Braddock laughed, went into the garden and lit a Marlboro.

30

JAMES

Jim Fosse sat in an armchair with a bowl of popcorn balanced on his ample stomach, as 'The Harry Lime Theme' played on the television. While *The Third Man* was not his favourite Orson Welles film – that privilege was reserved for *A Touch of Evil* – he relished the tinny soundtrack with its underscore of menace, and what is more he never tired of hearing Welles' cynical speech about humanity being little more than ants. It chimed perfectly with his own world view.

Welles may have made some stinker films, but his broadcast of *The War of the Worlds*, which had caused panic in the USA, was a work of genius. Jim Fosse appreciated anyone who could manipulate minds, and bend them to his will.

People were sheep. Stupid, routine-driven sheep, huddling together as if so doing would protect them from the circling wolves. And those who couldn't be scared could always be bought.

It was so difficult to find a worthy adversary, Jim reflected, whether it was at the negotiating table or in more personal situations. David Braddock had showed some promise in this direction, but now appeared to the American as just another mark, a source of amusement on an otherwise boring day.

Some popcorn spilled onto the floor and Jim tutted. He no longer had Monique around to clean up spillages.

Ah, the lovely, faithless and ultimately dim Monique.

For a woman with a first class degree and an MBA, she had proved to be naïve in the extreme. If most Western management consultants shared her inane predilections and inability to see danger when it was right in front of

211

their eyes, it was hardly surprising that the markets of Europe and North America were being gobbled up by the hungry entrepreneurs of Asia.

Jim swigged a beer and mused on how close he had come to messing up things with Laughlan Andrews.

As instructed by the Scotsman, Jim had deposited the attaché case at the Grand Hotel desk.

"Has Mr. Andrews checked out yet?" Jim had asked.

"Mr. Andrews checked out early this morning, sir," was the reply. "But he said he would be back later to collect this case."

Jim had been unable to control his curiosity about the pick-up, and had taken a seat in the lobby, concealing himself behind that morning's *Daily Telegraph*.

At just after eight-thirty, a young Indian-looking man wearing a hoodie, jeans and trainers, had appeared from the street and handed over a note. The hotel employee behind the desk had nodded, checked some detail with a senior colleague then passed the case to him. The man seemed oblivious to anything going on around him, and Jim put down his paper and followed him. The courier headed for the clock tower, swinging the case casually as if it were a matter of no concern.

After Jim had walked about a hundred yards, his cell phone rang and he fished it from his pocket. He didn't recognise the number.

"Mr. Fosse?" The voice was Andrews'.

"Yes?"

"If you insist on following the Indian gentleman, you and I will have a falling-out."

Jim stopped and scanned the street and buildings around him. There was no sign of any person with a bright red beard. But Andrews could be anywhere. At an upstairs window, in a doorway, anywhere.

A POISON TREE

The American could feel his heart beating hard and he realised how foolish he had been. Andrews was a hit man, for God's sake. What had he been thinking?

"I'm sorry, Mr. Andrews," he stammered. "I just wanted to make sure the case had been collected."

"Well, now you have seen that it has." The voice was emotionless. "Everything is in order."

The Indian man disappeared around a corner. Jim stood rooted to the spot.

"Go home, Mr. Fosse. And make sure you get on that plane tomorrow."

"I will." Jim had gulped and the line went dead.

Jim stuffed popcorn into his mouth and turned up the volume on the television.

But it's all turned out right in the end.

Andrews' *modus operandi* of having his target disappear, with no trace of the body, was efficient. But it was also inconvenient. It would take the life insurance company quite some time to pay up on Monique's policy, Jim was sure. This was in stark contrast to the death of his first wife, where the cash had been in his bank account within weeks of the poisoned mushrooms doing their work. But in the end, Jim would get the money, and aside from the unpleasantness of having to submit to police questioning and his crass and misguided attempt at tracking the attaché case, everything was on track.

Even the Braddock matter was working out to his satisfaction. There was more fun to be had there, doubtless, after which Jim would head east, kicking the English mud from his shoes with grateful abandon.

Tasks remained to be completed, however, before he could contemplate his next adventure.

Orson Welles lurked in the shadows, a sardonic grin on his face.

A POISON TREE

Jim was glad real life was not like the ending of so many modern Hollywood films. In real life the bad guys could win. And often did.

When the film finished, Jim packed a case.

Eleven o'clock.

Perhaps a celebratory trip to the Gold Club might be in order? He still had time. It was a while since he had visited, and any female flesh he would be touching over the next few days in Manila would be brown, not white.

He drove into Leicester and parked under a street lamp on the main road at Frog Island. The area was on the rough side, he considered, and he had no desire to find his car gone when he came out of the club.

Jim asked the madam if Adele was free, but was told she was not working that night. Instead he was offered an ample blonde named Leona. She would do nicely, he said.

They went upstairs to a room that, he noticed, had been recently redecorated.

"Do you have any lube, Leona?" Jim asked the woman.

"Yes, darlin'," she answered. "But I don't usually need it. And I'm sure I won't with you. I love Americans."

"Not even if I go up your ass?"

"I don't do that," she said, drawing back.

Jim patted her hand. "Ah, Leona, my dear. Life is one big adventure and you know we only pass this way once. We should try everything, taste all the fruits that are laid out before us."

Leona looked at him sideways.

"You seem unconvinced. Would another twenty pounds persuade you otherwise?"

Leona did the math. "I'll get the lube."

If they can't be frightened, they can be bought.

214

31

DAVID

Bill phoned me two days after our talk to ask if I could be at his house in Sheffield that evening. DCI Banks would also be attending.

I told Claire that Bill had asked me over to discuss the possibility of having an old boys' reunion.

"My, you're mysterious these days, David," she had said. "You don't have a girlfriend in South Yorkshire you need to tell me about, do you?"

"Not unless Bill is thinking of gender reassignment."

Bill's wife, Hazel, met me at the door of their home, which was on a modern, exclusive development outside the city. She showed me through to the lounge where the other men were waiting. From Hazel's demeanour and the friendly look of the two casually-dressed policemen, I judged she was completely in the dark as to why we were there. Once she left us, the atmosphere turned serious, and Banks was introduced to me formally.

"This meeting is not official, David, but the next one will be," Bill announced.

Banks stared at me. "I need to tell you, Mr. Braddock, I am unhappy with having an informal information-sharing session like this, but the Chief Inspector has vouched for your good character, so I am inclined to go along with it. But," he added, "I consider it most irregular." The DCI was a thin, careworn-looking individual. His dry, lined skin bore witness to too many cigarettes and an overly-long career in the firing line of public service. He shuffled in his chair.

"Take it easy, Martin. David understands what we say here is confidential. It saves me time if I tell you both together what I have found out. After that, I bow out gracefully. I am sure David will offer every co-operation to your investigation."

Banks' expression remained one of reluctance. "This is the *only* information that will be shared with you." This remark was directed at me. "And you will appreciate that it is not for me to disclose any details of our work on Mrs. Fosse's disappearance. There are rules to be followed about witnesses. So as far as I am concerned, this evening never happened. Is that understood?"

"Perfectly understood," I said. Banks relaxed a little.

Hazel reappeared with a pot of tea and some biscuits. Bill waited until she had once again closed the door behind her before opening the notebook that had been lying on the table.

"My friend in the NYPD came back to me much quicker than I expected. He has a colleague in North Carolina who proved to be very helpful. And what he had to say was extremely enlightening."

"We need to do all this officially in due course," said Banks.

"Yes, yes," replied Bill, with impatience. "We'll keep your paperwork straight, Martin. I do realise this is potentially a murder investigation, you know. Now do you want to hear this, or not?"

Banks gave a sigh of resignation.

"The officer in Greensboro knew all about our friend, Mr. Fosse. He investigated the death of Mrs. Fosse Number One, formerly Carol Quinn, who was born and bred in Greensboro. Mrs. Fosse, as you know, David, died from eating poison mushrooms.

"It seems Mrs. Fosse always did her shopping at the same supermarket. It was thought the mushrooms had been bought there, yet there were no other reports of poisoning in the area. The mushrooms at the supermarket were tested, and they were fine. The assumption was either Mrs. Fosse had deliberately poisoned herself or else the mushrooms in the fridge had been switched. Suicide by mushroom would seem an odd way to go." Bill paused while he drank tea.

"Did Carol Fosse have any enemies?" asked Banks.

"No. She was a friendly, unassuming woman whose life had been unremarkable up to that point. No family secrets, no skeletons in the closet, nothing. She was a popular schoolteacher, and a regular churchgoer."

Banks looked interested now. "So how about Fosse?"

"A watertight alibi. For the four weeks leading up to his wife's death, he had been in West Africa doing a business deal on an oil pipeline. Lots of witnesses, papers and visas checked. He never returned to the States until he was notified of her death.

"Fosse had taken out a large insurance policy on Carol about fifteen months before. A *very* large one. That, of course, is no crime.

"The local police smelled a rat, though. Fosse was cocky during questioning, and seemed unaffected by his wife's death. But they had nothing at all on him. You can't charge someone just because they show no emotion. Background checks produced nothing." Bill nibbled a biscuit.

"That's not the end of it, though, Bill, is it? Otherwise you wouldn't have asked us both over this evening."

Bill chuckled. "Just building a bit of tension," he said. Banks' expression turned sour again.

"Anyway," my old friend continued, "over the next month or so there were some curious happenings in Greensboro. Two weeks after Carol Fosse's death, a Mrs. Vivien Taylor was shot in the head at home while she slept. Three weeks after that, her husband, Hank Taylor committed suicide. Shot himself. He left a note saying he couldn't live with himself as he had killed his wife."

"I don't see the connection," said Banks.

"Taylor couldn't have killed his wife. He was on an oil rig in the Gulf of Mexico at the time."

"Two women killed and both husbands have perfect alibis?" I could feel my pulse quicken.

"Sound familiar, David?"

"Jesus Christ, Bill."

"The gun that killed Vivien Taylor was never found. Frank Taylor shot himself with his own gun."

Banks looked like he wanted to start making notes. "Did Taylor and Fosse know each other?"

"They were at school together."

"Fuck," I exclaimed. "My wife really is in danger."

Banks turned to me. "Why would you think that, Mr. Braddock? It's not as though you killed Monique Fosse, is it?"

"That's a stupid fucking question."

The two policemen studied me.

"Do I need a lawyer?" I felt like the room was closing in on me, like a zoom shot in some black and white movie.

"I don't know," said Banks. "Do you?"

I pulled an envelope from my jacket pocket. "This is the envelope Fosse gave me. Inside it is his travel schedule. I expect his fingerprints should be on it as well as mine. And here's something else." I laid a second envelope on the table while the two mean continued to observe me in silence. "Some months ago I received this anonymous note which suggests my wife was having an affair. There have been anonymous phone calls too, with the person speaking through an electronic gizmo to disguise his voice."

"Why didn't you mention this before, David?" Bill's face looked grim. "*Is* your wife having an affair?"

"Yes. I hired a private detective to tail her. I'm sorry, Bill. I should have told you before. I just ... ah, shit." My words dried up.

Bill was unamused.

"I have evidence bags in the car," Banks announced. "I need to put these envelopes into them."

"I know this doesn't look good," I said.

"You don't know the half of it."

"Why would Fosse tell you he was going to kill your wife if you hadn't killed Monique Fosse?" asked Banks. "That doesn't make any sense. Unless of course, you *did* murder his wife and you've changed your mind about having your own wife murdered. Panicked, maybe?"

"No."

"Perhaps your reasoning was that by getting the police involved, you would be off the hook?"

"No. I phoned Bill because I was worried about Claire."

Bill coughed.

"I think we should leave any further discussion for the formal interview."

"I agree." Banks rose to his feet. "And you will need to recall your movements during the time Monique Fosse went missing. Excuse me, I'm just going out to my car." He left the room.

Bill looked at me and sighed.

"Who do you think sent you the anonymous letter?"

"I think it might have been an ex-employee of mine called Mark Standish."

"We should talk to Standish."

"You can't."

"Why not?"

"He's dead."

Bill's mouth fell open. "People are dropping around you like flies, David."

"It seems like it, yes."

Bill was pensive for a moment. Then he said, "Before DCI Banks gets back, is there anything else you want to tell me?"

"No."

"You're not having an affair with anyone, are you?"

"No."

"Are you absolutely sure?"

"I think I'd know if I were having an affair, Bill."

"Don't try to be smart. You haven't been smart so far."

Banks returned and placed the envelopes with care into two see-through bags.

"Where is Fosse now?" Bill asked.

"According to that schedule I've just given you, he's in Manila," I said.

Bill turned to Banks. "You didn't pull his passport?"

Banks grimaced. "At this stage his wife is reported missing, that's all. We couldn't take his passport. We'd have the bloody American Embassy on the phone straight away."

"Fosse is out of the country for a few days. My wife is safe until then, at least."

Banks looked like he wanted to say something, but bit his tongue.

"You should talk to your wife, David. Come clean. Tell her what you know. You owe her that."

"Meantime, I'd like you to report to the station tomorrow, Mr. Braddock. Let's get all this recorded," said Banks in a flat voice.

"I'll give you the contact details for the States too, Martin. Your team should verify all this information." Bill tapped on his notebook. Both men looked down at their hands, as if unsure what to do or say next.

A POISON TREE

Should I tell them what I knew about Monique and Max meeting at that hotel? I reflected. *What happens if they need to check out my movements that weekend in London? Like who I slept with on the Saturday night, for instance?*

Best to keep silent. Every time I opened my mouth, the hole I was standing in got a little deeper.

Could things get any worse?

Then my cell phone rang and things did get worse. A lot worse.

And by the time the call was over, and the two policemen had averted their eyes, I knew that I would not be making my appointment with DCI Banks the next day, nor my lunch meeting with Anna.

Death has a way of clearing your calendar.

32

CLAIRE

For Claire Braddock, that Thursday had started like any other Thursday. There was nothing remarkable about it, least of all the drab, drizzling weather.

David had left for the office earlier than usual, and she wouldn't see him again until late that night after his trip to Sheffield to see his old school friend.

Claire was becoming concerned about her husband. For several weeks, his usually sharp mind had seemed distracted, as if he were focused on solving some intractable conundrum. He always cited work as the reason for his preoccupied state, but Claire was only half-convinced by this explanation.

She wondered whether he had found out about her liaisons with Jack, but persuaded herself that he had not. Like other spouses with secrets, her shield against discovery lay in the deep trust he placed in her. His inherent decency coated his eyes like cataracts. It both protected him from disappointment and heartache even as it provided a cloak for her dishonesty.

More and more, Claire was feeling uncomfortable in her own skin, and she had finally resolved to sever the relationship with Jack. If it continued, sooner or later, the truth would come out. She could not always rely on David's wilful unknowing. *Someone* would see her and Jack together, and when the news broke no amount of irrational thinking would help.

Claire Braddock had a lot to lose.

Moreover, some small voice told her that her husband needed her support now. Perhaps it *was* work that was troubling David – and he did work hard. Perhaps he was missing Katie. The house felt strange without her effervescent presence. Whatever it was, she was sure the man she loved was in a dark place, and *her* place was with him. The only time David relaxed was in the company of her sister. Anna was shouldering a duty that was Claire's. That situation needed to change.

But how and when to tell Jack?

The previous two days he had been in a foul mood, following some phone call that threw him into a state of incandescent anger. She had heard shouting, punctuated by obscenities, from his office – as had everyone within a fifty-yard radius – but he had offered no explanation afterwards and no-one had had the courage to inquire what had ignited the rage.

This weekend. Claire would call Jack and arrange to see him. Then it would be over. If things became awkward between them after that, she would change jobs. She knew of several companies that would be happy to employ her.

Then she could once more be the wife and companion she had been before a shadow had fallen between her and David. The shadow of Daniel.

Claire loaded up the dishwasher, locked the house and drove to the office, where most of her time was spent kicking the monthly accounts into order and mentoring a new starter on her duties in the accounts department.

Jack spent the whole day at Kettering on project meetings on engineering matters. These did not require Claire's presence.

When her cell phone rang around seven-thirty, she was at the big supermarket in town, filling a trolley with food supplies. The display told her the call was from Anna.

"Claire? Oh my God, something terrible has happened."

"What's wrong?"

"I've just called the police and the ambulance. It's – it's Max." Anna broke into wracking sobs.

"What about Max?"

Claire could not make out what her sister was saying. Anna sounded on the edge of hysteria.

"Anna, listen to me. Where are you?"

"At home." Between choking breaths, Anna managed to get the words out.

"Stay put. I'll be there in five minutes."

Claire abandoned her shopping, ran to her car and drove dangerously fast to Anna's apartment building. Other drivers sounded their horns as she weaved through the traffic. The drizzle was turning into heavy rain, and Claire switched the wipers to their fastest speed. She considered calling David on the way, but she had no real information to give him, and besides she worried that driving one-handed, she might not be able to keep the car on the road. She needed to get to Anna. David could wait. There was nothing he could do from Sheffield, in any event.

When Claire arrived, the entrance to the car parking area was blocked by a police car, its lights flashing, and two ambulances were parked inside. A second police vehicle screeched to a halt behind Claire's car, and two officers, one male, one female, dashed past her. Residents from the building stood around in the car park, and others craned over their balconies ogling at the activity below. Claire slammed her car door closed and, careless of the rain, rushed onto the driveway to scan the crowd for Anna.

She saw her sister sitting on the steps of the building. Anna looked dazed and soaked through. The female police officer was kneeling by her and holding her hand.

Claire sprinted over to her and threw her arms around her, but Anna barely seemed to register she was there.

A POISON TREE

Claire followed her sister's gaze which was directed towards the two crews of paramedics. One crew was loading a blanket-covered body onto a stretcher, while the second crew was working to resuscitate a man lying on the gravel. The man's limbs were splayed at unnatural angles and he wasn't breathing.

It was Jack Irving.

33

DAVID

In truth, we never know how we will behave in a crisis.

We like to think we will act with courage and fortitude, and that, guided by our unfailing moral compass, we will without hesitation step up to the mark and do the right thing. The pedestal of goodness awaits us. Our gold medals bear the inscription, 'Decency under Fire, Always'.

We may well discover, however, that we fall short of these exacting standards when calamity strikes, that our ethics are only shibboleths we spout when all is well with the world. As Leonato, a character in the Bard's play *Much Ado About Nothing*, observes, it is difficult to find a philosopher who can endure the toothache.

We do not know ourselves.

Entombed behind our wall of ego, selfishness and fear lurk, awaiting the appearance of a crack through which they can squeeze into the daylight. Then we see what we really are, glimpsing in that second the uncertainties and dreads that lie beneath our everyday actions, our delusions of valour. These are the monsters that drive us, we learn, and not some higher purpose.

We are all still children. We are afraid of the dark.

On Claire's instruction, I drove to our house. She had not been able to tell me exactly what had happened – in deference to the presence of her sister, I presumed – but I had gathered enough for sharp nails of worry to dig into my gut for the entire journey through the pouring rain. I chain-smoked while driving down the motorway, careless of the spray from lorries and the blinding stab of headlights. All thoughts of Jim Fosse and the police were exorcised from my mind.

I had to get home.

Natalie Holland's car was outside our house and Claire must have been watching for me because the door opened before I had time to insert my key.

Claire led me into the kitchen. "Anna's in the living room with Mum," she said. "I need to fill you in first before you see her."

"Of course."

My wife was pale and haggard and she trembled when I put my arms around her.

"Tell me," I said.

Claire took a deep breath. "Max is dead."

She sat down at the kitchen table. "Jack Irving turned up at Anna's apartment this evening. He had got wind of the fact that Max was seeing his daughter, Ruth. Anna said he was furious, out of control." She faltered, and I stroked her shoulders to reassure her.

Claire swallowed hard and continued. "Jack started shouting at Max, but Max refused to talk to him, turned his back and walked out onto the balcony. That's when Jack snapped and attacked him. There was a struggle, and they both went over the balustrade."

"Christ Almighty. Anna saw all this?"

"Yes." Claire swallowed again. "Max was killed instantly by the fall."

"And Jack?"

"He's in a critical condition at the hospital. They don't know whether he's going to make it."

I pulled Claire's head onto my chest. If I had ever entertained thoughts of revenge on Jack, they had all gone now.

Glad I see my foe outstretched beneath the tree.

Claire drew back from me. "Anna has given a preliminary statement to the police, but she'll have to make a formal one. The police have taped off her apartment, but they let Anna pack a bag. She's staying with us. I called Mum and she came straight here."

"Of course she's staying with us. How is she?"

Tears brimmed over. "How do you think? That shit of a husband, I'm glad he's dead."

Anna and Natalie were sitting on the sofa. Anna was still in shock. Her face was a ghostly white except for the redness around her eyes. She had one of Claire's shawls draped over her shoulders, but that wasn't enough to stop her shivering in spite of the fact that the central heating must have been on maximum.

I knelt in front of her and touched her hands. She didn't react.

"Anna."

"Hello, David." Her voice was a whisper. "I'm sorry about this."

"Don't be silly. None of this is your fault."

"Max is gone."

"I know, sweetheart."

In a closed system, the scientists tell us, entropy increases. The difference between hot and cold erodes away until equilibrium is reached, at which point no further change is possible.

Humanity is a closed system.

My sister-in-law wept, while the rest of us sat around and offered what support we could. The rain kept falling on the just and on the unjust fellow. The hands on the mantelpiece clock continued to move, reminding us that the flow of time is irreversible.

What's done is done. And we all have to live with it.

34

DAVID

Claire and I accompanied Anna to the police station the next morning.

With everything that had been going on, it had completely slipped my mind that I was supposed to have been going to Twickenham, but that was out of the question now and it was too late to offer my ticket to anyone. Besides, I had no desire to explain how it was I came to have a spare ticket.

My mother-in-law had argued that she too wanted to be there for her daughter, but we insisted she stay at home otherwise it was going to look like a family outing. Happily, I didn't bump into DCI Banks. That would have resulted in the solids hitting the air conditioning big time. There had been no sensible opportunity to say anything to either Claire or Anna about the Jim Fosse matter. To have spoken so soon after Max's death would have made an already dreadful situation worse.

That little slice of trauma would have to wait for another time.

The female police officer who led the interview opened by being solicitous and tactful. Her male colleague appeared bored, and to my eye looked like he'd been on the beer the night before. As the discussion progressed, the questions became more pointed.

"Were you aware that your husband was seeing Ruth Irving, Mrs. Harper?"

"I don't think that's an appropriate thing to ask," I said, feeling the outrage starting to bubble.

"We are just trying to establish the facts behind what happened, sir." The woman replied smoothly, but with a steel edge to her voice.

"Maybe you should have a solicitor present for this, Anna."

"It's all right, David," Anna responded. "I knew Max was seeing someone, but I didn't know who."

"So you don't know the Irving family at all?"

"No."

Claire and I exchanged a look, but remained silent.

"You don't know their address for instance?"

"She has already told you she doesn't know them," I said.

The male officer suddenly stirred. "Would you mind if we took your fingerprints, Mrs. Harper? This would be voluntary on your part, you understand."

Anna could see I was about to object, and she put a hand on my arm. "No, I don't mind," she replied. "Anything to help. Let's just get this over with."

"Thank you, Mrs. Harper. I realise this is an upsetting time for you. We will give you back access to your apartment just as soon as we can."

Once we had returned to the house, I took Claire to one side. "I don't like how some of those police questions were going."

"Do you think we should have said that we know the Irvings?"

"I don't think that would have helped. I'm struggling to see why any of that should be relevant. It seems pretty obvious what happened."

"Perhaps they are wondering if it was Anna who told Jack about the affair. It's a mess, David. Ruth is only seventeen, you know."

"I thought she was eighteen."

"Not until the end of this month."

"We don't know for sure Max had sex with her."

Claire raised an eyebrow. "Don't we? Knowing Max? It's not likely he was helping her with her homework."

I looked down at my shoes. "Do you want to go into the hospital and see how Jack is doing?"

A POISON TREE

"No. I have asked the office to ring me if there is any news. Eleanor will be at the hospital. My place is here with Anna. You go to work. We'll be fine."

I didn't go to work. There were things I needed to figure out. So I drove to Foxton Locks, parked the car and walked up the towpath. I needed solitude, and given the cold of the day, I doubted there would be many people around.

In the event, some hardy types were shuffling about and a couple of narrow boats were moving on the canal, but there was not enough activity to disturb my thoughts. I stopped at the place where I had taken that photograph of Claire all those years ago – the one I still carried in my wallet.

Fragments of Ian Kenney's bizarre take on Buddhist philosophy wafted through my head, and I tried to work out how any of that might be relevant.

Everything we do has consequences.

Was Max's death some kind of karmic payback for his misdeeds? Were Anna and Claire being punished too for their infidelities? And if so, when could I expect the sentence for my night with Anna to be passed down?

I sighed and lit a Marlboro.

This was no time to indulge in whimsy.

I parked all thoughts about Jim Fosse. He would have to wait. I had to work out first what had gone on in Anna's apartment, why the police were so interested in whether Anna knew the Irvings and why it was important that they had her fingerprints. Because something told me all these things *were* important and it was not only Braddock paranoia making an appearance.

Who were the good guys and who were the bad guys?

I lit a second cigarette from the stub of the first, feeling like a character in some pulp fiction novel.

Forget Jim Fosse.

A POISON TREE

Claire had slept with Jack. I had slept with Anna. Max had slept – I supposed – with Ruth, Jack's daughter. Jack had killed Max. *La Ronde*. What goes around comes around.

Jack was the pivot.

I went back to my car, started the engine and headed for the hospital.

The Leicester Royal Infirmary, which dates back to 1771 and is sited close to the centre of the city, houses the accident and emergency department to which Jack Irving would have been rushed the previous evening. By this time, I reasoned, he would presumably have been transferred from A&E to the Urgent Care Centre, assuming he was not still in surgery. Or in the morgue.

Two nurses of Indian extraction were busy shuffling papers at the reception desk. The area was bright, but lacking any human touches. The place was geared for processing efficiency, not for calming ambience.

Now that I had arrived, I was unsure how to proceed. Had I expected Jack to be up and about and ready to answer any questions I had?

The nurse in spectacles looked up from her desk and peered at me. "Can I help you, sir?"

"I'm here to see Mr. Jack Irving," I said. "He was admitted last night."

Her fingers moved over the keyboard and she squinted at the display screen. "Mr. Irving is in the ICU. Are you family?"

"No, but he's a good friend of mine."

"Family only, I'm afraid."

A voice from behind me said, "I didn't know you knew Jack that well."

Eleanor was standing holding a cup of coffee. She was dressed sombrely, as if she were already in mourning. She addressed the girl at the desk. "It's all right, nurse. Mr. Braddock is with me."

A POISON TREE

Eleanor Irving looked at me for a few seconds. Her expression was difficult to read. Anger? Puzzlement? Then she said, "Come to finish the job, David?"

"Eleanor, I am so sorry."

She made no reply. Instead, she indicated for me to follow her. We passed through double doors and turned into a corridor where a large glass window acted as a viewing port into the room that was occupied by Jack. "No-one is allowed in at present," she said.

Jack Irving appeared to have tubes everywhere. His breathing was being facilitated by a ventilator – a bad sign. His head and every limb were swathed in bandages. Such skin surface as was visible was covered in cuts and bruises. He looked like a broken doll. Banks of machines clustered at the bedside, and a nurse was moving around checking displays and drips.

Eleanor stared through the glass and sipped her coffee. "This is what it has come to," she said.

She sounded calm, but I could sense behind that still exterior something was waiting to burst. I felt a jab of guilt. Eleanor Irving might be a priggish and cold woman, but she was still a creature capable of feeling pain and sorrow.

I couldn't imagine what sensations and thoughts must be passing through her right now. I guessed she was still in shock, her system struggling to come to terms with what had happened.

"The doctors have warned me to expect the worst. They can detect no significant brain activity. I expect it won't be long before they ask me for permission to turn off the machines. They are the only things that are keeping Jack alive."

She turned to me. "Do you have any cigarettes?"

"Yes."

"Then let's go outside."

A POISON TREE

We found a quiet, sheltered spot in the hospital grounds and sat down on a bench. Eleanor took a cigarette from me and we both lit up.

"I didn't know you smoked," I said.

She gave a bitter laugh. "Why, do you think I've always been this dried-up, joyless, middle-aged woman?"

"I didn't –"

"You may find this hard to believe, but I was considered an attractive girl in my youth. I used to have fun." She stared at me in defiance. Then her bluster subsided and she looked away. "Tell Claire not to come in to see him. There is no point." She flicked ash from her cigarette and watched it blow into the bushes. "The man who was seeing Ruth, I understand he was your brother-in-law."

"Yes."

"How is his wife? I mean – widow?"

"Surviving."

"So what are you doing here? I should have thought it beneath you to come and gloat?"

"What do I have to gloat about?"

"Oh, *please*." She spat out the words. "Are you going to sit there, look me in the eye and tell me you didn't know your wife and Jack were seeing each other? *I* knew. You must have known too."

"Eleanor, this is not the time to talk about this."

"This is the perfect time." She smoked some more, then said. "Jack has always played around. All our married life. There was always someone. Until recent years, anyway."

I put my hand on her shoulder. "Why are you telling me this?"

I knew perfectly well why she was telling me. She had no-one else to tell. So much for the support mechanism of religion in times of trial.

234

A spasm of distress passed across her face, but she managed to keep control. "There is one thing you almost certainly don't know, however. Unlike in his previous dalliances, Jack and Claire never had sex."

"How could you know that?"

"Because it would have been impossible. Jack has been impotent for the last five years. A kind of poetic justice, I suppose. Then he goes and gets himself killed fighting with a man who was just a younger version of himself. Another philanderer."

"Jack's not dead, Eleanor."

"As good as. And they are going to ask me, a devout Christian, for permission to turn off the machines. Jack's last gift to me. So typically selfish of the man."

"You're in shock."

Eleanor looked away again. "I had best get back inside."

She stood up and all of a sudden looked old and frail.

"What did you mean when you asked me if I had come here to finish the job?"

"It doesn't matter."

"I think it does."

She made to walk away, but something stopped her. "A few days before it all happened, Jack received an anonymous phone call making disgusting remarks about our daughter. It put him in a terrible mood, but I thought nothing of it. Jack has been in business a long time and has collected some enemies along the way. But yesterday he received an anonymous letter giving details of Ruth's meetings with Max Harper. That's what triggered his driving over to Harper's apartment. My husband has always had a short fuse."

"An anonymous letter?"

"Yes." She paused. "I thought perhaps you might have sent it, given the circumstances."

"Jesus, no, Eleanor."

"Anyway, the police have it now. It's their problem. Whoever sent it, I hope they track him down and throw him off a balcony." She tossed away the remains of her cigarette. "Tell me, I'm curious. Does Claire know you know about her?"

I shook my head.

Eleanor snorted. "Well, good luck with that. And thank you for the cigarette. Smoking is every bit as disgusting as I remember." She walked back inside the hospital.

I lit another Marlboro.

The wind blew dried leaves around my ankles. I saw cars come and go from the car park and heard the big tree creak. The light started to fade.

Claire had not been unfaithful. Cumberbatch had been wrong. I had been wrong. With Jack, Claire had sought nothing more than the same comfort I had sought with Adele. She wanted a shoulder to lean on, a shoulder other than mine. She had taken matters no further than that, in spite of the superficial 'facts' in my private detective's report.

Claire was not the unfaithful one.

I was.

But there was more to this, much more.

I shouldered aside my feelings of guilt and self-loathing. There would be time enough for those later.

How often we fail to see what is right in front of us.

In some ways, it is unsurprising that connecting the dots is difficult. Every second of every day information bombards our senses. The more we take in, the more superficial our view. On the other hand, the more we concentrate, the more we miss, for when we direct our attention to one item, we ignore other things at the periphery. We need to be able to take in a bird's eye view and deploy a microscope at the same time. But our brain does not work that way. Meantime it corrupts the data, colouring it with our own experiences and prejudices. Therefore to solve an interconnected problem, we require an epiphany, triggered by a chance remark or the surfacing of some relevant memory. Where our forebrain fails us, we need a subconscious connection; something to shine a narrow spotlight on the place where we should have been looking for answers all along.

Epiphanies do happen. Sometimes they happen on a bench in the grounds of a hospital.

An anonymous letter directed at Jack Irving, to cause him trouble. That's what people would think. But I knew better. First the phone call, then the letter. The pattern that had been eluding me came into focus.

The primary purpose of the letter was not to wound Irving. It was intended to turn him into a weapon against Max Harper, the man who had slept with Jim Fosse's wife.

And then another piece of the jigsaw slid into place as I recalled a conversation I had with Katie in Bali. *Portfolio theory for the criminal mind,* were the words she had used. It explained many things.

I pulled out DCI Banks' card.

Given Eleanor's knowledge about Claire and Jack – and the fact that she might speak to the police about it, if she hadn't already – I was left with no choice but to raise the matter with my wife.

"I want you to know that I love you," I said.

"I know that."

"Sit down, Claire."

"What is it?"

"It's about Jack."

"Have you been to the hospital? Is he dead?"

"No. I mean, it's about you and Jack."

It was the last conversation I wanted to have, and much crying resulted. My wife was contrite but swore that although her liaison was conducted in an atmosphere of secrecy, no lovemaking had occurred even when she spent the night with Jack in London.

"Did you give him a blow job?" I said.

"No."

"A hand job?"

"No."

"Did he ask you to?"

"David, please."

I turned my face away, disgusted at my own brutality.

Claire knelt in front of me, resting her hands on my knee. I didn't pull back. My anger was directed inwards, not at Claire. She hadn't hurt me. I had hurt myself.

"You want the details, David?" She brushed back the hair that had fallen across her face. "You're entitled," she said, her voice hoarse. "He kissed me. I kissed him. He held me. I lay beside him. That is all that happened. I swear to you that is all. We talked."

"What about?"

"About lots of trivial things. But mainly about Daniel."

"You talked to him about Daniel, but you didn't talk to me?"

"That's right. I'm so sorry, David."

I reached forward, cradled her in my arms, and drew her against me. The tears came.

Claire had needed to unburden herself about our son, and about all the sensations of helplessness and futility his death evoked in her. I had felt the same need. I just hadn't acted on it in the same way. Things had developed from there, and gone too far. Listening to Claire, it was obvious that Daniel's death had affected her much more than I had realised. She was plagued by guilt and regret that she had not been able to reach out to me.

I believed everything she said. Even if her explanations had not rang true, given Eleanor's words, I would still have believed her. Because I wanted to. Because I needed things to be right between us. Because I loved her.

I told her I understood and that we would get through this.

If I could have confessed to Claire about Adele and Cumberbatch and Anna, I would have. But I knew I could not. It would have destroyed everything. The rest of our life together would have to be spent with those lies of omission; a stain on our relationship that would be visible only to me.

So as I reassured Claire that I forgave her, the hypocrisy of my words seared me like a branding iron.

When I related the Jim Fosse saga, Claire was concerned but content that at least now it was in the hands of the police. I think Claire's own feelings of guilt so consumed her at the time, it was hard for her to process the implications of Fosse's scheming. That was probably just as well.

Claire suffered.

I lied.

What a piece of work I was.

35

DAVID

It was around eight o'clock when I parked outside Jim Fosse's house. His car was in the drive and the downstairs lights were on, the curtains drawn. The pile of patio slabs was gone. As I approached the front door I could hear the sound of Mahler's 'Adagietto' from Symphony No. 5.

The door was answered after a few seconds. The man of the house stood there barefoot in a blue-and-white kimono, a glass of whisky in his hand.

"Ah, David." He did not appear surprised.

"I know what you've been doing, Jim," I said.

"Really?" he replied. "Well then, you'd better come in."

He ushered me into the sitting room where the theme from 'Death in Venice' played.

"Couldn't you just *die* for Mahler?" He twirled theatrically across the floor.

"Frankly, no. Can you turn the volume down?"

Jim looked at me as if I had just said something obscene. Then he picked up the remote control, pressed a button and the music stopped.

The silence felt loud. Jim Fosse regarded me for a few seconds.

"Please sit down. Would you like a drink?"

"No, thanks."

"Oh, please. Join me for a whisky. I'm getting myself a refill. From the expression on your face it looks as though at least one of us is going to need a stiff drink."

Without waiting for an answer, he swept into the kitchen and after a few moments I could hear the chink of ice. I took a seat on the large sofa and surveyed the room. It was completely different from the evening of the

240

dinner party. Lots of dark wood furniture and Asian artefacts. Expensive rugs from the Indian sub-continent. A large abstract bronze statue filling a corner. Japanese water colours on the walls. There was nothing to indicate the owner was American.

Jim returned with two whiskies on the rocks, passed me one and sat down opposite. He raised his glass.

"What shall we drink to, David?"

"How about 'just desserts'?"

"Or 'absent friends', perhaps?"

Jim sipped while I looked at my whisky.

He leaned forward and tapped me on the knee.

"It's not poisoned, you know. I wouldn't waste good Scotch. That would be a heresy. Or do I mean 'heterodoxy'?"

I declined to offer an opinion.

"This is a Campbeltown single malt," he said, as if that settled the matter.

I drank and put the glass down on the coffee table.

We looked at each other steadily for a few moments.

"I know what you've been up to, Jim. I worked it out."

"Aside from grieving for my missing wife, you mean? Aside from hoping she'll walk back through the front door?"

"You know very well your wife isn't coming back. Because you killed her."

Jim wrinkled his nose.

"And how exactly did I do that, David? I was in the Philippines when my wife disappeared. I'm sure the police have checked all this out thoroughly. My travel dates, passport stamps, airline bookings – and the fact that my wife was seen on several occasions after I'd left the UK."

He paused and raised the drink to his lips.

"I don't mean you did the actual deed. But I know that you arranged it."

"Actually, David, I thought that you might have done the deed; that perhaps you'd taken our drunken conversation at the Bell seriously, and killed my wife expecting me to kill yours in return."

"Cut the bullshit, Jim."

"You know, that reminds me. You haven't seen my new patio yet, have you? It took me a while to lay, but it was a labour of love. Do you want to see it?"

"No."

"I expect if the police are of your mind, they will want to dig it up to see if there is anyone underneath it. I guess that's all part of the game."

"This is not a game."

"No? Are you sure?" He sighed. "OK, David, set out your theory. But please remember you are talking to a man who is in an emotional state and go gentle." He winked at me.

I settled back in my chair. "I've been doing some checking up on you, Jim."

"How exciting."

"It seems the police in North Carolina are still very interested in you. They haven't yet closed the file on your first wife's death. Big insurance pay out, wasn't it?"

Jim was unfazed. "Yes, indeed. But if you have done your homework, you will know there was no evidence to charge me with anything. I wasn't even in the country when Carol died."

"Maybe not. But a gentleman by the name of Hank Taylor was. Just as you were in the country and *he* was abroad when his wife, Vivien Taylor was shot dead."

Jim raised his eyebrows. "My, you have been busy, David. I'm impressed. You're wasted in a car showroom. You should be a private detective. I can see you in a long coat, smoking your Marlboros."

"A wife for a wife."

"Ah, I see where you're going with this. But poor old Hank killed himself. Dead end there," he said, sounding apologetic.

"Convenient."

"Oh, David, where's your humanity? Here, before you go on, let me top you up."

Before I could refuse, he took my whisky glass and disappeared for a few minutes, then put a refreshed glass down in front of me.

"Please continue. I'm gripped."

"I figured out your method. Perhaps with Hank Taylor you got lucky. He was an old school friend of yours. So he may have been receptive to your proposal, although in the end he couldn't handle what he had been party to. At least he didn't feel he had to drop you in it. So instead, he assumed your guilt and took it with him to his grave."

Jim had been staring at his glass. "I'm listening," he said.

"Here in England, you would have to vary your approach a bit. Nobody knows you, so you would need to cast your net a little wider for a gullible fish. But you would have to be careful, couch your idea in a way that could be taken as a joke, if your target associate reacted the wrong way. Risky to approach several people, but the chance of your finding the right guy would be increased." I paused to let this sink in. "*Portfolio theory for the criminal mind.* Quite clever, I must admit. It would not occur to the person you approached that he was not the only one you were considering as a partner-in-crime. Whoever you talked to would be likely to keep quiet if they found out later Monique had died. They would not want to get involved: few people are that public-spirited. They're more concerned about self-preservation. They wouldn't want to talk to the police and have to explain they had had a discussion about killing someone. Neither would they want their wives to know. You are pretty shrewd on matters of psychology, and would have factored that in."

"And you know this – how?" he said.

"When I considered who else you might talk to, Mat Hoggard came to mind. When he also happened to be a dinner guest, it clicked into place. That was careless of you, Jim."

My companion said nothing, his mouth a thin line.

"Well, I talked to Mat," I continued. "It seems you did have a rather similar conversation with him to the one you had with me."

"So I have a rather black sense of humour, David. That's not a crime. If it were, half your English stand-up comedians would be in jail." Jim eyed me. "I will say, though, that you certainly have the imagination to be a *film noir* screenwriter, or even a private eye if you put your mind to it. However, if you want to play policeman, there is this thing called *evidence* to consider."

I picked up my whisky and drank while I waited for his move.

"So who killed Monique according to your hypothesis? Surely not Mat Hoggard. He wouldn't have spoken to you if that were the case. And, as I think we both know, he wouldn't have the balls for such an undertaking. Furthermore, if your theory were correct, presumably I should be killing someone else's wife round about now." Jim was enjoying the conversation. "Would you like to have a look around the house? See if I have any bodies lying about anywhere? Maybe it's someone else's wife under my new patio. What do you think?"

I straightened my back and looked him straight in the eyes. "I think you organised a professional hit on Monique. That's what I think. Your other plan is just too crazy to work. What is more, you've been fucking with my mind just for the fun of it. Or maybe to keep me quiet."

Jim gave a long, tired sigh. "So, no proof. All just theory. A pity. You had me interested there for a while."

"I haven't finished yet."

"Oh, good."

"You were the one who made those anonymous phone calls to me and sent me that poison pen letter alleging things about Claire. It was to get me stirred up. You did the same to Mat Hoggard. And you gave Jack Irving the same treatment, not because you wanted to get at *him*, but because you wanted him to confront Max Harper – the man who was sleeping with your wife. I saw you following Monique when she met Harper at a hotel. That Harper was killed must have exceeded your wildest dreams for revenge. Pity Irving had to be reduced to a vegetable at the same time. But then for you, that's just collateral damage, right? "

Jim appeared unruffled. "More supposition. Still, these are all good stories, David." He drained his glass. "Shall I tell you a story now?"

His calmness infuriated me.

"This is an entirely hypothetical story, you understand. But since you have transported us to some fantasy land already, let me continue in the same vein," Jim said. "If I were the cold-blooded person you assume me to be, do you know what I would have done? Let me paint you an alternative scenario. I would have printed out a letter from you to me which suggests we kill each other's wives. Then I would have made sure it had your fingerprints on it."

"And how would you have done that?"

He waved his hands in the air. "Oh, I don't know," he said. "Perhaps that night you came to dinner and I passed you the wrong piece of paper when we were out on the patio. Maybe that was the letter. You gave it back to me, remember? I guess I'd still have that somewhere." He smiled innocently. "Then do you know what I'd do? I'd serve you a Campbeltown single malt whisky, and when you'd finished it, I'd offer you another one. Meantime, I'd take your original glass with me and put it in my safe, and give you your second whisky in a new glass. The saliva containing traces of your DNA could then be transferred onto the gummed flap of an envelope containing the letter I mentioned earlier. That way, if there was any police investigation, I could produce the evidence which pointed to you originating this whole scheme for killing each other's wives. You'd be the prime suspect in Monique's disappearance then, wouldn't you?"

"You little bastard."

He spread his hands and assumed a virtuous air. "However, as I say, all this is just hypothetical. Still, best you not talk to the police, eh? They can be rather suspicious individuals and you never know which way they'll jump. Now if you would excuse me, David, I'm rather tired and I would like to listen to some more Mahler before I turn in. Give my kindest regards to Claire, won't you?"

I left Fosse's house and drove past the unmarked van parked just down the road. I stopped after a mile in a lay-by and called DCI Banks.

"I assume you're in the van with your team? I didn't think you'd appreciate my knocking on the back door," I said.

"Right on both counts." Banks sounded morose.

"Did you get anything usable?"

"No. None of this would stand up in court. Not the way Fosse was at pains to describe everything as hypothetical. It's almost as if he knew you were wearing a wire."

I removed my hidden microphone and transmitter and threw them on the passenger seat in disgust.

"He's smart. And careful," Banks continued. "You somehow expect a modern-day Bluebeard to be tall and wearing a pirate hat, and not some tubby little American who listens to Mahler." There was a pause. "If it's any consolation, Mr. Braddock, I am inclined to believe your version of events, not Fosse's. I don't think you're the guilty party in this."

"Thanks a million." I struggled to keep the sarcasm out of my voice.

"We will get him."

"When? On his third wife or fourth wife? Assuming he's even in England then. What about the forensics on that paper I gave you? You said you'd get back to me but never did."

I heard Banks suck in a deep breath of air. "There were fingerprints on the poison pen letter and its envelope, but I would guess none of those are Fosse's, though of course we will check. We will have to fingerprint your staff, I'm afraid, as well as you. No DNA evidence. The cell phone number that called you had a pay-and-go SIM card, so it's not traceable. As for the travel schedule that Fosse gave you, his fingerprints may be on that or its envelope but even then, that proves nothing."

"What about the anonymous letter that Jack Irving received?"

"Same story."

"In summary, then, you have sweet fuck all to link Fosse either to the poison pen letters or to Monique's disappearance."

"That's about the size of it, at present."

"At present?" I snorted. "He's run rings around you."

Banks sounded offended. "He has run rings around us all, Mr. Braddock, if I may say so. If Fosse does indeed have your fingerprints on an incriminating letter and your saliva on a whisky glass in his safe, you are done up like a kipper. Nice little insurance policy he's taken out there."

"Yeah, Fosse likes insurance policies. I should consider myself lucky you don't suspect me, shouldn't I?"

"That can change, Mr. Braddock. If something untoward were to happen to Mrs. Braddock, for instance, I might have to revise my opinion on your culpability."

A POISON TREE

Anger surged through me. "Nothing is going to happen to my wife."

"We must all hope not."

36

ADELE

After her job in the Bargain Mart ended, Adele managed to get a few hours' work each week at a new women's clothing store. It gave her some respectability, and would be seen as an 'authentic' occupation in the eyes of the churchgoers and the vicar of St. Mark's. She was aware, however, that it was a wafer-thin fig leaf to disguise her other, less socially-acceptable activities at the Gold Club. Even smaller than Eve's, she reflected. The meagre income she earned in the dress shop would not be enough to keep the eponymous financial wolf from her door.

She had therefore asked Miss Connie if she could work more shifts at the Gold Club, and the madam was happy to acquiesce. This made juggling her dual life more demanding, and the possibility of discovery more likely.

To make matters worse, her last regular client, Robbie, was having breathing-related health problems, which in turn had reduced the frequency of his visits to Adele's apartment. This further squeezed her finances at a period when her mother was becoming more demanding of her support.

All plans to visit Glasgow had to be put on hold as Adele could not afford the time off from work. If her situation deteriorated further, she mused, she might have to offer to sleep with her landlord who was making noises about increasing the rent.

Adele had remained in touch with Rosie Fletcher following her time in Leicester, and now had three people with whom she communicated by email. Rosie had gone backpacking in Central America, and sent her photographs from Guatemala and Belize. She was aiming to travel down to Peru to see the ruins of Machu Picchu if she could persuade her parents to fund the extended trip. It was the sort of adventure Adele could only dream about, and it caused her some pangs of envy.

So far as her other email correspondents were concerned, it was situation normal. Her old friend Moira continued to keep her posted on her life in "bloody freezing Aberdeen", and Ross was still country hopping. He was currently in Moscow, performing an unspecified security assignment for some Russian oligarch whom Adele had never heard of. She worried for his safety. In her book, men who carried guns usually came to a bad end, but she went on playing the charade with him that all was well, both as to his situation and her own.

And then there was Simon ...

The Reverend Simon Fletcher looked around the faces of his congregation. His expression was sad, unlike the cheery face he habitually presented to the world.

"This is a time of great trial for one of us here today," he said, his words echoing around the cold church. "You are, I am sure, all aware of the recent sorrows that have befallen our dear friend, Eleanor."

Only too aware, thought Adele from her usual place in the rear pew. Unless you didn't read the papers and never watched local television news, it would have been impossible to avoid the lurid, prurient reports of Max Harper's death at the hands of Jack Irving, and the latter's critical condition. The journalists had had a field day, and seemed to be competing with each other as to how salacious they could be in their outpourings on Max Harper's affair with the Irvings' schoolgirl daughter. Adele pitied Harper's wife, who appeared to have conducted herself with dignity throughout the media frenzy. Eleanor had clammed up and refused to make any comments to anyone. She had been forced to remove Ruth from her school. It had been besieged by uncaring *paparazzi* anxious to get pictures of the *Leicester Lolita.*

That morning the girl at the eye of the storm, Ruth Irving, was with her mother at church. They both looked as if they were only just keeping it together, and in spite of Eleanor's insufferable personality, Adele felt an outpouring of sympathy towards the older woman. Of course, she kept her empathetic response to herself. You never knew with Eleanor how she would react at the best of times, and to have expressed commiseration which might be misunderstood for pity, would have been to invite down the wrath of the proud upon Adele's undeserving head. So Adele avoided eye contact with Eleanor and hoped her demeanour alone would convey both sadness and support.

"At such times as these," Simon continued, "it is difficult to know what to say. It is hard to find the words that will bring comfort. Life sometimes deals some heavy blows. I know that for Eleanor her strong faith will be a great support. Our hearts also go out to her daughter, Ruth, who is with us this morning."

Adele saw Ruth's head tilt forward, but Eleanor remained straight-backed, unbowed in the face of adversity, her eyes fixed on Simon.

"I know that I speak for everyone here when I say that whatever help and friendship we can offer will be freely given. In the days of decision ahead, we will be here for you both, whenever you need us. And now, I should like us all to say a silent prayer for the Irving family, and especially we will remember Jack in that prayer." Simon bowed his head.

Although Simon spoke in vicar's code, Adele knew what was meant by *days of decision.* Jack Irving was on life support, being kept alive by machines. Eleanor had to make the call to switch them off, something which, Adele supposed, went against her deepest-held beliefs.

She studied Simon, as he stood, unmoving, exuding compassion.

A POISON TREE

He was a good man in a world where decency was undervalued. He was gentle, in a time when aggression and overarching ambition were the fashion. He breathed ethics in an atmosphere poisoned by the toxicity of self-interest and cynicism.

And Adele allowed in something she had been fighting for months. A realisation that could no longer be denied, despite its irresolvable implications.

She was in love with Simon Fletcher.

37

DAVID

Max's funeral, as one might expect, was a ghastly event.

Anna had moved in with her mother while all the sensational news reporting went on. Although she received sympathetic treatment, the presence of reporters and photographers served as a constant reminder of how her life had crashed and burned around her. At least at the farm there was nobody hanging around outside the front door with a camera, Natalie made sure of that.

The burden of making funeral arrangements fell on Anna, although Claire and I helped. There seemed to be a million things to do. The matter of the death certificate, the administration of Max's will and estate, further discussions with the police, and countless other tasks thrown up by the abrupt ending of a life, all served to pile further distress on Anna. All things considered, she coped well.

Then there was the time she and I had spent together in London. That had to remain secret. That hurt her too, I could see. When we found ourselves alone – and I deemed she could process the information – I told her everything about Fosse and the true facts of Claire's non-affair with Jack.

"Claire has been so supportive of me," she said, "and I have slept with her husband. She doesn't deserve that. She was faithful and I was faithless. I'm no better than Max when it comes down to it."

"Anna, it is entirely different. You're nothing like Max. If anything, this is all my fault. I'm the one who told you Claire was having an affair."

"Whether or not Claire misbehaved is irrelevant, David. The plain fact is that I wanted to make love with you. An opportunity arose and I took it. We might as well be honest about it with each other. If I can't be honest with you, I can't be honest with anyone."

I held her hands. "We both took the opportunity," I said. "I wanted it too."

"And do you know what's so awful? Even with everything that has happened, I would do it again. I must be a real psycho bitch."

"You're still in shock."

She looked away. "Yes, I must be."

Max's parents flew in from Australia. They did not know what to say, whether to apologise to Anna for their son's behaviour or to mourn with her. Anna was gracious and controlled and there were no angry scenes of recrimination. As soon as the sparsely-attended service at the crematorium was over, the Harpers got back on a plane to Sydney. Max was their only child. God knows what thoughts tormented them.

My father was uncharacteristically supportive during this period, and Nang made sure Anna knew she was always available. Somehow it brought the two families closer together. Nang and Natalie started spending much more time with each other and became Ladies Who Lunch. Katie made a couple of trips back from university to ensure all was well between her parents, and left reassured.

So many conversations went on that I lost track of who knew what details about the goings-on of 1999. But nobody found out about Anna and me, or even suspected anything so far as I could tell. If that news had broken ... well, everything would have been broken. The fabled tree Yggdrasil would have fallen in the most destructive manner imaginable.

Elsewhere, the police investigation into Monique Fosse's disappearance became bogged down from lack of evidence. Bill Munks kept his distance. Eleanor Irving consented to switching off the machines that kept Jack alive.

And one morning, Jim Fosse turned up at my office.

A POISON TREE

Sandra closed the door behind her, leaving me alone with the American.

"Can you give me one good reason why I shouldn't throw you through this window, Jim?"

"Probably not. Although I'd be quite heavy to lift. You might injure your back."

"What do you want?"

"Aren't you going to ask me to sit down?"

"You're not staying that long. What do you want?"

Jim emitted a deep sigh. "English manners are so overrated. I just stopped by to say my farewells."

"Oh?"

"I have a new assignment in Thailand. It's time to move on. The house is up for sale. It holds too many painful memories of my dear wife."

"I'm sure," I snorted. "Well, goodbye." I steered him towards the door, but he evaded my grasp.

"You know, it's a funny thing, but following your last visit to my house, while I was abroad, my house was broken into."

"Really? Did they get much?" I said, sounding disinterested.

"Some drawers had been opened and the contents scattered around, but the televisions and laptops were still there. They were obviously after the safe. They broke into that with a crowbar or something similar. I should have bought a more substantial one."

"Yes, you should have had an alarm system installed too. I couldn't help noticing you didn't have one. Careless of you. Overconfident, even. I suppose you relied on Monique to take care of things while you were abroad. But of course she's no longer around. Ironic, eh? It seems wives might have their uses after all."

His eyes narrowed.

A POISON TREE

"My lights were all set on a timer, so they'd come on at night. That way, anyone would think I was at home, even when I wasn't." He paused. "Of course, someone who had a copy of my travel schedule would know I was away."

"Unless they broke in during the day. Most burglaries occur around three o'clock in the afternoon, I understand."

Jim continued to squint at me.

"So what was in the safe, anyway?" I asked.

"Some letters, a whisky glass and two thousand pounds in cash."

"Maybe if you'd kept the whisky glass in the kitchen it wouldn't have been stolen."

He grunted.

"Oh, by the way," I added, "I heard on the grapevine that you'd made an anonymous donation of two thousand pounds to a charity looking after the victims of domestic violence. Well done."

"Thank you," he said sourly.

"What did the police have to say about it?"

"Nothing. I didn't call them in. I've had enough dealings with the police lately. Besides, I know they wouldn't investigate it properly. Even if they did, I doubt they'd be able to find any evidence as to the identity of the burglar. He struck me as a careful type."

A big smile suddenly lit up Jim's face and he extended his hand. "Very well played though, David. I underestimated you."

I ignored the hand. "As usual, Jim, I have no idea what you are talking about. Now get out of my office, you fucking psychopath, before I do something I would honestly not regret."

1999.

Quite a year, in retrospect.

256

A POISON TREE

The world did not end. Well, not for those of us still left, it didn't.

My world changed though, and I changed with it.

Maybe I lost whatever innocence I had left. I finished the year less optimistic about humanity, less open, more inclined to gallows humour, more able to lie.

Braddock Motors continued to thrive. Harry showed himself the man for the job at our Coventry showroom. England did not win the Rugby World Cup. Hereditary peers lost their right to vote in the House of Lords. Portugal returned Macau to China, and control of the Panama Canal reverted to Panama. The European Space Agency launched the XMM-Newton satellite, Information from which was to be handled at the University of Leicester. *Yay, Leicester.* Finally, something to shout about.

But as the crowds gathered worldwide to usher in the new Millennium, 1999 had one last surprise to throw at us.

Anna was pregnant.

2001: THE FELLING OF THE TREE

38

ADELE

The year 2000 had gone much better than Adele could have hoped.

To the churchgoers of St. Mark's, her secret life remained a secret, although common sense told her it was only a matter of time before the light of discovery would expose her dual existence. Since no one would believe a few hours a week in a dress shop would keep her fed and housed, Adele had invented an Internet marketing job working from home on her newly-acquired laptop.

She hated lying to Simon, but the alternative was far worse.

So she juggled.

She spent Sundays, Mondays, Tuesdays, and Fridays at the Gold Club; Wednesdays and Thursdays at the dress shop; Saturdays were free. Each Sunday morning she attended a service at St. Mark's. She saw Simon on Saturday mornings and Wednesday and Thursday evenings. They usually went out to dinner at modest, out-of-the-way establishments or ate at her flat. On such occasions, the vicar dressed in 'civvies'. They had not slept together, but while their relationship progressed at a snail's pace, there seemed little doubt in which direction it was headed.

Adele kept the brakes on commitment. She often agonised over the grand deception that made possible their growing affection for one another. She worried for his position in the community if the true nature of her employment became common knowledge. Yet she could not give him up. In a soiled world, he remained for her a beacon of decency.

Although religious belief failed to register on her dial of Things That Are Important, Adele had been adopted by the faithful of St. Mark's. She thought they viewed her as a kind of science project, an enigmatic member of their circle who would experience a Damascene conversion in the fullness of time.

Eleanor remained frosty, and continued her campaign to undermine Adele in unsubtle ways. Since her husband's life-support machines had been switched off, the older woman had thrown herself into her church activities even more, albeit her zeal had more to do with being top dog – or top bitch – than with the ideals of Christian charity. Her daughter Ruth had been packed off without ceremony to Durham University, lest she prove the cause of further embarrassment.

Eleanor Irving had more than her fair share of troubles, but her aloof, spiteful character made it difficult for anyone to have sympathy for her.

Ross had not been back to the UK at all in 2000. He had an extended assignment in Moscow for several months, working for a Russian 'family'. Some oil oligarch, Adele was given to understand. Whatever Ross' contract entailed, it required his travelling to Vladivostok and Dubai.

The arrival of winter found Ross in South East Asia, moving between Thailand, Cambodia and Vietnam. Whether he was still in the employ of the Russians was not stated. In one of his more chatty emails, there was mention of the establishment of a casino in Phuket. Adele had seen a television programme about rich Muscovites moving money into property in London, Spain and Thailand, so she reasoned the Russian continued as his paymaster. But you could never tell with Ross Gallagher.

He reported he had bought an apartment in Pattaya for rest and recuperation purposes. Knowing of the town's unsavoury reputation for girlie bars and general lewd behaviour, Adele deemed it wise not to enquire too deeply into this.

Something pulled Ross to South East Asia.

A POISON TREE

Whether it was to do with his father's death there, the laissez-faire lifestyle or the presence of a casual girlfriend – or multiple girlfriends – was unclear. But Adele could not blame him for staying away from his homeland unless family duty called. If she had the money to spend her days on a tropical beach, she would have done that too.

"Fuck," said Nina. She plonked her bag on the table in the back room of the Gold Club. "My boyfriend is driving me crazy. Do you know where I can buy some rat poison?"

"What's he done this time?" said Adele.

"He wants to buy himself a new motorbike. I am so glad we don't have a joint account. He'd bloody well empty it as soon as my back was turned." She sighed. "Fancy a cigarette before the rush?"

"Why not?"

The two women went into the yard.

For once, the February weather was kind.

The yard had been tidied and an old plastic table and two chairs had been placed there as part of Miss Connie's 'facilities improvements' for her girls.

Leona had stopped turning up for work at the Gold Club just before Christmas. Whether she had passed her law exams or given up, nobody knew. Girls came and went at the club, their final departure often unannounced. The half-Italian girl only lasted three months. It did not matter. The club had an inexhaustible supply of females looking to earn some tax-free cash.

The Gold Club's current favourite was a tall West Indian girl with dreadlocks and a model's figure. She possessed a fierce and unpredictable temper, and from time to time explosions occurred.

A POISON TREE

Up to that point, Miss Connie had only employed white girls, but with the arrival of more competition in the area, she had decided to 'go exotic'. Indian cushions and wall tapestries had appeared. The dungeon had a makeover.

A new establishment had opened a mile away. Asian Dreamland had Thai and Vietnamese women, and Adele thought the enterprise smelled of human trafficking.

There was also an Indian brothel in Highfields, but that was not part of Miss Connie's target market as it catered almost exclusively to clients of Asian origin.

Asian Dreamland, however, posed a serious threat to her livelihood.

"Ten more months in this dump," said Nina, puffing on a cigarette. "I've set December 2001 as my deadline, then I'm off to Hull to set up my art gallery."

"Will you have saved enough by then?"

"I don't care whether I'll have saved enough or not. I'm going. I'm sure there are guys in Hull who like to be spanked too. I've been looking into setting up a website. Maybe do some webcam sex. That looks like money for old rope."

It was a far cry from Nina's original dream. But life is full of compromises.

"I am not too concerned about your mother's heart murmur," said Dr. Stewart, "but I *am* worried about the state of her liver."

Flora Darrow glared at the GP. "Don't talk about me as if I'm not here."

He turned to her. "Much good it does when I do talk to you," he retorted. "This drinking is going to kill you. I can't be plainer than that. Perhaps your daughter can talk some sense into you. God knows, I can't."

Adele accompanied her mother home through Glasgow streets that were changing even as Flora Darrow remained trapped in a resentful past.

A POISON TREE

Adele tidied up the scruffy, uncared-for flat as best she could while the old woman complained at length about the state of the National Health Service and the price of cigarettes.

A panicky phone call from her mother two days before had brought Adele to her home city.

As she dusted, she reflected on how different this trip was compared to her last visit, when Social Services had grudgingly agreed to facilitate a meeting with Jamie under the auspices of his foster parents, the Martins. Without the Martins' kindness, such a gathering would have been impossible. They ignored the authorities' advice, for which Adele would be forever in their debt.

"A mother should have the chance to see her son."

They had given Adele the number of their landline, which meant Adele could talk to Jamie over the phone. She now called twice a month – enough to stay in touch, but not enough to disrupt his routine and make the little boy feel torn and confused.

Rebuilding their relationship would take time, but so long as the Martins remained amenable, it would happen. Hope forced its way up through a crack.

Adele stayed with her mother for two days, then caught the train south. No visit to Jamie this time. As much as her heart ached to see him, she had to do right by everyone. Also, she had to get back to work.

While her monetary situation had improved, Adele needed to keep her foot pressed on the cash pedal.

"You seem miles away this evening, Adele," said Simon. "Are you worried about your mother?"

"A little, I suppose. But Mam is a tough old bird. She'll survive."

"Are you thinking about Jamie, then?"

"Always," she said.

Adele reached across the restaurant table and held his hand. "I'm lucky to have such an understanding man."

"Does that mean I get to see you tomorrow evening too?"

"I can't." She pulled back her hand. "I have to work. Sorry. Saturday for sure though, OK?"

Colin was visiting her the following evening.

More juggling.

Adele pushed open the lobby door to her apartment block and tutted in annoyance.

Not only was the lift not working again, but the security access system was also out of commission, and had been for weeks. Adele had installed an extra chain on the door to her apartment after two of the ground floor flats had been burgled. The landlord remained unconcerned about security matters, even after one of the Indian tenants had led a petition calling on him to carry out essential maintenance on the building. The Indian's reward for his trouble was not having his lease renewed when it expired. Security of tenure might work in theory, but not in practice. Not with this landlord.

Adele trudged up the stairs to her flat, passing on the way a young family struggling to get a pushchair and baby downstairs. She was running late and just had enough time to shower and change before there was a knock on her door.

"Still no security, eh?" said Colin.

Colin's pronounced lisp made it sound like, *Thtill no thecurity*.

"No. We'll all be murdered in our beds one of these nights. Come in. Cup of tea?"

"Lovely."

A POISON TREE

Adele had met Colin a few months before at the Gold Club. It was shortly after she had lost her last special client, Robbie. The old Scotsman was in a bad way due to his worsening health problems, and had bid Adele a reluctant goodbye. With David also gone, Colin had caught Adele at a weak moment, and she agreed to let him visit her at the apartment.

Adele doubted 'Colin' was his real name, but aside from that predictable subterfuge he seemed genuine enough. She found his lisp endearing, and he made her laugh when he enthused about horse racing and betting. He told her he had recently moved to Leicester from Coventry, but did not elaborate further. This did not bother Adele. He was accommodating about visit times and saw her a couple of times a month, which suited her – although his time with her was always at the expense of Simon.

"Do you know," said Colin, undressing, ""I've had the most *th*urreal ex*th*perien*th* the la*th*t week. I keep bumping into thi*th* little old man with a mound of white hair. He remind*th* me of a leprechaun."

"Maybe he fancies you, Colin, but he's too shy to ask you out."

"You could be right. Now come here."

There was a loud hammering on the door. Colin and Adele both froze.

The knocking repeated, more insistent. A woman's voice shouted out, "Harry Dempsey, open this door. I know you are in there."

Adele threw on a robe and opened the door, keeping the chain in place.

A small, red-faced woman stood outside.

"I'm sorry," said Adele. "You must have the wrong apartment. There's no Harry Dempsey here."

"I don't care what name he uses with you, lady. I know my husband is in here. Now open this door or I'll make the sort of fuss you don't want your neighbours to hear."

Adele released the chain and the woman pushed past her into the bedroom, where a terrified Colin or Harry was desperately trying to pull up his pants.

"Violet," he said. "I can ec*th*plain."

"I rather doubt that, Harry. Now get dressed. You're coming home with me now."

The woman turned to Adele.

"Your name is Adele Darrow, isn't it?"

Adele stood still, unable to think of anything to say.

"I know it is. My private detective, Mr. Cumberbatch, has given me all the disgusting details."

Violet's errant husband appeared, shame-faced, from the bedroom, and she pushed him out into the corridor.

"If you ever go near my husband again, I'll get the police onto you, Miss Adele Darrow. Be warned, slut."

The door slammed behind her.

The encounter with Harry's wife frightened Adele.

The next few days she spent as little time as possible in her apartment, fearing a knock on the door. She cancelled her date with Simon, citing a migraine, and although she put in an appearance at church the next day, she did not stay around long after the service. Simon sensed something was amiss and called her.

"My mother has been drinking heavily and had a fall. She had to call out the doctor," she said. The lies came easily to her now. Practice made perfect.

"As long as that's all that's wrong," he said, sounding both sad and concerned.

"That's all. Mam's fine. Just bruises. I'm OK, Simon. Let's go out somewhere special on Wednesday. My treat."

A POISON TREE

"Now *that* sounds like an offer I can't refuse."

As the number of days since the incident extended into weeks, and the wrath of God – or of Violet Dempsey – failed to materialise, Adele began to relax. She was still shaken and mindful of how close she had come to exposure, but she convinced herself the matter was closed. Her disguise remained in place.

Until Easter Sunday.

As she made her way to St. Mark's on that morning, Adele felt light-hearted. The previous day she had spoken to Jamie, and accompanied Simon to the cinema for a pleasant, if forgettable, romantic comedy.

Then she saw Violet.

Harry's wife was on her way into the church, chatting with Eleanor as if they were long-lost friends. They hadn't spotted her. Adele stopped in mid-stride, then turned around and hurried home.

She bought a pack of cigarettes and sat in her apartment considering her options. She called Miss Connie, apologising she would not be at the club that day in view of a family emergency. Simon phoned her several times, each call going unanswered.

When darkness fell, Adele left the lights out so no one would think she was at home. At least the building access system had finally been repaired, so any visitor would have to buzz for admission.

That night, she hardly slept. She could not know whether Violet's attendance at the church was a one-off occasion. Neither could she know what the woman might say to Eleanor, if not now, then later.

As dawn broke, a resolution formed. Adele had to tell Simon everything, regardless of the consequences. If he had to learn the truth from anyone, it was best it came from her.

She showered and dressed.

A POISON TREE

At nine o'clock, she picked up her cell phone and called the vicar of St. Mark's.

"Adele, thank goodness, I was getting worried."

"Can I come and see you, Simon? There's something I need to talk to you about."

"Of course. When do you want to come?"

"Now."

Simon leaned forward on the sill, staring out through the vicarage window while Adele sat waiting for him to say something.

The silence stretched out interminably before he turned around to face her.

"So you are telling me you are a prostitute?" he said.

"Yes."

"And that all this time we have known each other – over a year and a half – you have been ... uh." His voice trailed off, but then he swallowed hard and continued. "You have been lying to me about it all this time?"

"Yes."

"Why?"

"Why do you think, Simon?"

He shook his head and slumped onto a chair.

"The only reason you are sitting here now is because you cannot cover it up any more."

It wasn't a question.

"Our new member, Violet, knows. You are afraid Eleanor might know too. You are compromised, so only now do you talk."

"I am concerned for you."

"Yet you were not concerned for me before."

"Of course I was."

A POISON TREE

Even to Adele's ears it sounded unconvincing. It was the justification of a selfish woman, one careless of others' feelings.

Simon stared down at the floor, unable to look at her. He seemed exhausted.

Adele stood up.

"I had better go," she said.

He rubbed a hand across his face.

"Yes. I think that would be best."

39

DAVID

About ten miles outside the city of Derby sits the Peak View Retirement Home.

Its title is misleading. It is not in the Peak District of Derbyshire at all, but overlooks pleasant, rolling countryside. Then again, perhaps the 'peak' referred to is a widow's peak, since the lady residents outnumber the men by a ratio of three to one. Women tend to live longer. Ian Kenney would say this is because there comes a point where married men want to die. They have had enough.

Peak View is an expensive, modern establishment with extensive grounds, and from the outside it has the feel of a hotel about it. Once inside, though, as shuffling residents heave into view, it takes on the characteristics of a hospital. Easy-clean surfaces, inoffensive prints on the walls, and straight-backed chairs create a Zen environment and one that may be less cosy than some of the inmates would like. I suspect for them it is a daily reminder the world has moved on from that of the homely, chintzy houses where they would have spent their earlier, happier years.

It was some time since I had last visited Jean, my great aunt. This was not something I was proud of, but I justified it to myself by the current domestic situation that was weighing on my mind.

Aunt Jean had phoned to ask when I might next be dropping by. She gave no indication why she might want to see me – and her calling was a rare occurrence – but nothing in her voice suggested a crisis. The mere fact that she had called at all indicated something was up.

It was on a bracing spring morning when I walked in through the main entrance of Peak View, and asked to see my eighty-seven-year-old relative. A somnambulistic male nurse showed me to her room. Such was his demeanour and general appearance that if he hadn't been wearing a uniform, he could have been mistaken for one of the residents.

Aunt Jean was sitting in her armchair watching a television show. She clicked the off button on the remote. "I don't know why I watch this rubbish," she said, a trace of annoyance in her voice.

Age had shrunk her, but even in her diminished form she retained the ramrod backbone of the Braddock family. Her blue eyes still had a twinkle in them and she continued to take pride in her looks and dress. Jean was not one to 'give up'. The departing nurse would have done well to have taken a leaf from her book.

I kissed her.

"Let's take a stroll, David."

"Are you sure? It's not that warm outside."

"It never is. But I could do with some fresh air." She grinned. "And you would like a cigarette, no doubt."

"True."

We took a slow walk around the well-kept gardens before sitting down on a bench which bore a memorial plaque. Aunt Jean wrinkled her nose at the brass rectangle.

"Fucking reminders of death everywhere in this place," she remarked.

Her habitual use of profanity always tickled me. It was so incongruous, juxtaposed with the image of that frail, silver-haired lady.

"Are you all right, Aunt Jean?"

"Why? Did my phone call spook you?"

"A bit."

She chuckled.

"David, you know you've always been my favourite. Your father and I speak from time to time, but we don't have that much in common these days. I love him, of course. He is my nephew, after all. But I wish he'd take that stick out of his arse on occasion."

"Yes, it would help."

"Things still difficult between you and the old bugger, eh? Even with how things are at home?"

"Same, same."

"Edward was always stubborn, even as a child. It's too late for him to change now. For you, on the other hand, it's not too late. When this business is over – and it *will* end, David – you need to do some living. See some of the world, have a few adventures, for Christ's sake. You're a long time dead."

"I can't think about any of that now, Aunt Jean."

"Well, you have to think about it sometime. Everyone else might tiptoe around you, but you know that's not my way."

We sat in silence for a few moments before she piped up. "Do you know how hard it is to get a fuck in Peak View?"

"Er – no."

"I had a boyfriend last year but I had to dump him. A toy boy, actually. He was only in his early sixties. Even so, he couldn't get it up. I told him to get some Viagra, but he wouldn't. Worried that with his high blood pressure it might give him a heart attack. Bloody wimp." She cocked her head to the side. "That reminds me, I must get some batteries for my vibrator."

"Thanks for that picture," I said. "It must be time for a cigarette now."

I lit up.

"I've left you everything in my will," she announced. "It's not a fortune, but it's not a small amount either. I thought you should know."

"Jesus, is that what you wanted to see me about? You're going to go on for years yet."

She ignored me and continued. "I've lived, you know, David. No complaints. Even if these days I am reduced to playing bloody bridge with old biddies. And when I had my Bohemian period, well, that was the happiest time, even if it did shock the family. Did I ever tell you I lived for a year with a negro in Jamaica in the sixties?"

"Yes, you did. Several times. In graphic detail. And, for the umpteenth time, we don't say 'negro' these days."

She huffed with impatience. "Samuel didn't mind what I called him, so I don't see as it's anyone else's business. He's the only man I ever truly loved. Nobody else even came close. He's the reason I never married. No point." A sigh escaped her. "God, what I wouldn't give to have that big, muscle-bound negro in my bed now."

"Political correctness has completely passed you by, hasn't it, Aunt Jean?"

She curled her lip. "I'm too old for all that fucking nonsense. In my day, having real respect for someone was what mattered, not mealy-mouthed epithets." She fixed me with a determined look. "Don't die in some piss-smelling home with a load of miserable old bastards, David. When I'm gone, use my money to have some fun, OK? Otherwise I'll come back and empty your bank account."

"Whatever you say."

"I'm serious."

"I can see you are. Though you're not going anywhere for ages."

"What did I say about using mealy-mouthed epithets?' She snapped at me. "I've told you I'm part witch, so I know what's coming. Recently, Samuel has been in my dreams a lot. It's like he's sending me a message that he's waiting for me; that it won't be long before we're together again."

Aunt Jean had never had much time for religion, so any reference to the afterlife sounded strange coming from her. But I made no comment. We all need beliefs, whether rational or not, to sustain us through dark days. And although my great aunt appeared, as always, resolute and fearless, perhaps behind that seeming-invincible exterior, she too was susceptible to terminal anxiety.

"Your great aunt sounds like she's still a game girl, a real trooper," said Anna.

"She certainly swears like a trooper. More than anyone else I can think of, in fact."

"Let me just check on Jenny." She set the coffee down on the table in front of me and went through to her daughter's bedroom.

I had thought – right up until after Jenny was born – that I might be referring to her as *our* daughter. But no. The fact that the baby was blood type A ruled out that possibility. Max was type A, Anna was the rarer type B, and I was a plain old type O. Jenny had to be Max's. Biology can be an exact science when it wants to be. My night with Anna was destined to produce confusion and guilt, but not offspring. Against all expectations, Max had finally done his duty by his wife.

I have to admit, part of me was disappointed despite the innumerable complications that would have ensued had I been the father. While a new, albeit secret, addition to the Braddock line would not have replaced Daniel, it would have given me something to hold onto as my old, comfortable life slipped away from me.

Jenny was a delightful baby. Claire doted on her, as did Katie during her visits home. She had the Holland red hair and, although I may be biased in this respect, the most beautiful eyes.

Anna was proving to be a natural as a mother, if that's not too clichéd a phrase. Jenny seemed to have given her the strength and incentive to put the events of the pre-Millennium behind her.

With everything that had happened, Anna's plans to move to London to join Bright Sparks Publishing had been put on hold. But, as Jenny's first birthday approached, this was being re-evaluated. If Anna could persuade Natalie to give up the farm and move south with her into more suitable secure accommodation, I felt sure she would go.

I gazed around the apartment as I waited for Anna's return. Whatever decisions were to be made about London, this place was already on the market. It would have been intolerable for Anna to go on living here.

Max had at least left her financially stable. His large life insurance policy made sure of that. The bastard had got one thing right, at least. Two, if you counted Jenny.

Anna reappeared. "She's still fast asleep. Do you want something to eat?"

"No. Just the coffee, thanks. I'd best get back."

She sat down beside me and stroked my arm. "You look tired, David. You need to take care of yourself, as well as Claire."

"There will be time enough for that later."

I sipped my coffee and attempted to look cheerful, even though I knew it would not convince my sister-in-law I was coping. It didn't even convince me.

Anna sighed. "We just never know what is going to happen in life, do we? However much we plan."

As it turned out, my Aunt Jean knew exactly what was going to happen. Her dreams proved to be prophetic, and a few days after my visit, she was dead. A tidy legacy was to be mine. A pot of cash to fund my own Bohemian lifestyle, if I followed her urging.

If only things were that simple.

40

DAVID

Somehow we made it to April 2001.

If 1999 had been characterised by suspicion and a sensation that all our old certainties were withering, 2000 was the year of the unwelcome surprise. Its milestones served as hard lessons for our family, reminders of the fragility of existence.

First there were the questions from Katie.

"Mum's going to be all right, isn't she, Dad?"

Of course.

"Do you need me to come home?"

No, we're fine.

"Can I talk to her?"

She's just resting now, sweetheart.

Then there were the statements from Claire.

"I'm going to beat this."

Of course you will. We will. Together.

"I'm fine, I just need a lie down."

It's OK, don't worry.

"I'm sorry I'm being such a nuisance."

Don't be silly, you're not.

Expert beyond experience.

Let's all pretend together.

A POISON TREE

And when the weariness comes and the nights are sleepless, we will tell each other stories of heroism and hope. We will feed on the memories of better times to fill our cold, empty bellies. We will strive to maintain the fiction of the journey without end, even as we see, in the distance, our final destination.

Cancer is not one disease but many.

We stuff it into a single box as if that somehow makes it more understandable, more controllable, less threatening. It is by this same magical logic that we imbue death with a personality and recognisable form, as if by our so doing his character becomes tractable and susceptible to reason. But neither death nor cancer negotiates. They cannot hear our pleas and silent prayers because they lack sentience. And because they lack sentience, they cannot feel compassion, and neither can they make allowances. Abstractions cannot experience, they just *are*. We may as well ask the night to be day.

Rationality will not, however, prevent us from seeing cancer as a spectre – a modern-day boogeyman – whereas its true self lies in dispassionate Aesculapian definition: a collective term for various types of abnormal cell growth. But that is not dramatic enough for us. We speak in hushed tones of the "emperor of all maladies", a phrase eloquently coined by a surgeon in the nineteenth century.

Some cancers are more virulent than others, I have learned. In the United Kingdom, lung cancer is the most common cause of cancer deaths in women, and in Claire's case, its unforgiving presence in her body announced itself shortly before Jenny's birth. Thus, as a debit entry was made in the ledger of life, a corresponding credit entry found its way into the shadow ledger.

I was the one who smoked. Claire was the one who contracted lung cancer. Fate no doubt considered this hilarious.

A POISON TREE

Survival times vary significantly, although two to five years is often cited, albeit with reluctance, by members of the medical profession. This range conceals a host of other statistics until eventually the numbers become lost in a mist of unknowing.

The reluctance of oncologists to be quoted on this matter lies in the many variable factors inherent in each incidence of the disease, but all will tell you that early diagnosis and treatment are essential to longevity. Therein lies the problem.

One of the reasons lung cancer is such an efficient killer is that there is no test to reveal how long it has been growing or indeed when it started. What is more, it tends to be fast-growing and it spreads early – especially if it is of the 'small cell' variety. It can take several years for a lung cancer to attain the size at which it can be detected on a chest X-ray. Symptoms may not be obvious, and diagnosis, therefore, late. That is why the prognosis is so poor.

With Claire, the symptoms manifested themselves in shortness of breath, minor chest pains and fatigue. It didn't seem like anything serious. But it was.

Expert beyond experience. Knowledge I could have done without.

New terms. "Adenocarcinoma". "Metastasis". "Distant recurrence". "Lymph node involvement". "Tumour grading".

Old terms. Disbelief. Fear. Pain.

"It's bad tonight, David."

"I know, darling, I'm here."

Spasms. Claire took a deep breath with difficulty and caressed my face. "You look so tired."

A POISON TREE

It was of no consequence to me how tired I looked. "It's Saturday tomorrow. No work. We can have a lazy day."

"I love you, David Braddock."

"I'm pretty fond of you too."

More spasms and retching. Some blood.

"Oh, Christ."

"Claire, it's fine."

"Look at the mess."

"I'll get a cloth."

A visit to the GP for what we expected to be a routine matter in the spring of 2000, led to further referrals and tests that revealed a shocking diagnosis. Claire's cancer was advanced and urgent chemotherapy was required to reduce tumour size prior to surgery. Post-surgery pathology of the diseased tissue confirmed the cancer had spread to other parts of her body.

The treatment reduced her in a short time from a fresh-faced, lively woman to a shrunken old lady, devoid of energy. Claire's oncologist was grim-faced about her prospects. Her form of the disease was aggressive. But the treatment continued.

Our reaction was to circle the family wagons, become closer. My concerns of the previous year appeared trivial compared with what now faced us. I started smoking more. It was a practice that Claire abhorred – not surprising given her condition – but after a while she ceased to comment on it. I guess she knew I needed some way to relieve the tension and worry, even if it was a stupid way to do it.

When autumn came, it arrived as another meditation on *anicca* – impermanence. The disappearance of the leaves from the trees was a marker, an aide memoire of the transience of life. The days grew darker.

A POISON TREE

"Cancer is a long goodbye," Anna said to me on one occasion.

She came to Bewden often – as did Natalie – bringing Jenny with her. On these occasions, my wife never failed to rally. We drank lots of tea and coffee.

At work, I made some changes to allow myself more time to spend with Claire. I moved Harry to Leicester, even paying for his relocation, so that he could assist with my duties and also take over the Leicester showroom, where our general manager had been poached by a rival. This unexpected promotion delighted him, even though it meant he had to sell his house. We shored up Coventry with a new hire. For once, my father made no comment and smoothed the process.

Last month – a few months after I moved him – Harry got himself into a scrape with his wife over some young woman he had started seeing. But that blew over, and I had no complaints about his work or commitment. Given what had happened to Mark, one might have thought Harry would have been more circumspect about playing around. But then, that was Harry all over. As a gambler, he could never resist the long odds.

I think I became a little manic, at least on the inside. Externally I maintained calm, while the strain of performing so many different roles fractured my personality. I swear I could have attended group therapy sessions on my own. I sought refuge in philosophy to relieve both Claire's and my own anxiety on matters of mortality, re-reading Epicurus and some of Nietzsche's more accessible aphorisms. It didn't really help. I couldn't get beyond the intellectualising, which seemed a poor defence against the emotional maelstrom threatening to overwhelm us. On a more practical level, I dug out all my old study material and course notes on hypnotherapy, and used interventions to help Claire to relax, although my efforts at assisting her with pain control were unsuccessful.

A POISON TREE

"We need to think about a holiday," I said. "How about Bali?"

"Let's just get Christmas over first. Then we'll see."

Impractical suggestions, graciously declined. Our world was contracting.

Whenever Katie came home, Claire was meticulous about her makeup and overly optimistic. She wore a wig over her bald head and became adept at concealing the agony chewing away at her body. These weekend visits always exhausted her. The play-acting was not sustainable for long periods. Katie, of course, was not fooled. But we all joined in the game. I realised for the first time how tough-minded my daughter was. In spite of our family drama – or perhaps because of it – she continued to excel in her studies. It was a point of principle for her to do well, not only for herself but also for us.

Our children form a large part of our Immortality Project. This is one of the reasons a child's death cuts so deep; some of the future dies with them. Through them and their descendants, part of us lives on forever, just as it does in the friends we touch and the ripples our actions cause in the world. All these effects are conscripts, earthwork defences against the finality of extinction.

For my part, I had no desire to live forever. But if I could have bestowed eternal life on Claire, I would have signed Mephistopheles' contract without hesitation.

I wrote letters to my wife explaining how important she was to me, how she had made me a happy and contented man. I never intended to give them to her. They were scripts for speeches I could never deliver. The mawkish sentiments expressed would have worsened an already overcharged situation, and drawn more attention to the approaching end game.

Besides, "I love you," is all that is necessary when it is said with honesty.

We visited Daniel's grave a few times, at Claire's insistence. These were no longer upsetting occasions for me, more like a routine. I had lost my connection with my dead son. It had only ever been an imaginary connection anyway. How could it be anything else? My only preoccupation now was with my dying wife. The idea that Claire would join Daniel in the darkness was anathema, as was the notion that one day soon I would have to compose a suitable inscription for her to be etched on some cold slab of marble.

Where death is, I am not.

Flowers, silence, departure.

The Christmas holidays came and went. We made the decision to end further treatment. Claire's cancer was too belligerent, too hostile to be mastered. It had put out its pestilent branches deep into her, and they continued to grow.

Palliative care was all that remained.

Claire's body showed itself to be contrary. While it surrendered readily to the disease, it proved resilient to the drugs designed to ease the pain. This had been a problem ever since the cancer had taken hold. She suffered constantly from background pain and, as matters progressed, more and more from flare ups – breakthrough cancer pain, or BTCP – which arrived unannounced.

The flare ups became more frequent. Weakened by nausea and diarrhoea, Claire no longer possessed the resilience to rise above her condition. She was stripped of both ease and dignity. Lacking energy to exercise, her muscles wasted. Her eyes sunk further into her head and her skin became the colour of papyrus. With the arrival of spring, my beautiful wife entered her autumnal phase, and April saw her back in hospital.

"Can't you give her more drugs?" I said to Linda, the nurse who tended to Claire.

A POISON TREE

"We can't, Mr. Braddock."

"Why not? She is in so much pain."

We were sitting in an empty side room. Linda looked at me with sad eyes. She must have had this conversation many times before.

We had come to know each other quite well over the months. Linda was, I suspected, sweet on Claire's oncologist, Dr. Dudley, and from what I had observed the feeling was reciprocated.

Linda explained with gentleness that since the notorious Dr. Harold Shipman's conviction for murdering patients through intravenous injections of diamorphine and other strong analgesics, the spotlight of officialdom was trained on any practices that might smack of euthanasia.

In this atmosphere, legal issues, politics and bureaucratic conservatism trumped concern for patient suffering. The strong opioids that Claire needed were top of the list of substances under scrutiny.

"We have to be careful these days," she said. Linda's sympathies lay on the side of mercy, but her hands were tied.

"David?" The effort of sitting up caused Claire to gasp.

"Yes?" I grasped her hand. It felt like paper.

"I've said all my goodbyes. I can't take any more."

She had been drifting in and out of consciousness for days, becoming insensible only when the cadence of fatigue took her. Each time she reopened her eyes the pain was evident.

The drugs don't work.

"Please get them to give me something. We need to end this."

"You don't know what you're saying."

"I do. Talk to Linda. She likes you. Tell her I need a big dose. Enough to stop the pain permanently." She looked at me, her eyes brimming with tears.

A POISON TREE

It's too soon. Anna was wrong about cancer being a long goodbye. This is still too soon. I'm not ready.

"Talk to Linda."

I went in search of the nurse. She knew from the expression on my face what I was going to ask her.

"Claire needs to die now."

She dropped her gaze.

"She is in agony. We wouldn't let an animal suffer like this."

"We can't give her any more, Mr. Braddock. We just can't."

"Please."

"We can't."

I returned to Claire's room. It was like a phantasmagorical dream from which no awakening was possible. Outside the window, the branches of a large ash tree swayed in the wind. The sky beyond was the colour of steel. Details. The smell of disinfectant. Irrelevancies bombarding me. Numbness. Unreality.

I shook my head, tried to keep the tremor from my voice. "Linda will come soon and try to make you comfortable. It's all she can do."

Claire struggled onto her side and pulled the pillow from under her head. It was her pillow from home, her 'comfy' one. She handed it to me, as another rictus distorted her face.

"You must help me, David."

"What? No."

"You promised you would, if it got too bad."

That had been hypothetical, like the Jim Fosse conversations. Not serious. Not real. She hadn't meant it. *I* hadn't meant it.

"Don't ask me to do this."

"It has to be you. Quick, now. Before they come."

A POISON TREE

I stood, frozen, as if the opiates were pouring into my bloodstream, rather than into my wife. My final role, my last service to Claire. Not carer, but killer. The woodsman chosen to fell the tree. The serpent beneath the root. My mind scrambled for an exit. There was none.

"I love you, David."

I saw the pleading in her eyes. Tears streamed down her face. Her breath was coming in ragged gasps. The pain had broken through her final defences and she was helpless.

I kissed her and tasted the salt of her tears.

"I love you too, Claire. I always will."

I climbed onto the bed, pressed the pillow over her face and held it there.

After a few moments she began to struggle. Something within her fought for life. I increased the pressure, applying more of my weight. Sweat ran off my brow. I pushed down harder, and tried not to imagine her face, her desperate attempts to breathe. Only a few seconds more. Extinguish the pain. Put out the light.

I set the pillow aside.

Claire was gone.

I waited for the Earth to stop spinning, for the rift to open and swallow us. Yet the ash tree remained framed in the window, refused to fall. Rain streaked the glass. Blood throbbed in my ears. Preternatural silence. The cruellest April.

I was not deceived. What I saw was *samsara*, illusion. The world had ended. I was sure of it. The seer's prediction was just off by sixteen months.

Nothingness.

Emptiness.

Free fall.

41

DAVID

Linda found me sitting by Claire's bed, stroking lifeless fingers, willing them to stir. The nurse examined my wife, then took the pillow and positioned it under Claire's head.

She put her hands on my shoulders.

"Go home, Mr. Braddock. Your wife has died. You have done nothing, do you understand?" She spoke slowly, as if to a child. "She died while you were here and that is all. You have done nothing. The cancer has taken your wife. She is at peace now. Go home. Come back tomorrow and ask for me. Will you do that?"

I walked out of the hospital and kept walking. A downpour whipped the streets but I felt nothing. People avoided me. It was almost as if they knew what I had done. My feet moved of their own accord.

I had no plan, no direction. I just walked.

Eventually, the rain slackened off. When I came to, and examined my surroundings, I found myself on a footpath outside a church. It had walls of blackened stone. Grills covered the windows.

I pushed on the heavy wooden door and stepped inside.

42

ADELE

Adele Darrow looked at the suitcase on her bedroom floor. A laptop bag and a bulging rucksack sat beside it. Everything she owned – except for the toiletries and cosmetics still in her bathroom – was packed into those three pieces of luggage. It did not seem much to show for twenty-odd years of life.

Travel light. Don't get tied down. Only rely on yourself.

Given her situation, these were sensible guiding principles, although she could not help experiencing sadness that after these years in Leicester, there were only three people to whom she had to say goodbye. Miss Connie and Nina had hugged her and told her to stay in touch, but she knew she wouldn't. At the Gold Club, when her clients asked for her and were told she had gone away, they would go upstairs with another girl. Flesh was replaceable.

Adele hesitated over her third farewell. She had not spoken to Simon since she went to see him at the vicarage. He had not called. Was that only a week ago? Seeing him again would be difficult, but she wanted to part on good terms with the man who had brought her security and self-respect, at least for a while. She owed him that. Sneaking away without closure struck her as cowardly. Perchance even at this late hour, she could undo some of the damage she had wrought.

Adele made a sweep of the room. In the bedside cabinet, she found a packet of condoms and some tissues. She stuffed the tissues into her coat pocket and dropped the condoms into the rubbish bin in the kitchen.

Outside, the heavy rain had given way to a light drizzle. Adele moved through the lobby of the building and opened up her umbrella.

A POISON TREE

She walked purposefully through the streets, avoiding puddles and the splashes from passing cars. The houses and shops appeared familiar, yet strange. She had never truly belonged here.

This time tomorrow I will be on a train, on my way to Aberdeen.

Her friend Moira had agreed to put her up until she could find a job and a place of her own. Moira had not asked too many questions, for which Adele was grateful.

Adele had no cogent plan, only the strong conviction that her time in the Midlands was over. She had outstayed her welcome. Perhaps she would find her father in the Granite City. Perhaps she would end up remaining on the game, serving the men from the rigs. Maybe that was her true vocation.

Whatever lay in wait for her, at least she would be nearer Jamie. She could not face the thought of living in Glasgow, becoming her mother's carer. That would be like death.

Adele's pace slowed as the church came into view, but she kept going. She shook out her umbrella on the porch of the vicarage and rang the bell.

What to say? How to begin?

She took a deep breath and composed herself.

Seconds ticked by.

She rang again. There was no reply.

Simon might be in the church.

Adele made her way through the churchyard and shoved on the big, pitted door, half-expecting it to be locked. It wasn't.

There were no lights on, and the interior of St. Mark's was dark and uninviting. Adele was about to leave when a movement in one of the pews caught her eye.

In the half-light, she could discern the shape of a seated man. He appeared to be sobbing. Her first instinct was not to approach, but his distress drew her forward.

A POISON TREE

"*David?*" she said.

The man looked up. His hair was wet, plastered to his head, and his clothing was soaked through. He squinted at her through red, swollen eyes.

"Adele?"

"Are you all right? What are you doing here?"

"I'm – I'm not sure. I needed to sit down. I've just killed my wife, you see."

"You've done what?" Adele stepped back.

David started to laugh, but it turned into a choking sob. He tried to breathe deeper, to fight the spasms in his chest. He doubled up against the pew in front, and for a moment Adele feared he was about to vomit. But he managed to steady himself. He stared forward, his breathing more regular. He held his hands before him and looked first at one, then the other, as if trying to understand something that eluded him.

"The tea is hot. The tea is cold. Claire is living. Claire is dead."

Adele wanted to run, but her legs were rooted to the spot.

"David, what are you saying? You're frightening me."

"I've killed Claire. My wife, Claire. At the hospital. She asked me to. She was ... I was there with her."

He raised an eyebrow in puzzlement and dropped his hands onto his lap. When he spoke again, his voice was quiet. His eyes had a faraway, lost look.

"She was in so much pain," he said, his mouth twisting at the memory. "Cancer. Terminal lung cancer. The King of Terrors. I put a pillow over her face. I put an end to the pain."

The words seemed to surprise him.

Adele suppressed her fear and sat down beside him. His body was limp, and he was in deep shock. She dared not touch him. It was unlikely he was dangerous, but Adele did not want to take any chances.

"Did you walk all the way here from the hospital? In the rain?"

A POISON TREE

David nodded.

"You're soaking wet. You need to dry off. Go home, David."

A bitter laugh escaped his lips.

"You sound like Nurse Linda at the hospital. She told me to go home. She said I'd done nothing wrong. I think she intends to cover up for me. Yet another wife killer to escape scot-free. Call me Jim. That would be appropriate."

Adele only half-understood what he was telling her, but replied, "I expect the nurse thought you and your wife had suffered enough."

"I don't care one way or the other. If the police want to get involved, let them. It doesn't matter anymore."

In spite of her nervousness, Adele laid a hand on his arm. David didn't react.

"Don't you have a daughter?"

"Yes."

"You need to think of her. You don't want the police involved. You must say nothing. You did a merciful thing, David. Don't punish yourself for it. Consider your daughter."

"Katie," he said, stirring. "I have to tell Katie."

"Tell her what? That her mother has died, is all you need to tell her. I doubt she could cope with hearing anything else."

"Yes," he whispered. "I must think of Katie."

For one mad instant, Adele wanted to throw her arms around him, to tell him to come away with her. But the moment passed. She could not know what would come of David's wife's death, or even what the circumstances of it were. All she had to go on were the words of a traumatised man. The last thing she needed was involvement with the police. She had her son to think of.

Yet she wanted to offer him some comfort. His situation put her own into perspective.

There is always someone worse off than you.

David looked at her.

"My wife isn't coming back," he said. "I'll never see her again."

A reminiscence pushed through into Adele's mind.

"You can still talk to her."

He snorted. "How? Through a medium? Via some priest? I don't even believe in God."

"Listen, David. When my grandfather died, my grandmother told me she used to talk to him often. She wasn't crazy. She said so long as her memory of him remained, so long as she could still converse with him, a part of him lived on."

Adele could not read his expression or tell whether he had understood her, but she continued.

"Do you remember the photograph of my boy you saw on my fridge? Until recently, I wasn't allowed to contact him. Social Services took him away. Yet I spoke to him every day in my head. I still do. We must never let our loved ones go. Not ever."

David wiped his eyes.

"You are a good woman," he said.

"No, I'm not. In fact, I'm so not-good that I can't stay here. I have to leave, to go back to Scotland."

"Why?"

Adele shrugged. "It's just how things are."

"So we won't meet again?"

"No."

"I see." He squeezed the cuff of his shirt and water trickled onto the floor. "I had better get home. There are things to do."

"Do you want me to find you a taxi?"

"No, I can manage. I'm sorry I'm so ... well, you know. Thank you for your kindness."

David rose to his feet and edged past her, moved to the door and pulled it open. He hesitated for a moment, as if there were something he had forgotten. But then he straightened up and walked out into the grey light.

Adele looked at the place on the pew where David had sat, and touched the pool of rainwater. Sadness for her troubled friend enveloped her. She became conscious of the dampness permeating the air of St. Mark's, and she shivered.

At the front of the church, the crucified Christ hung in the silence, watching her.

God knew where Simon was. But God wasn't talking to her.

Time to go.

"So long, Jesus," she said to the statue. "When you next talk to Simon, tell him I called round to say goodbye. I hope you'll do that for me."

43

DAVID

I was interviewed by the same two police officers who had seen Anna. We were even in the same room at the station.

"Thank you for coming in, sir," said the female officer. "I know this is a difficult time for you, but I assure you this is just routine. We already have statements from your wife's oncologist, Dr. Dudley, and from the duty nurse, Miss Linda Thompson. We are satisfied as to the circumstances of Mrs. Braddock's death. However, since you were there at the time, we are required to talk to you. I hope you understand."

"Perfectly."

The session was short and, in my opinion, rather half-hearted from the police side. I didn't fall to my knees and confess. I just answered their questions as dishonestly as I could.

When it was over, they asked me if I would mind staying a while longer as DCI Banks wanted to have a word with me. I voiced no objection. They left the room, taking their paperwork and their disinterest with them.

A couple of minutes later, Banks appeared and sat down opposite me. He dispensed with the niceties.

"In view of that business with Fosse eighteen months ago, when I was informed your wife had died, you will appreciate I was suspicious, Mr. Braddock."

"It's your job to be suspicious. But unless you are of the view that I've been smoking cigarettes around my wife with the specific aim of giving her lung cancer, I guess there is nothing further to discuss."

Banks fiddled with a pen.

"The hospital staff were unanimous about the cause of your wife's death," he said with care. "I am sorry. Her illness must have been a distressing time for you."

"You could say that. More distressing for Claire, however, and a lot more painful. I loved my wife. There was no way I would want to harm her. You presumably realise that by now."

Banks sniffed.

"Well, unlike our mutual friend in Sheffield, I really don't know you and I can't vouch for what your marriage was like."

"I wonder what sort of sentence I'd get for punching a policeman. It might be worth it."

He shuffled in his chair.

"Have you heard anything from Fosse since he left England?"

"No. But you never know, I might bump into him. I'm taking an extended trip to the Far East. If we do meet, he is owed a reckoning for all he's done. And it doesn't look as if the police are going to do anything about him."

Banks straightened his tie.

"You have never struck me as the type of man who dispenses vigilante justice, Mr. Braddock."

"Well, as you said yourself, Detective Chief Inspector, you really don't know me."

44

ANNA

Anna sat on the bed while David folded shirts and put them into his suitcase.

"Are you sure I can't help you with that?"

"No, you just sit there and look pretty."

"Sexist pig," she laughed.

It was good to see David even a little upbeat after the horrors he had endured in recent months. He had told her about Claire's death and the truth of what had happened. At first, Anna had feared that his heart might break, that his grief and remorse might propel him to a public admission of his guilt. But somehow he kept it together. For Katie's sake, Anna surmised. She could tell how much it hurt him having to lie to his daughter.

Adversity served to bring David and Anna closer together, and she found herself entertaining thoughts that were wholly inappropriate, given the circumstances. Even now, sitting in his bedroom – the bedroom he had shared with Claire – there was an easy intimacy between them. The urge to reach out and touch his hand was strong. But she fought her instincts, and reminded herself she was with a bereaved person, a man damaged by the loss of his wife. Her sister. Romance could not be on his agenda. The thought that she might overstep the line, and see him recoil in embarrassment, held her in check.

David's announcement that he was going off to live in the Far East for an indefinite period had come as a shock to Anna. She was yet struggling to come to terms with it.

"Is that your saxophone case?" she said.

"Yes. I thought I'd take my sax with me."

"I haven't heard you play it in years."

"That's because I haven't played it in years. I figured I might sit on a porch somewhere and make loud squeaking, honking noises, just to annoy the neighbours."

Anna's gaze moved around the room.

"So when do your tenants move in here?" she said.

"In three days. The agent is handling all the details, bless her. All our personal things are in storage. Everything you see still here is part of the furnished-property lease. As soon as I've packed this case, that's it. Any clothes that won't fit in can go out with the rubbish."

"Three days. Hmm. Where will you be then? In Bangkok?"

"No, I'll be in Bali. I'm going there for a few days initially. When I took Claire's ashes to Foxton Locks, I kept some back to scatter over the rice terraces outside Ubud. We had many happy times there. I'm sure she would appreciate that."

Anna felt a lump in her throat.

"You're a true romantic, David Braddock."

In spite of her resolution, Anna reached out and took his hand.

"Stop packing for a few minutes and tell me about your plans."

"I've already told you."

"Tell me again. I'm a woman. I only half-listen."

David sat on the bed and put an arm around her.

"Well, after I've been to Bali, I'm travelling to Bangkok to see a Thai guy that my father knows of. He owns a retail and export business in fine art and is looking for a partner. Braddock Senior thinks, since I no longer want to sell cars, I should at least have some business interest to occupy my mind while I'm away. He may be right. He's thinking of selling Braddock Motors, by the way. Did I tell you?"

"Is he selling up because you're leaving?"

"I doubt that. My father's decisions are based on money, not sentiment. He must have a good offer. You know, my relationship with the old bugger might improve when we're a few thousand miles apart. We'll see."

"Why Bangkok? Why not Bali?"

David sighed. "Too many memories. Bali is an island of ghosts. I might go crazy on my own after a while. Thailand is a much better option. There are lots of Western ex pats there."

"And lots of attractive Thai ladies too, especially in Patpong."

"That's the furthest thing from my mind."

And am I far from your mind too, David?

"Anyway, I don't see my living in Bangkok. It's too noisy and busy. I was thinking more of one of the islands, Phuket or Samui maybe. Then I can fly to the capital when necessary. I need to check them out and find somewhere so Katie can join me for the Christmas holidays."

Anna snuggled her body against him.

"You should get yourself a housekeeper."

Someone old.

"I suppose."

"Perhaps while you're in Ubud you should ask that nice spa lady you know – what's her name? Wayan? – to look after you."

"It's an interesting idea, but I can't see Wayan uprooting herself to Thailand for the sake of some mad Englishman. Besides, she has an elderly mother to take care of."

"You can but ask."

"I guess so."

"You can do whatever you like. You're a free agent now."

"I'll never be free."

David swung his legs off the bed and stood, his hands resting on the suitcase.

A POISON TREE

"I have misplaced myself somewhere," he said. "I have been taking stock of David Braddock. Who he used to be, who he is. I'm not sure I even know him anymore. In my twenties, I thought I was going to do things. I considered myself invincible, as the young are wont to do. There was always a quip on my lips."

He paused, searching for the words.

"When I step back and look at the last ten years, I've been on autopilot. I've lacked the motivation even to be apathetic. I've grown complacent and middle-aged. That wasn't anything to do with my family, it was me. My engine stalled.

"The last thing my great aunt said to me was I should have some adventures before it was too late. Be less afraid of life, and let death take care of itself. Over these last months, I've pondered on this more and more. Katie is making her own life, Claire is no longer here.

"I don't know what I'm going to do, if I'm honest, but I'm going to do *something*. And some force is pulling me towards South East Asia. I don't want to get all New Age about this, but I keep getting messages. I met a woman from Hong Kong on a train, Jim Fosse is in the Far East, this business opportunity in Bangkok. I have a Thai stepmother. Even Ian from the Bell has been ranting on about Buddhism."

"Promise me you're not going looking for Jim Fosse," said Anna, concerned.

"No, I'm not. I'm not yet so nuts that I'm prepared to set up my life so it becomes the plot of some *film noir*. Although now I come to think of it, when I get to Thailand perhaps I should open a detective agency. After all, I've had some exposure to that sort of work over the last couple of years, and it doesn't seem that difficult. Or maybe I should dust off my therapy training and put it to use at last. Then again, I could smuggle drugs, or open a refuge for abandoned dogs."

"You don't particularly like dogs."

"OK, scrub the dog refuge. I don't know what I'll do. This fine art business in Bangkok might work out, although what I know about fine art can be written on the back of a cigarette packet."

"You're resourceful. You'll think of something. But not the drugs, please."

"Only cigarettes. And I need to cut down on those."

"Oh, David. All these portents and this existential angst are all very well, but why are you going away and leaving us? Open a detective agency in Leicester instead." Anna tried to sound light, but she wasn't sure she pulled it off.

Leaving me.

"We're all leaving, aren't we? Katie won't come back to the Midlands once she's finished at university. In a few weeks, you'll be starting your new job with Bright Sparks in London."

It was true. Anna had, after much badgering and hints about Jenny, persuaded her mother to sell the farm. An old friend of Natalie's who lived in Bayswater had recently become widowed. Natalie would have a companion with whom she could spend time and she could see her granddaughter often. Anna would have an on-call babysitter just down the road, and an enthusiastic one at that. A child minder would be unnecessary.

It had all fallen into place so fast.

Time can move quickly when it loses its memory, or when there are no new memories to create. Reality's vulture flies down and picks at the bones of our dreams. David was slipping away from her. This gentle, wounded man was leaving. The thought ran through her like an electrical charge.

"You won't forget me, will you, David? You will stay in touch?" she said.

Tell him.

He looked at her in surprise. "Of course I'll stay in touch, silly. I am expecting you to come for holidays to Thailand."

A POISON TREE

Tell him.

"It's a long flight for Jenny."

"Let your mum look after Jenny for a week or two. She'd love it, and you can explore South East Asia with me."

Damn it, tell him.

"I'd like that."

David closed the suitcase and looked at his watch.

"We'd better be going soon. I'll just have a check around. I don't suppose that train will wait for me."

"Probably not."

But I will.

Anna dropped David at Leicester railway station.

"No long goodbye," she said. "Just give me a kiss and a hug."

"I'll call you as soon as I get to the hotel."

"OK. Go, before I start bawling my eyes out."

Anna's last image of David was in the rear view mirror. He was lighting a cigarette. It already felt like he was half a world away. A lorry pulled up in front of him and he vanished from her sight. It was then that she could no longer stop the tears.

She drove back to the farm to find her mother in the kitchen.

"How's Jenny been?"

"As good as gold. She fell asleep about twenty minutes ago. Did David get off all right?"

"Yes."

"Have you been crying?"

"Maybe a bit."

Her mother put her arms around her.

A POISON TREE

"You've always been close, you and David, right from the start. Sometimes I think –"

"What?"

Natalie shook her head.

"Oh, nothing. Ignore me. I'm a silly old woman."

Anna went upstairs to Jenny's room. Her daughter was sound asleep. Anna knelt down and whispered to her.

"I'm sorry, Jenny, I couldn't tell him. I couldn't tell David he's your daddy, not today. He needs some time to heal, you see, sweetheart. It wouldn't have been fair. Not with him going away. But I will tell him one day, I promise. I promise you, I will."

OAK

Well, Claire, here we are again at Heathrow airport.

Neither of us has ever really liked this place – it's too full of miserable people who should be happy – but it's always been a nuisance we were prepared to put up with as a prelude to something better: our trips to the Far East. And this will, after all, be a much longer trip. Maybe we will never come back to England. Katie can always visit us in South East Asia whenever she likes, legal career permitting.

I can't express, my love, what a relief it is to be able, at last, to tell you everything. No more secrets or lies or half-truths. We can once again be entirely open with each other, as we were in the early days. I know you understand, even about Anna.

Nothing can hurt us now.

Once we're settled in Thailand, I'll ship out our things and we can set about making a home there. A new start.

Life with you in the tropics, just the two of us. I can't wait.

Aren't you excited too?

Just a little bit?

David Braddock returns in

RUNNING ON EMPTINESS

The fourth book in the *Time, Blood and Karma* series,
to be published by Tention Publishing Limited.

Details of the first two books in the series are set out overleaf.

EVERYONE BURNS

It is January 2005 and the charred remains of two Europeans have been discovered on the Thai island of Samui.

Local Police Chief Charoenkul, sidelined by his superiors, enlists the reluctant David Braddock, a burnt-out private detective, to assist in an 'unofficial' investigation.

But Braddock has problems of his own, including his affair with the same Police Chief's wife ...

Peppered with irreverent humour and some pithy comments on everyday life in the Land of Smiles, *Everyone Burns* is much more than a crime novel. It is also a carefully-crafted psychological study of an anti-hero for our time.

HUNGRY GHOSTS

It is the spring of 2005 and the macabre 'burning murders' have ended. Life has apparently returned to normal for the Thai island of Samui.

For private investigator David Braddock 'normal' means finding a missing drug smuggler, sleeping with the Police Chief's wife and ensuring his office manager's latest money making scheme doesn't bankrupt him.

For Police Chief Charoenkul it means resuming his seemingly-endless wait for that elusive promotion to Bangkok.

However, the peace is destined to be short-lived. Unbeknown to both men, karmic storm clouds are gathering and murderous forces are about to be unleashed which could destroy them both ...

12625162R00184

Printed in Great Britain
by Amazon.co.uk, Ltd.,
Marston Gate.